Erin's hand paused on the Open sign.

Her attention was thoroughly captured by the sight of Remy unfolding his long, lean frame from the vehicle.

He'd held plenty of appeal the night before with his dress shirt plastered to his chest and shoulders from the rain. Today, clean and pressed in a gray suit with a pale blue shirt open at the neck, he was a whole different kind of handsome.

Remy lifted a hand in acknowledgment when he spotted her. Her heart rate jumped a little at his smile, a fact that irritated her more than she would have liked.

Opening the door, she concentrated on the fact he was just a client like any other. And he'd be on his way back to Miami before she knew it...

Dear Reader,

I fell in love with Heartache, Tennessee, in my last Harlequin Superromance novel, *Promises Under the Peach Tree* (September 2014). So much so that I just couldn't seem to leave! I hope you'll indulge me for a return trip to this fictional town south of Nashville where I've got another story to tell about one of the Finleys, Heartache's most prominent family. Things aren't going so well for Erin Finley when we meet her. But then Remy Weldon, the hero I sent her way, is having a hard time, as well.

Remy and his teenage daughter are both drawn in by small-town life in Heartache. I hope you are, too! Sit for a spell and enjoy the warm spring nights of Tennessee with me. The kids are all tucked in. The katydids are singing and the fireflies are just beginning to come out to light the evening with their magical glow. Best of all, two people are about to fall in love...

Happy reading,

Joanne Rock

PS—Follow me online at facebook.com/JoanneRockAuthor, or on Twitter, @JoanneRock6. I always love to hear from readers!

JOANNE ROCK

Nights Under the Tennessee Stars

HHARLEQUIN®SUPERROMANCE®

Recycling programs
for this product may
not exist in your area.

ISBN-13: 978-0-373-60907-9

Nights Under the Tennessee Stars

Printed in U.S.A.

www.Harlequin.com

While working on her master's degree in English literature, **Joanne Rock** took a break to write a romance novel and quickly realized a good book requires as much time as a master's program itself. She became obsessed with writing the best romance possible, and sixty-some novels later, she hopes readers have enjoyed all the "almost there" attempts. Today, Joanne is a frequent workshop speaker and writing instructor at regional and national writer conferences. She credits much of her success to the generosity of her fellow writers, who are always willing to share insights on the process. More important, she credits her readers with their kind notes and warm encouragement over the years for her joy in the writing journey.

Books by Joanne Rock

HARLEQUIN SUPERROMANCE

Promises Under the Peach Tree

HARLEQUIN BLAZE

The Captive
Double Play
Under Wraps
Highly Charged!
Making a Splash
Riding the Storm
One Man Rush
Her Man Advantage
Full Surrender
My Double Life
A Soldier's Christmas
"Presents Under the Tree"
My Secret Fantasies

Visit the Author Profile page
at Harlequin.com for more titles.

To all you romance-loving readers,

thank you for spending long hours
in front of the romance shelves at the bookstore
or on your ereaders!

I'm so grateful to you for thinking, like me, that
"happy-ever-after" is a story worth believing in and
worth reimagining again and again in the pages of
a book, in our hearts and in our real lives.

This book is for *you*, for daring to be romantic.
Thank you for your optimistic view of the world and
your belief that love conquers all. I hope this story
lifts you up, makes you smile, and reminds you of
the awesome power of love in our lives.

PROLOGUE

ERIN FINLEY HAD plane tickets, ID and her carry-on suitcase set for a romantic long weekend. Too bad the "romantic" part was decidedly absent, since Patrick was not at the airport as promised.

"Flight 8402 to Nashville, now boarding all rows," the airline's desk agent announced over a tinny PA system at the gate.

Damn it. Erin checked her phone—still no messages even though she'd texted him. Nervously, she toyed with the handle on her sticker-covered 1940s-era vintage suitcase, wishing Patrick's black leather duffel sat beside it. Her financial consultant boyfriend loved to tease her about her quirky fashion sense, which was inspired by her work as an antiques dealer and part-time boutique manager. Despite the teasing, he'd developed an artistic side since they'd met. He had taken up painting, a growing passion that he'd credited her with during a really awesome talk they'd recently had about their future. A future finally looking up for Erin. When they'd been in the shopping mall last weekend, she'd caught Patrick having a hushed conversation with a jeweler. She had every reason to think a ring might be in the works.

She checked her watch. They had traveled often in the past few months to make their long-distance relationship work, and he'd never been late for a date before. If anything, this trip should be easier than previous ones as she had stayed in Louisville, Kentucky, for a few weeks to work and he was based in Cincinnati, so, for the first time, they would be flying out of the same airport.

He'd been excited about their visit to Heartache, Tennessee, where he would meet her family for the first time. Staid, sweet Patrick didn't seem the type to get cold feet, even though he knew all about the strained relationships among the Finley clan, which was why she purposely didn't spend much time back home. She loved that Patrick shared her values, and she wondered if he might wait to pop the question until they were back in Heartache so she could enjoy the moment with her family—dysfunctional though they might be.

Her phone vibrated, and relief mingled with annoyance when she saw his number appear on the small screen. She thumbed the on button and tucked her cell to her ear.

"They're boarding now," she blurted. "Please say you're already in the airport and past Security." She stood on her toes to see farther down the concourse, hoping to spot his neat sandy hair and his quick, efficient steps.

"Who is this?" a woman's voice demanded on the other end of the call.

Confused, Erin sank down to her heels.

"Excuse me?" She held the phone away from her ear to double-check the number.

Patrick's digits were still on the screen.

"Who. Is. This." The speaker on the other end sounded tense. Angry.

The tone did nothing to improve Erin's mood when she was already stressed and nervous.

"I might ask you the same question," she shot back, raising her voice as the desk agent announced the final boarding call for her flight. "Where is Patrick and why do you have his phone?"

Had he left it behind at Security? Maybe some crazy woman had picked it up.

"You home-wrecking bitch."

The snarled accusation ripped into Erin's ear at full volume.

Thoughts of the airport, the flight and the romantic weekend scattered. Her focus narrowed to the call.

"Ex-excuse me?" An icy tingling started in her fingers and spread like a cold frost through her veins.

"Why are there twenty calls to you in my husband's phone in the last three days?" The woman had shouted the questions.

Husband?

Erin's heart stopped. Her gut plunged worse than any coaster she'd ever ridden. She walked away from her suitcase to stand at the window overlooking the tarmac. She needed a quieter place. Needed a second to make sense of what was happening.

"I don't know what you're talking about," she whispered, her voice failing her along with her brain cells.

Through the phone, she could hear a man's voice speaking quietly. Muffled arguing.

Erin tipped her forehead to the cold pane of glass and concentrated on the voices. It couldn't be Patrick. She knew everything about him. They'd spent almost every weekend together for months, ever since meeting in a remote Vermont town where they'd both been traveling for business. Since then, she'd coordinated several of her trips to coincide with his, never thinking twice about the fact she hadn't been to his home. He was never there, after all—one of the many ways she'd thought they were alike. They were in love. He was meeting her family for the first time because they'd waited until they were really sure about each other. Erin was a traditional-values kind of girl.

Maybe Patrick had a crazy stalker who had a

crush on him or something. A woman who wanted to get rid of the competition.

"Excuse me." Erin straightened, hoping she could resolve this mess before she had to listen to any more lunacy from whoever had intercepted Patrick's phone. "Are you still there?"

More muffled voices on the other end.

"Am I here? Hell yes, I'm here," the woman said. "I will *always* be here. You, on the other hand, are the intruding—" the string of expletives blistered Erin's ears "—who had better get out of my husband's life before I hunt you down and take care of you myself."

Erin shut out the threats and bad names. She'd grown up with a mom who suffered from severe mood swings, so Erin had plenty of experience withstanding tirades. The trick was to stay level, reasonable and get out of the conversation as fast as possible. Except what if this woman wasn't a stalker at all? She did have Patrick's phone.

Her stomach dropped to her toes as she grappled to make sense of this.

"Look, you may have picked up the wrong phone somewhere. My boyfriend is single—"

"Single?" A harsh laugh punctuated the word. "Is that what Pat told you? He has *kids*—two sons, eight and six years old—you slut. I'm hauling them to baseball games and birthday parties on my own every weekend so he can jet around the country as if he never made vows to *me*? As if a fancy diamond necklace would make me forget he's a cheating bastard who can't stay home with his family?"

The jewelry store.

He hadn't been buying Erin a ring. He'd been buying a gift for his wife. Something shifted inside her. Her knees wobbled and she slapped one hand on the window for support.

This woman did not have the wrong phone. They were not talking about different men.

The arguing in the background of the call became more heated. Still muffled, but there was a noticeable increase in fervency and volume. Every now and then, she could hear the man's voice more clearly. Patrick's voice.

Erin noted it in a marginal way, her main focus on the fact that her whole sense of self had just shattered into a million pieces. The fragments lay at her feet on the industrial gray carpet of the Northern Kentucky airport.

So much for traditional values.

"You want me to put the kids on the phone so you'll believe me?" the furious woman demanded suddenly. "Would you like to hear what Pat's children think of the woman destroying our lives—"

Erin's hands shook as she stabbed the disconnect button and missed. She pressed two more times before her finger made contact with the button and ended the call.

The sudden quiet hum of normal conversations around her felt jarring. Her ears still rang from the accusations and anger. When her phone rang again, her fingers were steadier as she turned the device off. She would never use that phone or that number again.

"Miss?" an older gentleman approached her, a kindly smile on his weathered face, a newspaper tucked under one arm of his corduroy jacket. "Don't forget your bag."

He pointed to her suitcase in the waiting area and she vaguely recalled he'd been seated near her earlier. They'd talked about the weather and the local baseball team. It seemed like a million years ago.

"Thank you." She nodded. Swallowed. Forced herself to put one foot in front of the other, her whole body numb with shock. "I'll go get it."

Patrick was *married*. The man she thought she loved had *children*.

Grabbing the smooth tortoiseshell handle of the suitcase—a suitcase she'd packed so carefully and hopefully—Erin strode up the concourse and away from the flight that would have taken her home. Away from the Finley family, who expected her to show up with Mr. Right just in time for dinner.

She should be embarrassed about being so stupid and blind that she hadn't known the love of her life had been lying to her every second they'd been together. He'd lied in the worst and most clichéd manner possible. He was married. She should feel ashamed to be an unknowing "other woman" in an era where most of her friends performed Google searches on any guy they dated.

But Erin wasn't ready to acknowledge any of those things just yet because most of all, she felt deeply sorry that she'd wounded an unsuspecting woman—a mother, no less—whose world must be falling apart faster and harder than Erin's today.

Focusing on the pain she'd inflicted helped keep some of her own fury at bay—at least until she arrived at her car. She dropped her bag in the trunk, then slid into the driver's seat. Once the doors were safely locked and the windows rolled up, she succumbed to the urge to pound her fist on the steering wheel and scream. She was done with Patrick. Done with men who had complicated lives and too many secrets. Life at high speed didn't suit her. Time to slow down. Regroup. And hope the day would come when she didn't feel the need to scrub her skin with disinfectant to get rid of the memory of Patrick's touch.

She needed to pack her rental place and get far away from the adulterous ass who'd done nothing but lie to her. Any other day it might have made her smile to think that what she really needed was to get back to Heartache.

CHAPTER ONE

Six months later

ERIN HANDED HER sister an airline ticket, her phone charger and her suitcase.

"I've got this, Heather. Go have fun." She nodded toward the door of their jointly owned boutique, Last Chance Vintage, figuring her organized younger sister would never get under way without a hard shove and possibly a crowbar. "You've been babysitting me too long. Time to let me do my own thing."

Erin and Heather were expanding the tiny shop on Heartache's main thoroughfare, taking over an ancient cobbler's storefront to make way for the new design. They'd done a lot of the labor themselves to save money, their DIY skills reasonably strong since their father had owned a construction business and their older brother still ran the family's building-supply store. Erin had finished sanding the hardwood floors in the new space two days ago. Even now, the pungent scent of a fresh coat of stain permeated the heavy plastic divider that sectioned off the workspace behind the front counter. Heather had tried to mask the scent with lavender chips in an electric warmer, but so far, the wood stain was winning out.

"Babysitting?" Heather dropped the bright teal suitcase on the rag rug, beside a display of necklaces artfully draped on the spokes of an old bicycle wheel. "As if. Last Chance is my store, too, you know. I can't help it if I want to oversee the redesign."

The freckles across Heather's nose aligned when she scrunched her face into a mad expression, a quirky characteristic no one but a sibling would notice. Heather and Erin had looked a lot alike growing up, so the freckle pattern was familiar from Erin's own reflection in the mirror. Her hair had been as red as Heather's once upon a time, too, but Erin had been dying it different colors since she was old enough to buy Clairol at the local drugstore without Mrs. Bartlett threatening to tell her mother.

Erin was almost done with the Goth-girl black on her lopped-off curls, knowing she looked way too much like a caricature of a pissed-off woman. But the inky shade sure did suit her mood lately. The store expansion had been her brainchild, prompted by a sudden desire to wield a sledgehammer.

She put her hands on her hips. "I've got the redesign well in hand, and you know it. The expansion is no excuse for you sticking to me like glue these days." Erin kept her voice low even though there was no one else in the store, and probably wouldn't be, since closing time was five minutes away. After her mother's legendary tirades, Erin tended to keep a tight rein on how she displayed her emotions. "You have to admit you've been hanging out at my house every day after closing time. And we never talk about the store."

Erin loved her hometown for a lot of reasons. But the shoulder-to-shoulder proximity of her brother's, mother's and sister's homes was not really one of them. However, since the Finley land had been free for building and gifted in parcels to each of them, that was exactly how things had panned out. A couple of acres separated each house, and the farmland nearby was still mostly vacant.

"So sue me for preferring to share a bottle of wine." Heather rearranged the silk daisies tucked inside the bicycle basket, her hot-pink manicure showing off metallic emerald stripes. Erin had painted her sister's nails earlier in the week while sharing one of those bottles. "It's been nice having both of us in town for a change. I get tired of doing the dutiful daughter thing here by myself."

For years, they'd traded off time in Heartache to keep tabs on their mom's health. It was no different now that they owned the store. They each traveled to scout new items for the store or to sell on their website. Last Chance Vintage had cornered a niche market on antique linens and silverware, catering to numerous independent decorators who liked doing business with smaller companies. Sometimes, in their flea market scouring, they found genuinely valuable antiques, as well, and they'd been in business long enough that they knew which of their clients would love them.

Still, Erin knew she'd done the lion's share of the traveling in the past two years while Heather had been at home to weather more of their mother's crises. Heather deserved to get out of Heartache more often. She'd stifled her own dreams as a musician for the sake of a job that kept her in town.

"I'm planning to stay closer to home in the future, so I'll be here when you get back. And clearly, someone needs to do some buying if we're going to fill the new floor space." She gestured at the heavy plastic sheet hanging between the old store and the new expansion. "It's definitely your turn to rack up the frequent-flier miles."

It was stupid, but the thought of setting foot in an airport again practically made Erin hyperventilate. She hadn't left town since returning six months ago. She'd methodically cut every reminder of Patrick out of her life, from giving away the landscape painting he'd done for her to dumping every card, memento and shared concert ticket in the trash. After chucking her cell phone and changing her number—overkill, but that was how she rolled these days—she'd also gotten rid of her landline in the

Heartache house because Patrick had that number, too. She had planned an extended hiatus from dating and men since she didn't trust her judgment anymore.

Sometimes, she woke up punching her pillow in a fury, and it had been half a year since she'd found out he was a lying cheat. If she hadn't loved him—hadn't thought for sure he'd been about to propose and seen for herself how gooey and blind that had made her—she might have been able to control the anger better. But knowing she'd been played for a fool, that she'd been in love with an illusion, rocked her.

"I know." Heather sighed, removing one of the silk daisies to wrap around her wrist in an impromptu bracelet, an accessory that actually looked pretty cute with her sunshine-yellow blazer and jean capris. "But I'd gotten into a good groove with my students here and part of me worries you're only sending me out to shop because you don't want to end up on the same plane as Patrick or something weird like that."

A gifted singer and musician, Heather had never pursued her love of music other than to give lessons to locals. Erin hoped that one day her sister would make the trip north to Nashville to live out her own dreams.

"That *is* very weird." Although no stranger than hyperventilating near airports. "And totally untrue. Patrick's wife probably has him on a choke chain these days. For all I know, he changed jobs or moved." She shrugged, genuinely not caring about her former lover's life. She cared more about his kids, whom she'd never met. The guilt sneaked up on her at odd times.

"Okay." Biting her lip as she studied Erin, Heather turned back to the bicycle basket and plucked another daisy. "I'm going to go." She wrapped it around Erin's wrist. "And I'm not going to think about you spending 24/7 on the store expansion, which I know you're going to do without me around to force you to go home. You love that sledgehammer too much."

Erin smiled in spite of herself while Heather took a photo of their matching wrists with her phone. Her sister might be bossy, but she meant well. Heather was practical, organized and the business mind behind Last Chance Vintage. She also happened to be much better with their mother—a calming presence that soothed Diana Finley's fractious nerves. Erin had always envied Heather's ease with their mom.

"Awesome." Erin gave her a quick hug. "If you leave now, you can still grab a coffee for the road. Plus, I hear there's a storm coming in tonight. It would be good to stay ahead of it."

Heather peered outside at weather that had gotten more overcast as the day had gone on.

"Right." Heather frowned, tucking her phone back in her shoulder bag. "I just worry you won't follow through on the promotions I've set up."

Erin suppressed a groan, and instead recited the mental list. "Dress sale on the first Tuesday of the month, free champagne for shoppers during Friday lunch hours and thirty percent off anything spring-related next week."

"Yes, fine." Heather nodded absently, her heavy turquoise earrings rocking against her curtain of long red curls. "But I mean the press releases about the grand reopening for the updated store and the social media presence I'm trying to maintain. I've sent out a lot of feelers to try and attract some media attention. We need to bolster that stuff to support the expansion."

Erin tried not to grind her teeth. She and her sister could not be more diametrically opposed on this issue. The last thing Erin wanted was to turn a kitschy small-town boutique into some regional shopping mecca. But retreading old ground now would not get Heather out the door.

"I will probably not do as good a job as you, but I will try." She stretched her lips into what she hoped passed for a reassuring smile.

She held her breath.

"Fair enough," Heather said finally, and surprised the hell out of Erin by picking up her suitcase. "Austin, Texas, here I come."

When Heather swished out the door, the welcome bell ringing in her absence, Erin slumped against the front counter. She was too mentally exhausted to celebrate that she'd ousted her sister before Heather's wise eyes had seen through the Goth-girl hair and the sledgehammer-wielding nights to the truth that Erin was still a broken mess and not really over a lying scumbag she should hate with a passion.

How long would it take for her brain to get the message Patrick's wife had delivered so succinctly six months ago? He was the antithesis of everything Erin hoped for in a man. But some days, it was hard to reconcile that image of him with the guy she'd fallen for, possibly because she'd never confronted him about it, had purposely avoided any interaction with him ever again. She'd never gotten to see his expression as she called him on his lies, never gotten the chance to see the charming facade fall away.

Maybe that would have helped her to hate him more.

Okay, she actually hated him quite a bit.

And that was the whole problem. She wanted desperately not to care.

Until then, she would simply keep moving forward, building her new life here and hoping that by walling out the rest of the world, she'd finally find some peace.

REMY WELDON HAD never seen fog like this. It had come from out of nowhere in the past two hours, causing his visibility to shrink. It looked as though someone had dumped a few metric tons of wet cotton balls along the back roads of central Tennessee. In theory, he was scouting locations for one of his shows that was floundering in ratings—*Interstate Antiquer.* But since he couldn't see what street he was on, he didn't hold out hope he'd see much of the shop he'd been searching for, Last Chance Vintage.

In his six years as a TV producer, he'd never had a show plummet in viewership so fast, but then, he'd never had a successful show's host walk away midseason to make a documentary on a turn-of-the-century American painter. As if that film project would lift the guy's career more than Remy's show? Either way, Remy was at his wit's end trying to patch together the rest of the contracted shows with guest hosts while doing the heavy lifting himself on everything from location scouting to script development.

Everything sucked. Much like the thick gray fog that cloaked the headlights on his crappy rental car. Much like life since his wife had died two years ago and he'd relocated from Louisiana to Miami to escape the memories. There seemed to be no end to gray fog and suck-age.

"Arriving at destination," his GPS informed him with obnoxious cheeriness, her electronic voice sounding smug at having landed him in a downpour thick with rain, fog and inky darkness.

If he was truly near Last Chance Vintage—one of ten businesses he planned to scout this trip—there was no sign of it outside the car window. Then again, he could barely see the road in front of him as he braked to a stop, the headlights picking up a drain in the street where water rushed from all sides. He must be near a curb.

Shutting off the engine, Remy sat for a minute, letting the stress of the drive slide off his shoulders. He'd been away from his home in Miami for three days already—long enough to be apart from his adopted daughter. Liv's daughter. His first priority should be—and was—taking care of Sarah until she finished high school and started college. But since her mom had died, he'd struggled with being overprotective to the point of overbearing. He was trying to return to a more regular travel schedule even though being away from his daughter made him uneasy after what had happened to his wife.

In fact, if he thought about it too long—knowing full well Sarah was staying with extremely responsible friends of the family—he stood a very real chance of a panic attack while sitting on the side of the road.

She was safe. She was safe. She was safe...

The mantra didn't work as fast as Remy needed it to, memories of his wife's death—while home alone—returning too fast for him to block them out. Two years wasn't too long to grieve. Not when

Liv's death had been Remy's fault. He hadn't been home when two drifters had shown up, targeting their home for easy-to-pawn goods and cash. They'd known about the house thanks to a shared jail cell with Sarah's biological father, Brandon, who was doing time at a medium-security facility for some kind of hacking crime. The guy had bragged that his ex-girlfriend had struck it rich when she had married, spilling details about the new house Remy had built in Lafayette, Louisiana.

The weight on his chest increased, the air in his lungs leaving in a rush of breath and fear.

Feeling along the passenger seat in the darkened car interior, he found his cell phone and punched in the speed dial code for his daughter. He'd be all right once he heard her voice. God, let her be okay…

Dialing. The device showed it was dialing. And dialing.

Then the call screen disappeared and returned to his home page. Remy punched in her number again. Only to repeat the process.

How far away from civilization was he that he couldn't grab a cell signal? The delay did zero for the onslaught of panic. He snatched up his phone and keys and shoved open the car door, heading out into the rain. A stupid idea. Except he needed to get in touch with Sarah. Now.

Torrents of water streamed from the sky, soaking him instantly. The street was a rushing river, filling his shoes and plastering the hem of his pants legs to his ankles.

He was a dumbass. This fear was irrational. And so real he didn't give a shit. Maybe he'd get a better signal if he got out of the rain.

Crossing the street, he could make out the shape of buildings—red brick and clapboard side by side. A few awnings shielded him from some of the rain, but not enough that he trusted using his phone without ruining it. He cursed the rain, his luck and the growing fear in his chest. He picked up his pace and sloshed along the cobblestones, hoping to see a pay phone. Talk about an antique… What were the chances he'd find one?

Thwack! Thwack!

A series of sharp sounds cut through the rumble of the deluge. *Thwack! Thwack!*

He tracked the noise to his left and saw a dull glow from a glass storefront with a bicycle in the front window. Last Chance Vintage was painted in purple-and-red-striped letters. Relieved to finally find the place after hours of looking, he tried to remember what he'd read about it. His notes had said the business was owned by sisters, but he didn't recall much more than that. Probably two old maids with blue hair and double-stranded pearls.

Thwack! Thwack!

The sound definitely came from inside, and judging by the light emanating behind an opaque sheet of plastic near the register, he guessed a construction crew was doing some work after hours. He lifted his fist to bang on the door with one hand while he pushed the brass doorbell with the other. Whoever was making that racket inside might not hear otherwise—

Shadows moved behind the plastic sheet, but Remy's eye was already on the corded phone on the counter right near a cash register circa 1920. When the sheet moved, a woman emerged in overalls and safety goggles, carrying a bright orange nail gun. No doubt that accounted for the noise.

Remy lifted a hand in a sorry excuse for a wave. He hoped he didn't scare her away. He probably looked like an intruder. His throat closed up tight as the young woman pulled off the safety goggles and strode toward the door. He half wished she wouldn't let him in—what the hell was she thinking opening the door to a total stranger after hours?—but he needed to call Sarah. Some days were worse than others since Liv's death and this was turning out to be one of the worst ones.

It was difficult traveling away from home.

The door opened and the woman stood back to admit him. The scent of wood shavings and stain was heavy in the warm interior air.

"Can I help you?" She fixed him with knockout blue eyes, the soft color a surprise feminine detail next to the baggy jean overalls and shapeless dark tee underneath. Her jet-black hair was purposefully shaded and cut in a razor-sharp line just above her shoulders.

Definitely not an old maid.

"I can't get a cell signal out here." Remy didn't cross the threshold despite the open door.

His wife had been murdered during a home robbery while he was away from home for work. Seeing this total stranger, this *vulnerable* stranger, open the door to him was messing with his head.

"Come in!" The woman waved him forward impatiently. "You're getting rain all over the floor."

"I can give you the number," he offered, his feet feeling as if they were stuck in concrete. "You could make the call for me, if you'd feel more comfortable having me wait outside—"

"I am *most* comfortable not having the hardwood ruined." She stepped forward to grab the door and gestured emphatically for him to come inside.

He forced his feet to move, grateful to get out of the rain.

She shoved the door closed and toed the welcome mat closer to him. "Here. I'll get you a towel and you can use the phone." She rummaged in a basket beneath one of the display shelves and retrieved a couple of rumpled terry cloth rags. "I'm Erin Finley, by the way. One of the owners. You must be from out of town?"

"Remy Weldon, from Miami." He mopped off his face and hands, knowing the rest of him was a lost cause. "Sorry to bother you—"

"It's no bother." She was already grabbing the phone and yanking free some extra cord so she could bring it to him while he stood on the mat. "I'm glad I could help. It's a small-town thing, you know? Be nice to strangers and all that."

She shrugged a shoulder as if it was no big deal, and something about the gesture hinted at the feminine curves beneath the overalls, catching him off guard. He hadn't noticed women in anything but the most detached way in a long time.

Dropping the heavy, old-fashioned phone into his hands, Erin gave him a fleeting smile.

Remy swallowed hard, his thoughts all over the place. The anxiety in the car had spiraled into worries about a total stranger opening the door to him, and now this surprise awareness of her. He gripped the phone tighter.

"I didn't mean to stand outside and let the rain in for so long," he said finally, his brain clearly short-circuiting. "I—ah—didn't think…"

And then no words freaking came. Remy Weldon, who'd built a career on his ability to get funding for any show and sweet-talk talent into any role, gaped like a fish out of water.

Not that Erin seemed to notice. She was too busy running a hand over the wooden molding on the front of the checkout counter. Pressing a thumb over one raised spot, she lifted her nail gun to the wood and—*thwack!*—put the trim back into place.

She looked at him. "I figure it's safe enough to let a stranger inside when I'm the one carrying the air nail framer with enough compression power to staple your hands to the wall." Her mouth stretched into a smile that he bet some guys would find intimidating. "That is, if I needed to."

"Awesome. Good thinking." He liked Erin immediately. Not only because she thought about a weapon to bring to the door, but also because she didn't seem to notice the fits and starts of his speech that had plagued him the past two years. Bad enough to be caught thinking about his wife in the middle of a meeting and have everyone's expression turn embarrassed, impatient or—worse— pitying. But then, to stumble over his own words or realize he'd lost his place in the conversation completely? He hated that.

Dialing his daughter's phone number, Remy already felt his heart rate slowing. Some of the weight stopped crushing his chest.

"Daddy?" Sarah sounded surprised. "It's late."

He checked his watch and realized it was midnight. Crap.

"Sorry." He lowered his voice even though Erin was halfway across the store, her fingers traveling over more molding around a set of bay windows. "I didn't realize how late it was and I had trouble getting a call out in a storm. Everything okay there?"

His daughter's exasperated sigh sounded more like a growl. With teens, the intonation of a sigh could be all you had to decode a mood sometimes.

"Fine. Everything is fine as always, and you can't call in the middle of the night to check on me or you might wake up Mr. and Mrs. Stedder—Unless you're calling to invite me on your scouting trip?"

She sounded so hopeful Remy hated to say no. She'd been asking that a lot lately. Why did his work travel suddenly interest her? She'd resented it mightily when he had stayed home for over a year after Liv's death, needing to keep tabs on their daughter. Going back to work hadn't been easy.

"Not this time, Sarah. And I thought you had a big field trip with some kids from school this week?" He wasn't home as much as he'd like to be, but he tried to pay attention to her school activities.

"Right. Whatever. Dad, I'm tired of being at the Stedders all the time. I could help you—"

"Tomorrow, okay?" He didn't want to get into a disagreement now, not after how worried he'd been. He just needed his life to feel normal again tonight.

"Tomorrow? While I'm on an overnight field trip?"

"When you get home." He wished he could get on a flight home. Now. "I promise."

Disconnecting the call, he hoped Sarah understood. She'd been through so much.

He'd love to surprise her and show up in Miami by the time she was back from the field trip. Except he hadn't scouted jack squat for locations unless Erin Finley could be talked into a spot.

The nail-gun-wielding store proprietor would be a great guest. Everything about the store was perfect, too, except he didn't see many antiques besides those used as decor.

He set the store's phone on a shelf—a shelf that used a tarnished silver cake stand to display an assortment of brooches from cameos to cubic zirconia cartoon cats. The store seemed to be a hybrid consignment shop where used and new items rubbed elbows comfortably. On second glance, he realized the "shelf" was actually a repurposed plantation shutter.

He definitely wanted to discuss the show with Erin, but dripping wet on her floor at midnight didn't seem like the best way to make a pitch.

"Thank you," he called over to her.

"All done?" She finished driving a few more nails into a piece of trim around a window casing and then strode over.

"Yes. Guess I need to try and find a hotel." He turned back toward the glass door and stared into the darkness. "Sounds as though it might be slowing down."

"Wishful thinking. And you might have to head back to Franklin for a hotel. Heartache just has a bed-and-breakfast, but Tansy Whittaker might not answer the door at this hour if you don't have a reservation." Erin carefully switched the safety on her nail gun and set the tool on a peeling green apothecary cabinet. "She told me she runs a white-noise machine at night because it masks the sound of the most, er, enthusiastic newlyweds' vacations."

"Right." He wondered vaguely if she was flirting with him. No. The risqué reference was just normal conversation. "That makes me all the more grateful you heard when I knocked."

"I don't like surprises anymore." Her voice had an edge to it as she leaned down to reach for something alongside him, her sudden proximity bringing the scent of her perfume and freshly cut lumber. She had a tattoo of a bluebird at the top of her spine just below her hairline. "Here."

He looked at what she had handed him. A plain black umbrella. His gaze moved to the wrought iron stand near the door where two other umbrellas remained.

"Thanks, but I don't want to take yours—"

"You're a tough man to help, you know that?" She rested a hand on one hip and surveyed him through narrowed eyes. "All of those umbrellas have been there for at least a year, so I assure you, no one will be back to claim it now."

"Then…thank you." He tucked it under his arm. He didn't have trouble accepting help. Much. "I might try the local place first, but I appreciate the tip about Franklin. Would you have time to meet tomorrow? I actually might be in the market for some specialty antiques."

He liked to play it safe when interviewing prospective guests for a show. That way, if something didn't pan out or they didn't have the right temperament for television, there were no hard feelings afterward. But damn…if he could firm things up with Erin's place and two more dealers, he could justify the trip and head home.

"Sure. Stop by anytime. If you want to block out some uninterrupted time, though, we'll have to meet after five. We close early tomorrow, but I'm the only one here until then."

"Great. Five sounds good." He had made business appointments hundreds of times in his line of work. But this one felt oddly personal. Partly because Erin didn't know the real purpose of his visit and might assume he simply wanted an excuse to see her again. But maybe also because they were alone at midnight with the steady hum of rain drowning out the rest of the world.

"Until then, safe travels, Remy Weldon." Erin

stuck a hand out to save him from his stupid line of thinking.

Right. This was business and he was just over-tired. He took her hand and shook it. A brief, warm contact that was there and then gone.

"Thanks for everything." He really did owe her big-time. If there was any way that *Interstate Antiquer* could put her store on the map and improve her business, he planned to make that happen. He owed her that much for her kindness.

But as he turned to head out into the storm—a black umbrella now sheltering his head—he wasn't thinking much about her business. Instead, he saw cornflower blue eyes and the wry smile of a sharp, self-possessed woman who didn't play games.

It made him uneasy to think he wasn't going to put her out of his mind anytime soon.

CHAPTER TWO

THE STORE WAS surprisingly busy the next day, keeping Erin on her toes all morning and well into the afternoon. She hardly had time to think about her visitor from the previous night, which was just as well since Remy Weldon had occupied far too much mental real estate the night before.

Just when she thought she'd beaten her libido into permanent submission, a compelling stranger had to enter her store with a cleft in his chin and a trace of a sexy Cajun accent. She told herself he was just a test of her new powers of restraint—a six-foot-plus hazel-eyed handsome man dropped into her path just so she could prove to herself she'd learned her lesson about attraction to men from out of town. But it unsettled her that a shared smile could make her pulse flutter.

"Miss?" a woman called from behind one of the dressing room curtains shortly before closing time. "Could I get your opinion on an outfit?"

Erin was only too glad to shove thoughts of Remy to the farthest reaches of her mind.

"Be right there." She excused herself from another customer—a thrifty local who came in mostly to barter and browse—and hurried over to the middle of three curtained dressing areas. "Should I come in or do you want to step out?"

"If you could come in." The curtain was swept partially aside and Erin noted the woman's thin hands and worn nail polish.

A tiny size two at most, the customer had been in the store for about twenty minutes and had spent a long time searching through the clearance rack. Erin saw now that she had five items on hangers while a too-big dress slouched on her trim frame. From her worn shoes and scuffed bag, Erin guessed maybe she was an overworked mom looking for a bargain outfit to spruce up her wardrobe, but Erin tried not to make too many assumptions about clients. Sometimes the ones who dressed the most humbly or spent their money the most carefully were the secret millionaires.

"Would you like me to look for some smaller sizes?" Erin offered.

"There aren't any." The woman bit her lip. "Not on the clearance rack, anyway."

Something about the dark worry in her eyes made Erin wonder what the dress was for.

"We're having a dress sale, though. Thirty percent off—"

"It's not enough to make anything else affordable." She shook her head and turned to face herself in the mirror. She pinched a handful of fabric at her waist to pull the blue cotton jersey tighter to her body. "But I sew well enough. I can take this in."

"Oh." Erin tried to picture the simple shirtwaist dress with a few adjustments. "If you can do that and maybe trim the bodice a little—"

"Do you think it's right for a job interview?" Worry lines creased her forehead.

"For what kind of job?" Erin tried to keep one ear tuned to the sales floor in case anyone else needed her help. At least she didn't have to worry about theft since Heartache was a safe small town where the local police spent more time directing traffic at church functions than they did solving crimes.

"Finleys'—the home building supply store— advertised for a bookkeeper."

Erin smiled. "That's my brother's store. It will be Scott or his wife, Bethany, who interviews you." Her smile faded as she remembered why they probably needed a bookkeeper. Their marriage had been teetering on the verge of divorce this year. Bethany normally handled the books. "I think this will be a great dress for an interview, although if you have a jacket—"

"I *don't* have a jacket." The woman's voice was tight as she shook her head, a limp strand of pale blond hair sliding loose from the tight ponytail. "I can't afford more than the dress. This is a lot to spend on a job I might not get."

"You definitely don't need a jacket," Erin blurted, sensing she'd touched a nerve. "I think you could style this a lot of ways—"

Her customer slumped onto the small wooden stool in one corner of the dressing room. "I don't even have shoes to go with this. Or a bag." She covered her face with both hands and shook her head. "Don't mind me. I didn't mean to have a meltdown in your nice store."

"It's okay." Erin's heart went out to the woman, whatever her story. Erin had been blessed. She had never had those kinds of financial worries, and she hated to think she had neighbors who fought battles like that. "Can I get you a tissue or—"

"No!" Her head lifted, and although there were tears on her cheeks, her eyes blazed with a fresh determination. "God, no. I am *not* crying over my rat bastard ex-boyfriend who took everything when he ditched his son and me to screw his home-wrecking whore of a secretary."

She swiped her face fiercely to get rid of all trace of moisture while Erin reeled from her words. Even six months after finding out she'd accidentally cheated with a married father of two, the accusation of "home-wrecking whore" jabbed her chest as sharply as if it had been meant for her.

Kind of like this woman had peeked into Erin's personal ghost closet.

"I—" Her voice faltered. "I'm sorry to hear that."

"I'm sorry to live it." She stood abruptly, brushing over the skirt of the dress with her hands. "And I didn't mean to make myself at home in the dress when I haven't even bought it. It's lovely, but maybe I'd better think it over before I buy anything."

Erin wanted to help the woman even more than she'd wanted to assist Remy Weldon the night before. She'd given Remy a helping hand out of common courtesy. But the need to give something back to this woman went deeper than that—a personal need to soothe over some of the guilt in her heart.

"The store is actually hosting a big Dress for Success event later this month," Erin lied, unsure about the name, but remembering an article describing an organization that provided professional attire to disadvantaged women. She'd thought about doing something similar in the past but had gotten busy with renovations. "I've been collecting clothes for it for weeks."

That wasn't true, either. But personal pride could be a hard-won commodity, and she didn't want to injure this woman's by making it sound as if she wanted to give her a handout.

The woman tilted her chin at Erin, her thin arms folded tight. "I've never heard of it."

"It's an event that gives women who've had a

hard time the chance to choose a nice outfit for a job interview. You know, help them get ahead?" She tried to gauge the woman's expression. "It's exactly for women who have rat bastard exes in their past."

"Is that so?" Pushing at the sleeves of the too-big dress, the blonde smiled. "It would definitely save me a lot of time if I didn't have to take in an outfit. Do you think you'll have any smaller sizes?"

"I'm positive we do." Erin's brain worked fast to calculate how long it would take her to pull off something like this and make it a success. "I planned to unveil the project later this month, but since I've already got inventory for it, why don't you come back and take a look at it—when is your interview?"

"Monday."

Erin would have to shuffle aside everything else in her schedule to research this. She had off-season inventory at home, and she could raid friends' closets.

"Why don't you come by Friday after the shop closes and you can take a peek at what I've got in the storeroom?" The toughest part would be coming up with enough shoes, bags and accessories to make it look as though she'd been collecting for a while. "Er, what size shoe are you?"

"Seven and a half." The woman extended her hand. "I'm Jamie Raybourn, by the way. This is really kind of you."

"Erin Finley. And it's no problem. You'll do better at the interview if you feel happy about what you're wearing, and the cool thing about this program is that women can come back for work clothes once they land a job."

"Really?" Jamie's one raised eyebrow suggested she was skeptical, and it made Erin sad to think the woman didn't believe she'd ever get a break. She fiddled with the price tag on the dress she still wore.

"Yes. It's a great program." Or it would be when Erin got done with it. "I'd better get back to the front counter. But you'll be here on Friday?"

Erin wanted to help. Needed to help. Even if she wasn't desperate to somehow alleviate the guilt she felt about another mother with a bastard for a husband, Erin had been raised to be civic-minded and care for her community. Her father's long stint as Heartache's mayor had instilled that kind of community awareness in all the Finleys.

Jamie smiled and shrugged narrow shoulders out of the blue jersey dress. "I will. Thank you so much."

Erin sidled out through the gap in the curtain on one side, careful not to flash her half-dressed customer. She worried a little about pulling off a small clothing drive in the next few days, let alone organizing the storage area enough to allow a client in there to browse some inventory. Expanding

Last Chance Vintage meant a lot of furnishings and display items were tucked in storage to stay out of the way of drywall, sanding and painting projects.

Renovation work would have to wait a little longer because right now, Erin had a more important focus. Maybe helping Jamie—and other women like her—would put Erin on a more positive path to forgiving herself for being a blind idiot about Patrick.

And if not? At least she was doing something constructive with her time, unlike all the months she had wasted loving some guy who'd done nothing but lie to her.

Ducking behind the front counter, Erin grabbed her cell phone and sent out her first SOS text to start collecting clothes. If she acted fast, maybe she could coerce some friends into cleaning out their closets tonight and she could make the rounds in the morning to pick things up. Too bad her sister-in-law, Bethany, was one of the few "size two" women Erin knew. She couldn't let Jamie walk into an interview with Bethany while wearing her sister-in-law's former clothes.

Erin was just closing out the register and flipping the sign on the front door when Remy Weldon pulled up in a white sedan with out-of-state plates. Her hand paused on the Open sign, her attention thoroughly captured by the sight of him unfolding his long, lean frame from the vehicle.

He'd held plenty of appeal the night before with his dress shirt plastered to his chest and shoulders from the rain. Today, clean and pressed in a gray suit with a pale blue shirt open at the neck, he was a whole different kind of handsome. Something about the suit and the crisp shirt cuffs peeking out from the sleeves as he moved reminded her of Patrick and all the things she'd once admired about him. His sharp, professional appearance. His travel wardrobe that could fold down into the smallest possible roll-away bag.

Remy lifted a hand in acknowledgment when he spotted her. Her heart rate jumped a little at his smile, a fact that irritated her more than she would have liked. Opening the door, she concentrated on the fact he was just a client like any other. And he'd be on his way back to Miami before she knew it.

"I hardly recognize you when you're not sopping wet," she called by way of greeting. As soon as she said it, she had a schoolgirl moment where she panicked the words could be construed as having a sexual undertone.

But no. Just because her *thoughts* had sexual undertones didn't mean her words did.

"That's a coincidence." He paused a few steps away from her and seemed to take her measure, his hazel eyes doing a slow tour. "Because I hardly recognize you without the overalls and safety goggles."

He wasn't flirting. Probably just being amusing. But his attractiveness skewed the conversation in a weird way, and it didn't help that she didn't have the goggles and overalls to hide behind. Suddenly self-conscious, she turned and headed inside.

"Come on in," she called over her shoulder, hoping she was behaving normally and not like a junior high school girl. "I have a table in the back where we can discuss what you're looking for."

She heard the shop bell ring behind him as the door shut, sealing them inside the empty store. Alone again, just like the night before.

"I appreciate you making time for me today." Remy's tone had shifted to all business as he followed her past the open pie safe full of vintage linens. He gripped a dark leather folder in one hand. Was he going to take notes? Or maybe he had pictures to show her the kinds of items he collected.

"Antiques are my business." She switched off her phone since it was already buzzing with incoming texts, no doubt replies from her friends about the last-minute clothing drive. "I'm happy to help."

She gestured to an old kitchen chair repurposed with a leather seat that was pulled up to a high workstation with drawers full of swatches, samples and assorted cabinetry hardware. Occasionally, she refinished furniture here or re-covered old lamp shades with new material.

"You seem to be involved in a lot more than

antiques," he observed, gesturing to the racks of vintage clothing dotting the store just outside the alcove where they sat across from one another.

"I have a wide variety of interests." A quality she'd inherited from her mother.

"Everything from construction to retail." He winked at her, but the charm felt a little too practiced.

She knew she was a cynic, but she had an odd feeling about this meeting. Why the added charm if he wasn't flirting with her?

"Can you tell me what you're looking for?" She folded her hands on the scarred wooden surface of the worktable, trying to keep the meeting on track.

"I'm the producer for a television show called *Interstate Antiquer.*" He slid a business card across the table with the logo of a show she recognized from one of the home improvement cable channels. "I'm on a scouting trip this week in central Tennessee, hoping to line up some stops for our host."

Did that mean a big sale for her store? She was even more curious now and also grateful for the new barrier to her attraction for him. She couldn't act on the attraction if they were working together.

"You need antiques for the show?" She tried to recall the format of the program but wasn't sure if she'd seen it.

"We need stores to feature. We would film at least a full day's worth of footage in Last Chance

Vintage to give our viewers a chance to see you work with the customers and what kinds of things you sell or trade—"

"Is that why you were in the rain outside my store last night? As part of your scouting trip?" It reminded her of the telemarketing calls where the sales rep launched into a friendly chat as though you were old friends before identifying himself. "You drove through here to find antiques shops?"

Any flirtation she'd imagined on his part had been an illusion. He was here only on business. She should be grateful she didn't need to worry about any romantic distraction—he would not test her willpower regarding handsome men. But irritation niggled.

"Last Chance Vintage was on my list of places to see. Yes."

"Yet you didn't mention it." Was it too much to ask for people to be forthright about who they were and what they wanted? Even knowing that she was overreacting didn't stop her from feeling… deceived. "I thought you were here on business."

"I am here on business." He reached into his folder and pulled out a piece of paper.

"Television is your business, not mine. I'm renovating the store while my sister is out of town, and I have to run daily operations, too. That doesn't leave time for much else." She scooped up her cell phone and stood. "Maybe when my sister returns, she could do it. She has more personal charm than me and I'm not really what you'd call viewer-friendly."

"Wait." Remy rose, as well, his lean height and well-tailored suit making her feel short and frumpy. "These spots are usually very good for a store's bottom line, Erin. Did you want to check with your partner before you say no? She's the one who brought your shop to our attention. And we can't reschedule our whole central Tennessee spotlight until she returns."

He handed her the piece of paper he'd withdrawn from the leather folder, and she recognized the Last Chance Vintage logo at the top of the letterhead. A note from Heather. No doubt her sister had worked hard to gain this kind of exposure.

Heather would kill her for turning down an opportunity like this just because Erin felt deceived that Remy Weldon hadn't been forthright. Heather was always working on promo opportunities from the store, a part of the business Erin gave little attention.

"I don't understand." She stopped. Setting Heather's letter aside, Erin folded her arms across her chest. "Why didn't you tell me last night that you were in town to look at Last Chance Vintage for the show?"

"Two reasons." He tipped one shoulder against the doorjamb, looking oddly at ease in spite of the hand-sewn floral aprons fluttering in the breeze from an oscillating fan nearby. "First, I don't always advertise my business in case the store I'm researching turns out to be a glorified junk shop or the owners are difficult to work with."

She supposed that made sense.

"And two, I was a road-weary zombie last night when I walked in here. I wasn't thinking straight." His smile returned, the one that made the cleft in his chin deepen. "I got distracted by the nail gun and figured we could just sort things out today."

What was it about his Cajun accent that slid along her skin like a soothing touch?

"I don't want to be on camera." She had survived childhood as one of five children by learning never to be the center of attention. It was an MO that worked for her.

Her mom's battles with bipolar issues had given her a big personality that overshadowed the rest of the household. For Erin, being the center of attention meant someone might notice her shortcomings, so she had always taken behind-the-scenes jobs in the family. The habit had rolled into the rest of her life. Heather kept things organized, Erin tried to help quietly on the sides and their youngest sister, Amy, had bailed on the family at the first opportunity, declaring herself an emancipated minor at seventeen and never looking back.

"So where's Heather?" Remy peered around the shop as if she might walk out of a back room at any moment. "Maybe she can be the voice of the store on the show."

"She's on a buying trip. She won't be back for four to six weeks." Erin hated to let her sister down. She felt she'd been one disappointment after another to her family lately, starting with not showing up for that dinner with Mr. Right six months ago. She'd kept a low profile ever since, using store renovations as an excuse for skipping out on family events. "How soon will you want to film a spot?"

He frowned. "Normally, I'd have a longer lead time. But my host quit a few weeks ago and some of the spots pulled out when he did."

"Meaning?"

"I just tentatively confirmed with a store in Franklin for next week. I could do the shoot with Last Chance Vintage right afterward. Maybe nine days from now?" He pulled out his phone as if to give her a date.

"No way," she blurted. "I know Heather would love the promo, but not with the store still draped in plastic." She was relieved, actually, because the renovation provided a concrete excuse for saying no, instead of being camera shy.

Or afraid her ex would see her on television and try to contact her.

"You're sure?" Remy straightened, his fingers pausing over the screen on his phone.

"The store expansion isn't complete. Plus, I just

committed to holding a big Dress for Success event here. It's an initiative to help make sure disadvantaged women have help putting together a wardrobe for job interviews and transitioning back to work," she explained. "Which means I need to really focus on that instead of finishing the store renovations."

"You can't get me out of your hair fast enough, can you?" Grinning, Remy pocketed his phone and slid the leather folder under one arm. "I won't pretend I'm not disappointed, Erin, because you've got a really unique place here. And we could have increased your clothing drive donations by about one hundred percent." He extended his hand to shake hers. "But I respect your decision."

Her mind still stuck on the "one hundred percent increase" remark, Erin held out her hand before she braced herself for Remy's touch. The warm strength of a male hand wrapped around hers made a feminine instinct quicken inside her.

Damn him. She pulled her hand back quickly.

"Good luck with your show." She was sure he'd find another store to take her place, although her pride in her business also forced her to admit that his second choice couldn't possibly be as good. She'd worked hard to make Last Chance Vintage unique.

He nodded, still smiling. A handsome man who could surely find dozens of store owners who'd love to invite him into their place of business for a few days. Watching him walk away, Erin wondered if she would be able to handle the guilt of knowing she'd just refused the best possible assistance for her Dress for Success event.

Double damn him.

REMY WASN'T THE kind of guy to gloat.

But he hadn't gotten this far as a producer without knowing how to read people. And he was almost positive that Erin Finley wouldn't let him drive away. He'd seen it in her eyes when he'd told her his show would have improved her chances of a successful clothing drive.

Erin showed the world a tough exterior with her overalls, nail guns and the inky-black dye job. But those pale blue eyes of hers were a window to a whole different woman inside.

"Wait." She called to him just as he shoved open the front door, the welcome bell still chiming over his head.

And even though he wasn't the kind of guy to gloat, he made sure to keep his features neutral before he turned, because he needed this too badly to screw it up now. He'd had wealth to spare at one point in his life, but he'd personally financed a manhunt and a reward for his wife's killer. Between that and unloading their extravagant Louisiana home for well under market value simply to get rid of it, he wasn't in the same place financially as he'd been a few years ago. Plus, with private-school bills for Sarah and college just around the corner, he couldn't afford a failing show.

"Yes?" He hoped like hell Erin would say yes. Viewers were going to love her, and he needed that kind of ratings spike to keep the show afloat into next season. He still had two other successful shows to his credit, so he'd find a way to make things work personally. But a lot of other people counted on this show for their livelihood and he refused to let a good program fail just because his host walked away.

"You really think an appearance on *Interstate Antiquer* will boost the Dress for Success event that much?" She wore a long black ballerina skirt and a white T-shirt with a cartoon monkey on it.

How could he *not* smile at the thought of her—dressed like that—being so concerned about a clothing drive meant to put struggling women into professional business attire? She was made-for-TV perfection. He still knew what made for good TV, even if he hadn't been flexing his creative muscle the past two years.

"I do." He dropped his folder on the raised platform that held the store window display of an antique bicycle, vintage picnic basket and an assortment of mismatched dishes. "Shops that do this show get calls from all over the country about pieces in their stores—not just items we feature. Viewers see random stuff in the edge of the frame and decide they have to buy it."

Erin nodded slowly. "That means I could sell a lot. How do you know people will donate a lot?"

"On one episode, we had a shop owner in a dated wheelchair who had some trouble navigating it around his inventory. He had three new chairs show up the next day and twelve more offers for upgrades by email within the week." That show had been a turning point for Remy's anger during his grieving for Liv. Seeing the outpouring of caring had restored some faith in humanity. "Wheelchairs are expensive and we never suggested the guy needed a new one in the show. Can you imagine the kind of support you'd get on a drive where we invite people to be involved?"

He watched her flip her phone from hand to hand, thinking it over, obviously still full of reservations. He was surprised that someone who seemed so sure of herself could be this nervous about being on television. In the era of selfies and YouTube, he didn't meet many people who were afraid of the camera anymore.

"What about the repairs?" she asked. "Will you try not to show that my store is all torn up?" She stalked toward the front counter and eyed the heavy plastic dividing the current store from the space she was renovating.

"We can avoid shooting it if you want." He followed her, telling himself he was only curious about what was behind the curtain. "But viewers aren't interested in seeing perfect places or perfect people. They respond to what's real. They relate better to people who work hard just like they do. Seeing the process of building the business can be a part of the appeal."

"Is that so? That hardly explains why every other show on TV is about Hollywood wives or teenage billionaires." She set her phone down on the front counter and ran her fingers over a basket of polished gemstones sitting by the register.

He picked up a smooth green gem. They were worry stones with sayings on them—*luck, happiness, joy*. As soon as his hand went in the basket, hers darted away.

"Erin, people don't watch those shows to see Hollywood wives being happy and pampered, though, do they? They want to see catfights and back-talking kids. They want to see the reality behind the glamour." His hand stalled on a stone that read "Wisdom" and fought the urge to pocket it.

He had the feeling spending more time with Erin would not be wise for him.

"There will be no catfights in my episode," she announced, walking away from him toward the construction area. "I'm putting that in my contract."

"I don't imagine anyone would mess with you

after they've seen you with a nail gun anyhow." He followed her to the plastic sheeting. "But I'll make a note of it just to be safe. Although you never know what might happen if two people are drop-dead set on getting the same item. Think about those wedding dress reality shows."

"Will you be staying in town until the shooting begins for the Franklin store?" She pulled aside the curtain to show him the other half of Last Chance Vintage.

"It depends how fast I can bring on a third business to feature." He whistled at the space she'd unveiled. "Wow."

The adjoining room looked like a turn-of-the-century general store, the walls lined with open shelving, drawers and bins. A waist-high counter stood a few feet in front of the wall shelves, the dark wood polished to a high sheen. A rolling ladder leaned against one set of shelves. An antique sewing machine sat on a black tea cart and an ancient cash register was parked on one of the counters. A few cast-iron lanterns hung from rafters.

"Pretty cool, right?" Erin was the most relaxed he'd seen her all day. "This was the candy store when I was growing up. Well, I guess they sold cards and drugstore stuff, too. But all those shelves were full of candy jars."

Her eyes sparkled at the memory, as if she had come alive. He could see what drove her work on the renovations. Maybe what drove the whole passion for antiques.

"Sounds like kid heaven." He followed her across the polished hardwood floor that looked recently refinished. Or maybe it was just the scent of wood stain that still hung heavy in the air.

"We would spend half a Sunday afternoon debating how to best use fifty cents." Smoothing a hand along a countertop, she spun to a sudden stop.

"We?" He paused right behind her, close enough that the top layer of her ballerina skirt brushed against his leg.

"My brothers and sisters and me." She propped her elbows on the counter and watched him with a steady gaze.

"How many would that be?" He pulled open a shallow drawer under one of the countertops.

"Five in all. Two brothers, two sisters and me. But, er—here." She popped open one of the bins on the front of a shelf, her shift back to neutral topics an obvious scramble away from anything personal. "I'm going to use some of these spots for the smaller architectural pieces—cabinetry hardware, vintage doorknobs, keys and switch plates. Modern home owners love stuff like that."

They stood close together to look at the drawer, close enough for him to catch a hint of Erin's fragrance. Amber… The realization distracted him from the conversation and took him back to Liv's studio, where she had developed her own perfumes. Half the reason he'd bought that mammoth new house in the middle of nowhere had been to accommodate her plans to expand her business. She'd been so happy with the workspace in a separate building at the edge of the property…

"Remy?" Erin's voice tugged him back to the present. "Everything okay?" She frowned at him. "I have spinach stuck between my teeth, don't I?"

Her comment surprised a laugh out of him, her easy diffusion of the moment a welcome relief even if it didn't chase away the weird guilt that came with this heightened awareness of her. His own wife had once told him that a woman's scent acted on a man's sexual desires even when she was nowhere around, so it bugged the hell out of him that he couldn't stir up a sense memory of Liv, although he could probably recite the damn chemical recipe.

"No spinach, I promise." He needed to get out of this store. Away from Erin and a rogue attraction he didn't want to feel. "Sorry. I just—ah—remembered I need to follow up with some stores tonight to try and nail down the third spot for my central Tennessee show."

"Of course." She tucked a stray dark hair behind one ear and swept toward the gap in the plastic divider, her black tulle skirt floating along with her. "You'll be in touch to confirm the day and time you'll want to shoot?" She dug under the front counter and produced a business card. "All my contact information is on here."

"Great. I'll have someone from the shooting crew call you to go over all the details." He took the card, careful not to let his fingers brush hers. "I'm glad you're going to do this, Erin. I hope it's really good for business."

"I'm not going to lie." She straightened a few pillboxes on a display near the register. "I hope we get a ton of great clothes for women who need them."

He wondered how she could be so blasé about the store's bottom line but not enough to linger in her amber presence to ask about it. His gaze had returned to her mouth a few too many times in the past five minutes.

"Me, too." Normally, at the close of a meeting like this, he'd shake hands and walk away. But she didn't seem any more inclined to make contact than him. She was sticking close to the register.

And the fact that she was as wary as he was only made him more curious about her. He backed up a step.

"Good luck finding that third business." She picked up her phone and turned her attention to the screen.

"Thanks, Erin." Remy recognized he'd been dismissed.

It was what he'd wanted—to get out of the shop

before the attraction ramped up higher. He pushed through the door and slid into his rental car, feeling oddly let down. He'd felt the spark of a connection, and he knew she did, too. In another lifetime, that might have been a cause for some joy. Pleasure.

Today, it made him determined not to go back.

CHAPTER THREE

SARAH WELDON WAS so dead.

Cranking the volume on her car stereo as she drove from Gainesville to Nashville, Sarah hoped the throbbing bass would drown out her own thoughts since she usually tried not to think about that idea.

Dead.

Her mother had been murdered two years ago in a house break-in while Sarah had been overnight at a friend's home. So death was a real, sickening reality for her. In fact, her father would have a fit if she said the words out loud—*I'm so dead*.

But then, her father was stuck in his grieving. Even *she* knew that, and she was just barely eighteen and in imminent danger of being kicked out of high school. There was a lot Sarah didn't know, yet she was rock-solid certain that her father was more wrecked in the head than she was when it came to her mom. Sarah coped by trying new things, taking new risks and pushing her boundaries. Running fast and hard helped. She'd moved on, right? Her father, on the other hand, was stuck in the past and big-time overprotective of her.

Which was why she couldn't tell him about the letter that had arrived for her last week. She rested her hand on her purse where she'd tucked the note, wishing it would magically disappear.

Squinting in the dark at the sign for Chattanooga, she merged onto Interstate 24 East just as her phone rang. She prayed hard it wasn't her father. Or the family she was supposed to be staying with while her dad worked. Or the school field trip chaperone who would probably get fired for losing track of Sarah during the overnight visit to the University of Florida in Gainesville.

"Bestie," chirped the Bluetooth automated voice, reporting the contact in a way that had made Sarah and her best friend, Mathilda, laugh for an hour when they'd given all of Sarah's friends nicknames in the address book.

Taking a deep breath, she pressed the connect button on the call so it came through the car speakers.

"Don't be mad at me," Sarah blurted, her eyes glued to the road and the taillights of a semi she'd been behind for nearly an hour.

"Are you insane?" Mathilda whisper-shouted. "Where are you?"

Sarah pictured her friend in the hotel room where she'd seen her last, sitting on the king-size bed they were supposed to be sharing on the field trip.

"If I don't tell you, you'll be able to answer honestly when Ms. Fairly grills you tomorrow about where I went." She chewed her thumbnail. It had been practically impossible not to spill this plan to Mathilda, but she didn't want her to get in trouble.

Sarah had caused Mathilda enough problems in the past two years, dragging her to parties she didn't want to attend and convincing her to sneak out after their curfew so Sarah's father wouldn't know she wasn't at home. Sarah couldn't help that she liked to have more fun than Mathilda, but she'd been doing better lately. Behaving herself.

"That may be the dumbest thing you've ever said," Mathilda hissed in the same urgent whisper. "I'm your best friend in the world, and if you've done something stupid, you need to tell *someone* about it so they know when to worry about you for real, Sarah."

"See? That's why it's been so hard not to tell you the plan. You're so smart and I knew you would think of all the details I forgot." She was nervous enough about her decision to sneak away.

Students weren't supposed to have cars on the campus for the trip, but Sarah had planned a week in advance, paying a boy to follow her all the way to Gainesville from Miami the weekend before so she could leave the car in the lot. Boys would do anything for the chance to attend a big-deal college basketball game, and Sarah had helped him do just that—although she'd probably also given him the impression she liked him, which she hadn't meant to. Still, it had been a way to drop off her car ahead of time so she'd have it for her escape. She'd told her father she'd left it at Mathilda's, not that he'd asked. He thought mostly about work these days.

"What plan?" Mathilda pressed. "Seriously, I love you, but I'm about a minute away from ratting you out because I'm scared you're doing something dangerous. You know you're not supposed to go running at night by yourself."

If only it was that simple.

Sarah watched the trucker's signal light flip on to pass the car ahead and she turned on hers, too. It was nice having someone to follow through the dark.

"Don't tell on me. I'm eighteen now, you know." The Stedders had made her a cake to celebrate when her father had been on a location shoot in Georgia a couple of weeks ago. "What can the school really do to me at this point?"

For a long time she'd been waiting for the day where no one could tell her no. Even with the careful planning and occasional sneaking out, she still felt suffocated by her father. After her mom had died, he'd taken a leave from his job for over a year. He'd spent the time staring at Sarah as though she was going to be the next person to be murdered. It was enough to creep anyone out. Worse, she missed the old him. He used to be so much fun.

"Do *not* play that 'I'm eighteen' card with me,"

Mathilda huffed, probably mad her birthday was still six weeks away.

"Fine. I left a couple of hours ago right after you fell asleep. I'm driving to Tennessee to see Dad and help him on his business trip." And hide from letters that arrived from state prison.

She hadn't opened the one that her so-called biological father had sent. Ten times over, she'd debated just burning it and pretending it had never existed. But what if he'd already mentioned her to his cell mates the way he'd talked about her mom? Thanks to him, her mother was dead. And while the guys responsible were in jail for life, that didn't mean her sperm-contributing relative would stop talking.

Bastard. Did he want her dead next?

"Does your dad know?" Mathilda referred to Remy, of course, who was Sarah's father in every way that mattered.

"Of course not. He's going to kill me when I get there, but I'm going anyway."

The fact that Mathilda was silent for a few seconds reassured Sarah. If her friend thought it was the worst plan in the world, she would have berated Sarah instantly.

"I don't know why you couldn't have just asked to go with him and gotten permission. Ms. Fairly is going to flip out."

Sarah slid back into the right-hand lane behind

the truck, her GPS reassuring her that she'd make it to Heartache, Tennessee, in time for breakfast.

"But that's where the plan gets really good." She tucked a long, brown strand of hair behind one ear and wished she had an elastic to hold it back. "I'm going to arrive at Dad's bed-and-breakfast before the morning orientation meeting at the hotel. I'll have Dad call Ms. Fairly and tell her that he picked me up last night for— I don't know. Urgent family reasons." She couldn't keep the bitterness out of her voice.

"Sarah—"

"What?" she snapped, tired of tiptoeing around anything and everything that had to do with her mother's death. "You know she'll forgive him as soon as the words are out of his mouth. Poor Remy Weldon who lost his wife can do no wrong. Ms. Fairly practically drools on him every time she sees him."

"It *is* gross," Mathilda admitted.

"Agreed." She rolled down her window for a little fresh air. She wasn't tired, but she planned to take every precaution to make sure she didn't feel sleepy. Two energy drinks rested side by side in her cup holders, but so far, adrenaline was keeping her going.

"Text me when you get there, okay? I have to know you arrived safely."

Sarah's throat itched from the sudden lump in

it. Her friend didn't try to "mother" her, but sometimes, when she said stuff like that, it made Sarah miss having a mom. It also made her super grateful she'd managed to keep one good friend during the hell of the past two years. She'd met Mathilda during a dark time in her life and Mathilda liked her anyway.

"Of course." She cleared her throat and popped open one of the energy drinks.

"I can't believe you're not going to look at UF with me." Mathilda wanted to be a Gator at the University of Florida in the fall, and she'd wanted Sarah to be one, too, but that wasn't happening.

Sarah had no idea what she wanted to do. She'd spent half her high school years in mourning for her mom and then—later—for the dad who'd checked out on her, too. His parenting these past two years was a weird combo of being smothering or—lately—being absent. It sounded impossible, but he managed it well, sticking her with the Stedders, who were old enough to be her grandparents and twice as nosy. Then there were the freaked-out phone calls that came when he was away. Did he think she didn't know he was terrified she'd get shot in the head someday, too, even though they'd moved nine hundred miles away from where her mom had died?

It was completely disturbing.

"Mathilda, no matter what happens in the fall, it doesn't change that we're friends." She said it automatically, a response she'd trotted out a half-dozen times since Mathilda had forced her to fill out the paperwork for the college application.

Sarah already knew she hadn't gotten in. Her standardized test scores were crap and her course grades were average at best. She'd only tried for the past two years because she had wanted to stay in classes with Mathilda.

"I know we'll still be friends, Bestie," she said, using the nickname from another era of their friendship. "But it makes me sad to think we won't hang out as much. I can't even imagine how much trouble you're going to get in without me."

Mathilda was only half teasing.

"Starting now." Sarah stepped on the gas to pass the truck she'd been following, in a new hurry to get to Tennessee and hit the reset button on her life that had gone off the rails. "If Dad yells at me for making this trip, I'm going to tell him I'm dropping out of school."

Her friend gasped. "You wouldn't."

Sarah pulled back in the right-hand lane and locked in a cruising speed faster than she'd been driving before.

"School has been a waste of my time for two years straight. I absolutely would." Besides, she was scared of returning to Miami, where a letter had found its way into her mailbox from the man she hated most in the world.

She shuddered and hoped her dad would make everything okay again.

"Be careful," Mathilda whispered into the phone. "I mean it."

Sarah downed the last of the energy drink just as she crossed the Tennessee state line, wondering how it would taste with vodka. Not while driving, obviously. But later, maybe.

She needed something to forget about that letter burning a hole in her purse, and running for hours hadn't come close to making her forget.

"Will do," Sarah lied just before she disconnected the call and turned up the radio again.

This time, she had no intention of being careful.

"EVENTUALLY, I WANT to do caramel with ombré highlights." Erin pointed to a picture in a magazine while her favorite stylist, Trish, worked on her hair at The Strand salon the next morning.

The salon opened early on Tuesdays, making it easy for her to change her hair color before she needed to be at Last Chance Vintage. She wasn't the only one who appreciated the extended hours. Daisy Spencer—soon to be her brother Mack's grandmother-in-law—was seated at the manicure booth getting a gel coat of bright pink on her toes. Her boyfriend, Harlan, read the paper in the waiting area.

Erin sighed. Mrs. Spencer navigated the dating world better at eighty-plus years old than Erin ever had.

"That will look fantastic on you." Trish nodded while she skimmed the blow-dryer over a section of Erin's hair, smoothing the newly bronzed strands around a fat round brush. "But I think this color is pretty hot, too. Or maybe I'm just glad you let me pull out that black. How long have I been telling you that color is too strong for your features?"

"Six months." Not that she'd been counting the days since the guy who'd lied to her with every breath had turned her into the kind of person she'd never wanted to be. "Ever since I came back to Heartache."

"So what made you finally change your mind?" Trish turned down the setting on the dryer as she began working on the front of Erin's hair.

"That clothing drive I told you about?" She had already posted flyers in the salon and asked Trish to mention it to her clients. "I'm going to get some television publicity for it and I didn't want to look like—you know—super scary."

Personally, Erin thought she'd rocked the black hair, but her whole style lately screamed "don't mess with me," and she wasn't going to risk it costing her any clothes donations. She was committed, both feet in, to making this thing a success.

Trish frowned as she shut off the dryer and set it aside. "I was hoping the new color might have something to do with a certain gorgeous someone I saw leaving your store after hours yesterday."

Remy.

Just thinking about him stirred a mixed bag of feelings that she wanted no part of—curiosity, suspicion, undeniable attraction.

"Definitely not, but—" She was about to say more and then decided the less said the better.

"But?" Trish twirled Erin's chair around and handed her a small mirror so she could see the back of her hair.

"But that was the producer for the TV show *Interstate Antiquer*. Last Chance Vintage is going to be featured on it. He said they will cover the clothing drive so I'll increase my donations." And the way Remy looked at her didn't have a damn thing to do with her hair color.

Something unspoken, but definite, had passed between them while she'd been showing him the space she was renovating. A look, maybe. She hadn't imagined that moment of mutual awareness any more than she'd imagined Remy's reaction.

He hadn't been able to leave fast enough.

"So you'll be working with him?" Trish met her eyes in the mirror.

"No. It sounds like I'll be working with a production crew that makes the actual episodes—a show host, a couple of camera people." She had the impression Remy wouldn't be back in Heartache if he could avoid it. Something about his hasty retreat almost made her wonder if he was married.

An honorable guy would walk away fast if he felt a stray attraction to someone else, right? She wanted to believe that, but that was about as far as she'd come in getting past the Patrick ordeal—an acknowledgment that she still held out hope for some marriages.

She just didn't hold out much for herself.

"That is so exciting." Trish beamed as she admired Erin's hair. "You'll look fantastic on television. And this will be so good for Heartache."

Standing, Erin checked her watch and noticed she was a few minutes late opening the store. Digging out her wallet, she called goodbye to Mrs. Spencer and Harlan, then followed Trish to the checkout register.

"It will be great to rake in lots of clothes. I'm really excited about the chance to help out women who—" had been cheated on by two-timing bastards "—need an extra hand."

"Yes, well, for that reason, too." Trish rang up the cost of the services. "But I meant this will also be good for the rest of us. A nationally broadcast show with your adorable store featured? It's going to put Heartache on the map for tourists. Your sister must be turning cartwheels."

Something about the way she said it made Erin stop.

"I don't think it's a show with *that* much reach."

Interstate Antiquer was geared toward a niche audience.

"Are you kidding me?" Trish ran Erin's credit card and printed the receipt. "I've watched it, and I don't know anything about antiques. People tune in for the slice of small-town life to get a feel for a place. It'll definitely bring tourism to town. Your father would have loved this, Erin."

Erin's father had passed away eighteen months ago. He had been the mayor of Heartache for over a decade, helping to bring the town out of a recession. The Finley name was practically synonymous with Heartache. While Erin was proud of her town, she didn't want any part of expanding tourism and bringing lots of outsiders in. She was a behind-the-scenes woman, for one thing.

And for another? She liked things here the way they were—Heartache was a place that still felt a little isolated from the rest of the world. It didn't even have an airport. That time she'd planned to bring Patrick to town with her they'd had tickets to fly into Nashville.

"We'll see," Erin said finally, when she realized Trish had been waiting for some kind of response. She took her receipt and jammed it into her purse, wondering if she'd made a huge mistake by saying yes to Remy.

"Hey, isn't that your producer friend now?" Trish pointed out the window where they could see the front of Last Chance Vintage. Where Remy Weldon stood, back against the glass storefront, cell phone pressed to his ear.

The fluttery feeling that started in Erin's chest would have been exciting if she was sixteen. Right now, it felt ominous. She took a deep breath.

"Guess I'd better open the store." Erin scrawled a quick signature on the receipt.

"You said it." Trish's eyes remained fixed on Remy. "Go get him, tiger."

Erin shook her head. "Seriously. Not interested, Trish, but thank you for the great hair."

Her friend winked at her.

Main Street held only a handful of local businesses. Her shop. The sandwich place. The Strand. There was a gas station farther down, and a pizza parlor. Then at the corner, she could just see Lucky's Grocer and the village square. She liked it this way and she didn't want to see four new fast-food chains pop up if tourism increased.

"Looking for me?" Erin called as she crossed the street.

Remy tilted his head sideways as he tucked his phone into his pocket. "I don't know. Is that you?"

"Of course. I don't look that different." Her heart beat too fast and she didn't want to talk about her appearance. "Figured I'd better spruce up the locks if I'm going on television. Don't want to embarrass my mom."

Remy leaned a shoulder into the doorjamb, far too close to where she needed to insert the key in the dead bolt. But then, he seemed distracted by her hair.

"What was wrong with your color?" His eyes wandered over her in a way that seemed more like a professional assessment than a personal inventory.

That was, until his gaze reached breast level. It would have been laughable at how fast his chin shot up except that he seemed...*pained.* Feeling that she'd witnessed some private part of him, she turned her attention to the lock.

Remy stepped back to give her room, taking all his lean good looks and masculinity a few inches away.

"Black wasn't my natural color." She let herself in and he followed slowly, closing the door as the bell jingled. She flipped on the lights. "See that photo of Heather and me?" She pointed to a shot her mother had taken of them on the front porch when they were about nine and ten years old, sharing a bowl of raspberries and wearing matching blue dresses. "That shade of red is my color. Heather still looks exactly the same, by the way."

"That's a great picture."

"My mom has always been good with a camera." It was one way Erin had been able to relate to her mother since Diana saw the world differently through the lens, where her perceptions weren't quite as frenetic. Erin fired up the computer and turned on some music. "I'm surprised you're here. I thought for sure I'd seen the last of you yesterday after you sprinted out the door."

"About that—" He shoved his hands in the pockets of his sleek dark trousers. His white silk T-shirt probably meant it was a casual day for him, but since he wore it with a gray jacket, he still looked extraordinarily well put together. "I wanted to apologize. I've had a lot on my mind lately and—" He shook his head as if he wasn't sure where to go with that next.

"It's no big deal," she said, leaping into the conversational void to save him, or possibly herself. She didn't need to hear anything overly personal about Remy. "I can imagine it must be difficult traveling away from home so often."

Her eyes went surreptitiously to his left hand, bare of a wedding ring. Was it her imagination, or could she see a hint of a tan line there?

"That's no excuse for bad business." He reached into his jacket pocket and withdrew a sheaf of papers. "I figured I'd deliver this personally so I could apologize. This is the contract and some information about how we film and what to expect."

"Nice." She reached for the papers, grateful for the counter between them. "I will look it over tonight."

There was something incredibly appealing about

his jaw, which sported a few days' growth of beard, scruffy enough to keep him from being movie-star handsome. She wondered how many women threw themselves at him in his line of work.

"Erin." He didn't let go of the papers, his eyes locked on hers. Confusing the hell out of her.

What was this push-pull game he was playing and not just with the contract?

The bell on the shop door rang, the entrance banging open as a crying teen stepped inside the store. Erin and Remy jumped apart. Erin was about to ask the girl what was wrong, but the young woman's green eyes landed on Remy.

"Daddy!" she wailed, rushing toward him. "Where have you been?"

CHAPTER FOUR

REMY COULDN'T PROCESS what he was seeing. His daughter, Sarah, inside Last Chance Vintage. Three states away from where he'd left her. She had held herself together better than he had after Liv's death, so seeing her in tears stopped him cold, making every protective urge fire to life.

"Sarah? What's wrong?" He opened his arms to her and she flew into them in a swirl of hair ribbons and high drama. "How did you get here?"

He met Erin's shocked eyes briefly over his daughter's head.

"I drove!" Sarah's voice was high and impatient. She got angry more easily now than she had... before. "What matters is that Ms. Fairly will kill me for leaving the field trip unless you call her *now* and tell her that I'm with you."

Sarah thrust her cell phone at his face.

Erin's lips pursed in a disapproving frown. Who was she to judge his daughter? Or him, for that matter?

"Why did you leave the field trip?" He withdrew the phone from his daughter's shaking fingertips while the store's welcome bell chimed again. He glanced over. An older couple was entering Last Chance Vintage.

"Feel free to use my office if you want to talk more privately," Erin offered, gesturing to the area where they'd met the day before. Excusing herself, she walked over to greet her customers.

Leaving Remy with his crying teen and completely out of his depth. Damn it. He'd struggled to force himself back into a routine after Liv had died, convinced something would happen to Sarah if he left town again. But Sarah's counselor had been adamant that he wasn't doing the teen any favors by coddling her. Yet, look what happened when he left?

"Sarah, come sit." He drew her toward the back room. It wasn't totally private, but he didn't want to go to the car and be on display on the town's main street. Plus, driving anywhere right now was out of the question. He couldn't believe his just-turned-eighteen-year-old daughter had traveled well over five hundred miles by herself. Without telling him, let alone asking his permission. Hard to believe the girl who had once texted him eight times from cheerleading tryouts with updates on the final cuts would not even bother to discuss this trip with him.

He'd asked Sarah's grief counselor about her risk-taking behavior a year ago, but at the time, the woman's professional opinion had been that sporadically cutting class, lower grades and one nightmarish episode of underage drinking were "normal" teenage incidents. As a parent, how was he supposed to tell the difference?

"Can you just call Ms. Fairly?" Sarah blurted, twisting the end of her long, brown braid where it rested on one shoulder. "I thought you'd be at the bed-and-breakfast, so I went there first, hoping you could contact her before she found out I was gone. But now it's getting late. I'm going to be in so much trouble unless you tell her I'm with you."

Frustrated and trying his damnedest to keep a lid on it, he placed his hands on Sarah's thin shoulders. Was it his imagination, or did Erin's eyes track the drama in the back room while she helped her customer?

"In a minute. I'm not calling your teacher until I have the answers to the questions I know she's going to ask me." He set Sarah's phone on the wooden counter that Erin used for a workspace. "Like why did you leave the field trip without my permission?"

She could have broken down on the way to Heart-ache. A pervert could have stopped under the guise of helping...

Remy's chest constricted.

"That's the thing." Sarah swiped her eyes, which were a different shade of green than her mother's had been. Her biological father was a high school classmate of Liv's and he'd wanted nothing to do with Liv or Sarah after he'd found out Liv was pregnant. Later, the guy had used his computer skills to hack a system that should have been secured by the Department of Defense, and had been in jail for as long as Remy had known Liv. "Just tell her I *had* your permission. Like it was a family emergency or something and you left a message that she must have just missed."

Remy heard Erin making small talk with her customers and greeting a few more who walked into the store. He watched her stride off toward the back to retrieve something off a nearby shelf. He kept his voice low as he spoke to his daughter.

"If you're going to ask me to lie, I think I have the right to know why." He'd really thought Sarah was on track with school after the bumps in the road at the end of her junior year.

Mouth falling open, she gave him a look that suggested he needed a brain transplant for asking the question.

"To see *you*!" She jabbed one finger onto the wooden workstation as if making a point. "How many times have you said you wished you could stay closer to home for your work?"

Guilt pummeled him even as he felt Erin's gaze on him again. "It's not easy, Sarah—"

"I get that." She shrugged at him. "So I made it easy for you. I don't need to be on that field trip since I don't care about college. I want field experience in television and who better to shadow for a week than my own dad?"

Remy had spent enough years on the winning side of a conference table to recognize when he'd been beaten. Either his daughter had a great point or she'd just played him extremely well. But at this moment, it truly didn't matter. She was here—five hundred miles from where she was supposed to be—and he didn't have time to leave the job and personally escort her home. Just thinking about all the things that could have happened to her on the road alone threatened to send him back into another panic attack. His forehead broke out in a cold sweat.

"Remy?" Erin called from the other side of a clothing rack. "Can I talk to you for one quick second?"

He glanced up, in no mood to think about anything but Sarah at the moment.

Erin waved him over.

Stepping away from his daughter, he regretted having this discussion with Sarah here. He wasn't thinking clearly.

"What?" He was terse, but not nearly as terse as he felt.

"I have no right to make a suggestion, but I'm going to advise you not to lie for her or she'll never learn how to be accountable for her own actions."

Remy shook his head. "Seriously? You're giving me parenting advice? Do you have kids?"

She frowned. Bristled. "You looked like you were drowning. I thought I'd send you a lifeline since you didn't seem to know what to do."

And didn't that just get on his last nerve? How many times had he struggled with not knowing how to string words together in the year after Liv had died? With losing his train of thought in the middle of talking? He thought he'd kicked both those problems pretty damn well, so it ticked him off that Erin was finding fault when he was holding it together just fine.

"I know what I'm doing," he said between gritted teeth.

Her shoulders straightened. "Fine. I'm sure I know nothing about teenagers since I have no kids of my own."

She stalked off, back ramrod straight.

He'd won that battle, but now he was going to have to make nice with Erin all over again if he wanted her to stay on board for the show. He turned back to Sarah and drew her deeper into the back room.

"Daddy, please," she started, her pleading tone grating when he had already decided to do what she'd asked.

He just wasn't going to lie for her.

"This discussion is not finished," he barked at

her. "I'm going to call Ms. Fairly and deal with that end of the problem, but I have a major issue with you deciding to leave school on your own. You may be eighteen, but you're still under my roof, which makes you accountable to me for your actions. We'll revisit that later."

The relief on her face—her wide smile exactly like her mom's—reminded him of when he'd first met Sarah as an outgoing eleven-year-old. She'd charmed him even then, inviting him to her dance recital after he'd applauded her pirouettes on Liv's kitchen floor when he had visited their place to buy an original painting from the up-and-coming local artist—his future wife.

Later, her art had expanded to gardening and then perfumes, her creativity knowing no boundaries. Remy had wanted to give her every opportunity she'd never had growing up or while raising Sarah alone, so he'd tried to help her develop her talents.

On impulse, he leaned over to brush a kiss on Sarah's forehead.

She maintained a weary, indulgent smile. "Seriously, though. My teacher will freak out unless you sweet-talk her."

While Sarah punched in the number and dialed, Remy's eyes found Erin. She was accepting an armful of clothes on hangers from a woman wearing a bright orange caftan and head scarf. He wondered what drove Erin to be such an activist even as he told himself to stay away from her. She was going to be on one of his television shows. Nothing more.

He didn't appreciate her telling him how to parent his daughter when she had no idea what Sarah had been through. Bad enough the girl had a felon for a biological father. Now she had no mother and her adoptive father was coming up short on the parenting front.

He switched into father mode as Sarah's teacher answered the call. He made excuses and apologies for Sarah's absence, keeping his explanation as vague as possible until he'd had time to talk to his daughter's counselor about their next move. He didn't doubt for a minute that the school would expel her if she got into any more trouble, especially considering some of the stunts she'd pulled the year before. He would talk to her about it. Make sure she was level or send her back to the counselor.

Maybe it was just as well she was here where he could keep an eye on her since he was spending half his time worrying about her anyway. He couldn't afford anything happening to her while he was gone—like another drinking episode. If Sarah was this serious about needing his attention, he planned to make certain she had it.

By the time he finished speaking to the teacher—

assuring her he'd come in for a meeting to discuss the issue as soon as he returned to Miami—he noticed Sarah had her head down on the table, arms folded.

"All set," he told her, passing back her phone.

Only to realize she'd fallen asleep right there.

Crap. Now what?

A stress headache promised to level him any moment now. He gripped his temples and squeezed tight.

"Everything okay?" Erin asked, appearing at the open entryway between the back room and the rest of the store.

She stared at Sarah and then at him, her new bronze highlights catching the overhead light. He told himself to pull it together. Now that Sarah had passed out on Erin's table, there was no pressing need to get out of the store.

"I suppose everything is all right. Until the next crisis that comes with having a teenager." He tucked Sarah's phone in his pocket for safekeeping. "Sorry I didn't get to introduce the two of you before she conked out. That's my daughter, Sarah."

Erin watched him with a wariness that he hadn't seen in her before. She carried an armful of clothes on hangers.

"You're married?" She spoke the words carefully, enunciating each syllable with an awkwardness that felt uncomfortable.

Or was that just his imagination? Sometimes he felt as though the whole world must know he was a widower, as if that grief had been permanently etched into his features at all times. He knew he should probably get out of Erin's store and take Sarah with him, but finding out what his daughter had done had thrown him for a major loop. He was exhausted, and it wasn't even noon yet. Besides, Sarah looked as though she could sleep for three days straight, her right arm pillowing her head and her braid draped over her chin.

Poor kid.

"I *was* married. My wife died two years ago." Because of him. Even then, he'd been on the road too much. Was the answer to quit his job? To make sure Sarah was safe and stayed out of trouble for the rest of her senior year?

Too bad he couldn't come close to affording it. He needed to work to bring his finances back in line to pay for Sarah's college tuition.

Erin's expression shifted in predictable ways. Empathy, sympathy, a trace of pity.

He'd become adept at picking out all three in people's faces. More so once they'd heard *how* she'd died.

Something he would not be sharing today as he was still recovering from the shock of seeing Sarah. He brushed a hand across his forehead, the skin cold and damp.

"I'm so sorry." Erin laid the garments on a credenza. "That must be hard for both of you."

Her eyes went to Sarah, for which he was grateful.

"I thought she was doing better." He watched his daughter's shoulders rise and fall ever so slightly with each breath. "It's tough to tell what behaviors are normal teen drama and what things are in reaction to her mom's death—the things I should be watching out for."

"So she drove herself all the way up here?" Erin filled a coffeepot at a utility sink against one wall. "From Miami?"

He noticed she hadn't apologized for butting in regarding his parenting. Then again, maybe she wasn't sorry.

"She was in Gainesville on a school trip." Was Sarah really serious about wanting experience in television? He'd dismissed it in the past when she'd asked to join him, assuming she was merely trying to take a few days off from school. "That put her several hours closer. But still…she had to have been driving for nine hours."

"No wonder she's exhausted. Thank goodness she made it here safely. Want some coffee? I don't know if you're going to move her anytime soon." Erin spooned coffee grounds into the machine, the storefront quiet for the moment except for Sarah's light snores coming between measured breaths. "I'm surprised she knew to look for you here."

"I gave her a rough itinerary before I left." Thank God she was safe. He wanted to just stare at his daughter and rejoice in that fact. "And I did mention stopping by here to the woman who runs the bed-and-breakfast." His voice was gravelly with exhaustion after these past few days. "And please, no need to make any coffee for me. I'll get out of your hair as soon as I recover from the heart attack of seeing Sarah."

"You're staying at Heartache B and B?" Erin asked, flipping the switch that turned the coffeepot to brew. "Just so you know, telling Tansy Whittaker spreads news faster than Twitter in this town."

The dry note in her voice made him smile in spite of the crap kind of day he was having.

"Today, that turned out to be a good thing." He didn't need Sarah getting any more upset. Her tears and worry were painful for him.

"Amen to that." Erin nodded slowly, her blue eyes resting on Sarah again. "Is she your only child?"

"Yeah." The sound of the coffee percolating filled the silence as it stretched, strangely comfortable, between them. He wished he hadn't snapped at Erin, even if he hadn't appreciated her advice. "I adopted Sarah when I met her mom. Actually, maybe Sarah adopted me first. She's got a powerhouse personality. She's all in when she likes someone."

"My father was like that—very magnetic. He was the mayor of Heartache for almost fifteen years before he died." Erin's gaze shifted to his. "I always admired that charismatic side of him."

"You were the mayor's daughter while you were growing up?" Sarah's phone buzzed with incoming messages, so he reached into his pocket to turn it off.

"Just during my teenage years." Erin's expression closed. She definitely wasn't one to talk about herself. "So what are you going to do with her now that she's here? Will you have to return home sooner than planned?"

"No." He knew that much from discussions with her counselor in the past. It didn't help the situation to adjust his life to suit her, even though families healing from grief sometimes did just that in an effort to ensure their kids never experienced any other obstacles. "I'm fortunate to have maintained my job despite long absences after Liv's death. I can't shortchange the show now."

It was true enough, and it spared him from having to discuss the show's loss of ratings and the need to bolster it to keep it afloat.

"At the risk of having you accuse me of overstepping, was your daughter having problems at school? Is that why she drove all this way to see you?" Erin reached into an overhead cabinet and pulled out two mismatched mugs and a sugar container.

"No. Actually, I don't know. She's been asking me not to travel as much, but I thought that was because she liked being at our place instead of staying with an older couple when I leave town." Did he really know what had been going on at school lately? Maybe he had just figured no news was good news. "But now she says she doesn't care about college and she wants to go into television, so it makes sense to watch me work firsthand. She does have spring break coming up, so…"

"Are you sure you don't want some coffee?" Erin asked, pouring a cup for herself before the whole pot finished brewing.

"No, thanks. I should settle Sarah back into her own room at the bed-and-breakfast, I guess. I had checked out this morning, thinking I'd find a place on the road closer to my next stop, but maybe now that she's here, it'll be easier to make this my home base for a few more days. I can't take her with me everywhere." It wasn't feasible. Sarah should understand that.

"Heartache makes a nice home base." Erin added sugar to her cup.

Damn, but parenting was difficult.

"I know I overreacted when you were trying to help before—"

Erin narrowed her eyes. "Just because I don't have kids doesn't mean I'm clueless in the ways of teenagers."

"Right." He told himself not to get defensive. She hadn't said his parenting sucked. Just that she wanted to help. "So now I'm asking for your opinion." He needed to make nice with her, for one thing. And for another...he really was curious. "Do you really think her driving all the way up here means something's wrong at school? I know you don't know her well. I just wonder about your gut reaction. Does that sound like a red flag for a teenager?"

"I don't know if it means problems at school, but if you want me to be totally honest..."

"Please." He grabbed the empty coffee mug and poured himself a cup after all. He might need the caffeine to get himself through this day.

Erin stepped out of his way, giving him access to the sugar.

"Then honestly, it shouts red flag in my book. If not school issues, there could be friend trouble or boy problems. My niece went through a rough patch last year and I know that stuff causes kids a lot of stress. As we get older, we forget how life-and-death everything is at that age—the emotions, the fears..."

Remy gulped the scalding coffee.

"You're right." Damn it, he needed to figure out what was going on with his daughter.

"But I think it's great she wanted to see you." Erin sipped her drink out of a stoneware mug that looked as though it had been hand painted. "A lot of teenage girls wouldn't turn to their fathers for help."

Something about the way she said it suggested she would have never turned to her own father—the father beloved by all of Heartache. What had it been like growing up in such a small town in a well-known family?

He sighed. "Maybe she just knows who the pushover is." He didn't appreciate Sarah's insistence that he "sweet-talk" the teacher. Worse, it bugged him that he'd done exactly that.

"I think it speaks well of your relationship." Erin's rings clanked against the mug handle as she set down the cup.

She wore a black dress today with a black vinyl apron that suggested she planned to do a bit of crafting. The short sleeves on her dress exposed a brightly colored tattoo. Vines twisted around one arm and disappeared up into her sleeve.

He must have taken too long to answer because he became aware of her staring at him.

"Is there anything else I can do?" she asked, making him realize he'd stood there too damn long, taking over her store and her office with his personal problems.

It must be the odd thread of attraction he experienced that had his feet rooted to the floor, but it had been nice having someone to talk to about Sarah's behavior. Someone who wasn't a shrink and didn't connect everything in their lives back to Liv. A year ago, that thought would have felt disloyal to her memory. But now he owned it for what it was—plain and simple truth.

"No." He set down the cup and straightened. "I'll wake Sarah and get out of your hair."

"There's no rush—"

"I've imposed on your goodwill enough in the past few days." He jammed his hands into his pockets to make sure things didn't become more personal than they already were. "I'm glad you're going to do the show, Erin. I'm not going to risk scaring you off now."

He tested out the smile that worked with other people, but, true to form, it seemed to fall flat on Erin. She frowned.

"Remy, I'm scared off by slick, big-city manners, so please don't feel you need to pile on the charm for my sake. If we're going to work together, I'd rather know the real you than the television sham."

And wasn't that a wake-up call in his day?

"I've got a whole lot more real where this comes from." He shook his head. "Too much." He laid a hand on Sarah's shoulder and squeezed gently. "Come on, Sarah. Time to go."

His daughter blinked slowly and lifted her head as if it weighed too much.

"If you're still in town on Friday, Lucky's Grocer and Restaurant is having the first outdoor dance of the spring." Erin flipped through the pile of clothes she'd stacked in one corner while she sipped her coffee. "The whole town will be there for dinner and dancing on the village square. I can introduce Sarah to my niece and some other kids her age."

"A dance?" His daughter's ears perked up.

"We might be able to get a flight out by then. But thanks." Remy didn't need the temptation of seeing Erin Finley in her dancing dress, let alone the entanglements of getting to know a small-town community.

There was a reason he'd chosen the anonymity of Miami after Liv's death.

"Just keep it in mind." Erin followed them out through the store, Sarah walking in a sleepy daze as she touched a few of the hangers with vintage motorcycle jackets and plaid wool miniskirts.

"Your store is so cute," she murmured as she shuffled along. "Daddy, I hope we stay for the dance."

Remy tried not to glare at Erin over his daughter's head, but why had she brought that up?

"We'll see," he muttered, knowing his lame

comeback made him sound like the clichéd over-whelmed single father he was.

"Good luck today," Erin told him as he opened the door for Sarah and then held it for a customer walking in with another armful of clothes.

"After that kind of start, things can only get better." He stood in the doorway with Erin while Sarah trundled toward her car.

"You can work on my store renovations if you're feeling stressed." Erin winked at him in a conspiratorial way. "Nothing gets out frustrated aggression like sledgehammers and air nail guns."

"Except sex." The words rolled off his tongue as easily as they might have a couple of decades ago. It surprised the hell out of him.

Thankfully, Erin didn't take them flirtatiously.

"I'm guessing that's not a remote possibility for you, any more than it is for me." Her blue eyes met his for an unguarded moment. "Damn shame."

CHAPTER FIVE

"So TELL ME all about *Interstate Antiquer.*" Erin's sister-in-law, Bethany, sorted through a pile of women's shoes in the tent that Erin had rented for the next two weeks.

It was Friday. She hadn't heard from Remy since he'd left the store with his daughter on Tuesday. She'd spent all her free time researching affiliations with the Dress for Success national organization and making sure she met the guidelines for an event. If she was going to be on national television, she wanted it to serve a good purpose. Helping others while she tried to fill the gaping hole of guilt inside was a good start.

Today, Bethany had come over to the store to help her with all the donations she'd collected already. Bethany's teenage daughter, Ally, had early dismissal from school, so she was watching the register for Erin while the older women worked.

"It was Heather's idea." Erin sorted stained clothes into a recycle pile and hung the items she planned to keep on rolling racks. The tent stood off to the side of the parking lot behind the store. There were canvas sides to keep out the elements, but they'd opened one of the walls to allow in a spring breeze. She still needed to sort by size and steam a few things in Jamie Raybourn's size before the woman arrived later for her private preview of the big event. She also needed to set a date shortly after the filming to allow time for—she hoped—donations to arrive.

"That doesn't surprise me." Bethany rubbed at a scuff on a black patent pump and added it to a bin for cleaning. "Your sister is determined to make that store a showplace after all the hard work you're doing to renovate it." She sorted the shoes with the same quick efficiency she brought to everything she did, including managing Finleys' Building Supplies.

Erin wished her oldest brother, Scott, would get his act together in order to keep Bethany in the family. Their marriage had lasted seventeen years. They'd tied the knot right after college graduation when Bethany was pregnant. Erin had always thought the couple was rock solid. They were in counseling, but neither talked much about each other or their relationship. If those two couldn't stay together, Erin wondered why she'd thought she'd ever had a chance.

"I guess I didn't realize how serious she was about it until the producer showed up on my doorstep." She had thought about Remy too many times to count this week, a fact that was making her irritable when she should be celebrating her newfound direction with her good-works initiative.

She wondered if his daughter had stayed in town with him like he'd planned, but she wondered a lot more than that. Like how his wife died and if the daughter was getting enough help to deal with it.

"I hear he's really cute." Bethany held up a pair of pink sparkly sandals and put them in the donation bin since they were keeping only business attire.

"Word travels fast in a small town." Erin did not want to envision Remy's face again, yet she found herself remembering the line of his jaw and the golden-brown scruff of beard that made her want to run her fingers along his cheek to test the texture.

"So you don't deny it?" Bethany poked her in the knee from her seat on a stool beside her.

"Everyone in television is attractive. I'm more concerned with how I'm going to face a store full of cameras when they film this thing."

Bethany was quiet for so long that Erin stopped sorting to peer over at her. Her sister-in-law grinned from ear to ear.

"You like him," she announced, sliding a brown leather mule onto some open shelving they'd brought outside to show off the wares.

Erin sighed. "I don't know him well enough to like him or not like him. He just is. Cute, I mean." What was it about a handsome man that made women so eager to matchmake? "And who's been yammering around town about how cute he is? Maybe that person likes him and not me." She felt a rant coming on and couldn't quite stop herself. "Just because I'm single doesn't mean I'm desperate to meet a man, okay? I broke up with a guy because I needed some time on my own. I have no desire to jump back into dating yet."

She hadn't told her family the real reason behind her breakup with Patrick. The truth mortified her, and she wasn't a woman who embarrassed easily.

Bethany held up both hands in surrender.

"Message received. It was Trish at The Strand salon who mentioned how cute the guy was, but she's a happily married woman, so she won't be making a play for the producer." Bethany busied herself with straightening a row of purses above the shoe shelf while an old convertible sedan pulled into the parking lot nearby, music blaring at full volume with the top down.

"Yes, well, all I meant to say is that she could if she wanted to as I'm not going to pay any more attention to Remy Weldon than is strictly necessary." Erin watched the boys and girls hop out of the car, laughing and shoving as they headed toward the back door of an ice-cream place. Even as a teenager, she hadn't been the kind of girl to hang out with tons of friends, sticking close to her family until she'd been old enough to leave Heartache. She didn't envy Sarah Weldon trying to find her way in the world as a teen without her mom.

"Remy Weldon." Bethany sighed. "That sounds very French."

"Cajun, actually," Erin found herself saying. She folded a stack of camisoles with new speed, embarrassed to know way too much about him. "He's got that warm honey accent to prove it."

"Oh my, that sounds nice. You'll have to excuse an old married lady for occasionally eyeing the hot young men in town." Bethany picked up a bottle of leather cleaner from the ground beside her folding chair. "Scott has barely noticed me in the last year and it gets tough—"

Her voice cracked a little. Erin set down a stack of silk blouses so she could give her a hug.

"I'm so sorry he's being this way." Erin squeezed Bethany's shoulders. "I wish I knew what to say or how to help."

"Me, too." Bethany tipped her forehead to Erin's for a moment before straightening. "But it's like I'm out of words when it comes to him. I don't even know anymore if it's his fault or mine. We just don't ever have anything to say to each other, and when we do, it's always so full of old resentments. It's like we have this mean-spirited language we speak that only we understand and the subtext is full of unhappiness."

Erin still found it hard to believe that Scott and

Bethany—once the town's Harvest King and Queen and longtime golden couple—could have drifted so far off course in their marriage.

"I just keep remembering how happy you both were when Scott took over Finleys' and you left your teaching job to help." Erin had worked part-time in the afternoons at the store while Bethany overhauled inventory and rearranged shelves to make them more appealing. "I know I was just a kid, but I recall thinking there was nothing you two couldn't accomplish. You seemed like such a great team."

"Once upon a time maybe we were." Bethany straightened the last pair of shoes she'd cleaned. "Speaking of which, I'd better get going so I'm not late for today's family counseling session."

"Right. I'll take over at the counter for Ally." Erin knew that had been the deal when Bethany agreed to help out. "Thank you so much for being here."

"We're still family. That's what we do." She tugged the strap of her purse up her shoulder.

"Damn straight, we're family." Erin might have issues with her mother, but being away from Heartache had made her appreciate this place and these people all the more. Small-town was exactly her speed these days, even if she occasionally missed the access to more stores and restaurants. More culture.

As they exited the tent, Erin noticed a few kids

on bicycles pull into the parking lot, loaded down with backpacks and gym bags. The local high school must have let out for the day.

Bethany helped her secure the one canvas wall so the clothing and accessories stayed safe inside. While they worked, a bicycle tire rolled into Erin's peripheral vision.

"Ms. Finley?" Sarah Weldon, Remy's teenage daughter, perched on the seat of a yellow three-speed bike with a woven brown basket on the front. The logo for the Heartache B and B—a pink heart with a crack—was stenciled on the front. "I love the highlights in your hair."

The girl smiled and Erin remembered what her dad had called her—a powerhouse personality. Sarah might not be Remy's flesh and blood, but she sure had his charm.

She wondered how deep it went or if it was the kind people put on for show.

"Thank you, Sarah." Erin extended a hand to the girl. "It's nice to see you again." She introduced Bethany and noticed Sarah's basket contained a big green garbage bag. "How are you enjoying your time in our little town? It's a far cry from Miami, I know."

"I love it!" She planted green tennis shoes on the pavement and steadied the bike by the handlebars. "You can bike everywhere without fearing for your life from crazy drivers, which was a good thing for me since I've been grounded and don't get to drive my car again until tonight." She held up her fingers to show that they were crossed. "I've also been researching some online coursework so I can keep up with classes while I'm here, and that's kept me busy. But everyone around Heartache is so *nice*."

"I like that about it, too." Erin was glad to hear that Remy had coughed up some kind of punishment to keep his daughter accountable for her actions. Not that it was any of her business, as he'd been quick to point out.

Yet the intimacy of that quiet conversation with him, talking about his problems with his daughter while Sarah slept and the coffeepot gurgled… Something about it had stuck with her, reminding her of all Erin was giving up by turning her back on dating.

"Let me see if Ally can step outside to say hello," Bethany suggested. "Sarah, she's a senior in the local high school. I'm sure she'd like to meet you."

"That would be great!" Sarah's sunny disposition didn't hint at any problems back home, but Erin wondered what it had been like to lose her mom as a teen.

Erin had been a straight-up mess at Sarah's age, and she hadn't lost her mother—just struggled to stay level in a household where her parents' ups and downs dictated everything in the Finley family. Although when Diana locked herself in her room for weeks straight and didn't answer no matter how hard they knocked and pleaded, sometimes it felt as if her mother had died.

"Here." Sarah thrust the big green garbage bag at her, pulling Erin out of old memories. "Dad said you were collecting women's career wear, so I asked the innkeeper and a couple of her neighbors for donations. There's nothing great in there, but I did score a couple pairs of barely worn leather pumps that will last someone a lot of years."

"That's fantastic." Erin peeked in the bag, impressed at the energy and initiative from someone so young. "Thank you so much for doing that."

"No probs!" She waved off the thanks. "But you know, put in a good word for me with my dad that I'm not a total screwup? I wanted to go with him on a meeting with his camera crew in Franklin today, but he didn't even wake me up when he left this morning."

She rolled her eyes and laughed it off, but Erin heard the frustration beneath. Why was he leaving his daughter alone in a strange town if he was worried about her getting into trouble? It didn't make sense.

"I'm sure he knows you're not a screwup." Erin set the bag on the ground as the pack of teens returned to their convertible on the other side of the parking lot.

One of them whistled and Sarah's attention was already zeroed in on the boys in the front seat.

"Yum," she said aloud before covering her mouth with one hand and giggling. "That is—sorry, Ms. Finley. I just figured as long as I'm in town I might as well go to that dance."

Sarah's attention wandered again as Ally and Bethany emerged from the back of the store.

"Sarah, this is my daughter, Ally." While Bethany made introductions, the girls arranged to meet at the village green later, where Lucky's Grocer and Restaurant would host the first Outdoor Night of the season.

The local market backed up to the village square, and the town council had given Lucky's Grocer special permission to set up outdoor tables that spilled into the park at the center of town. It occurred on only one night a week during the warm months, but everyone looked forward to the Friday nights. Families arrived early and brought their food to the playground. Teens stayed late and took over the swings after the younger crowd cleared out. For everyone else, there was beer and ribs and dancing under the stars to live music.

Bethany winked at Erin while the girls chatted. "I pulled Ally off the register. We waited until the store was empty, but I can run back inside—"

"No." Erin picked up the bag of clothes. "You've

got your appointment. I'll head in and maybe I'll see you at Lucky's later?"

"You're going?"

Erin shrugged. "Might as well. It's an easy way to see people and I've stuck close to home since I've been back in town."

Bethany nodded, a thoughtful look in her eye. "I've noticed. I'm glad you're getting out more." She touched the ends of Erin's hair, the strands that were newly colored warm bronze. "I don't know what happened with that former guy of yours, but I'm glad to see you're coming back to life."

Erin's chest ached at the reminder. It sucked to be someone's fool.

"How about you?" she asked, eager to deflect the conversation from her failed relationship. "Will you be there?"

Bethany shook her head. "I try not to ask Scott for dates. We're not there yet, and I don't want to put too much pressure on him." She swallowed hard. "I'm trying to give him space and time to see what we had and what we could have together again. But it's not easy."

Erin nodded. "I don't imagine it would be."

As Sarah and Ally finalized plans to meet later, Bethany headed toward the heavy-duty pickup truck she drove with the Finley store name painted on one side. Erin watched her go, wondering how a woman could pour so much of herself into a marriage and a man—a good man, for all Scott's flaws—and still feel so lonely.

Her heart broke for them. But it made Erin all the more certain of her decision to keep her boundaries in place where Remy Weldon was concerned.

OBTAINING ALCOHOL AT eighteen years old was ridiculously easy. And since her father wasn't around anyway…why not?

Sarah patted the six-pack on the passenger seat of her car now that she'd reclaimed her driving privileges after putting in her time being grounded. She congratulated herself on another successful liquor store run.

Four days in Heartache, Tennessee, and she was already working the town like a local. She had a place to go on a Friday night, and a fun new friend to hang out with. Sure, her dad had blown off her every attempt to work with him this week, citing her punishment of being "grounded," but honestly—screw him. She knew he didn't care about being a father to her now that her mom was gone. He might have cared once, but now? Every day that he made excuses not to hang out with her only made her feel worse. If he wasn't looking out for her, who would protect her?

There'd been a time when they did stuff together every weekend. But maybe that had only been to impress her mom. Too bad Sarah had really bought it. Ever since her mother died, Remy was stuck working and being sad all the time. He'd moved them out of that gargantuan house he'd built in Lafayette, Louisiana, and transplanted them to Miami, which she hated. Then he'd just retreated from her and everything else. Except for work. Oh sure, he pawned her off on people all the time. Responsible adults like the Stedders who could watch her 24/7. This was the first time in two years she'd pushed his hand to spend time with her and he was running away every chance he got.

If he couldn't be bothered with her, she'd find someone, or something, else to entertain her. Like a dance under the stars, a new dress and the name of the cute driver of the hot convertible she'd seen in the parking lot behind Last Chance Vintage today. Lucas Maynard.

Yum.

Ally Finley had warned Sarah to steer clear of him in a text she'd sent earlier. He had a girlfriend, apparently. But after the way Lucas had looked at Sarah, she had figured the girlfriend couldn't be serious. The beer on the front seat had his name on it, in fact. Because really, the drinking thing was only a little bit for her. Mostly it paved the way with boys, who were always impressed and grateful at her ability to secure the goods.

Steering her car around the village square once to get the lay of the land, Sarah smiled with pleasure at how easy it had been this time. She'd sat outside the liquor store until a young guy pulled up alone. He hadn't been supercute, but then, that was just what she'd needed. The guys who were a little sloppier looking were all the more surprised and flattered that a girl needed help. Guys loved to play hero when she explained her "I forgot my license" dilemma.

She cranked her tunes as she spotted Lucas's convertible. Sarah checked her lip gloss in the rearview mirror. Adrenaline pumping, she could almost forget about her dad ignoring her and the letter still hidden away in her purse. She pulled into a parking space behind the convertible and told herself that after some beer and some Lucas Maynard, she wouldn't care any more about those things.

Tonight, she planned on having the time of her life.

IF NOT FOR his daughter, Remy would have never shown up in Heartache's small-town square that night.

Exhausted from a killer week of work, he'd spent all day on the road scouting locations, constantly on the phone trying to confirm the guest host for the remaining episodes. Remy had been looking forward to a quiet night at the Heartache B and B and—finally—a real conversation with his daughter about what was going on in her world, maybe over a nice dinner. But she'd requested a video chat at midday, reminding him that her four-day grounding was supposed to be over. Since he'd been in a meeting, he'd rescinded the punishment—a stricter one than what he would have done in the past, but Erin's words about forcing Sarah to take some responsibility for her actions had resonated. He'd been glad to give his daughter back the car privileges, confident she'd learned her lesson.

Unfortunately, he'd returned to town to discover a note that she'd gone here—to the dance Erin had mentioned on Tuesday.

Remy stood on the fringes of the mayhem that spilled out of Lucky's Grocer and Restaurant. A bluegrass band worked their banjo strings with a fierceness that a Louisiana boy could appreciate— if only he'd been in the mood. Remy wanted to find Sarah and get out of there.

Simple.

Except the first person his gaze found in the crowd of people dancing under the stars happened to be Erin Finley.

He told himself that was normal enough. She was practically the only person he knew in town besides Sarah and the lady who ran the Heartache B and B. Wouldn't it be human nature for his eye to gravitate toward a face he recognized?

Too bad he didn't fool himself for a second. Especially when he hadn't *seen* her face yet, not when she danced with her back to him, her arms around a smiling dude old enough to be her grandfather. Remy had recognized her silhouette in a floral sundress paired with a dark denim jacket and cowboy boots. He recognized the way she moved—more functional efficiency than traditionally feminine. And, yeah, he realized exactly how much that revealed about the amount of time he'd spent thinking about her.

Cursing himself and his stupid level of observation, he plowed through the crowd toward the dance floor. He'd ask her if she'd seen his daughter and then he'd get out of here.

A few swirling skirts brushed against his legs as he moved through the dancers. He tried not to scowl when two-stepping couples forced him off the direct path to Erin and her dancing partner. Remy didn't know what tipped the guy off, but the gray-haired man seemed to know who Remy had in mind as a target, and by the time he reached them, the old-timer was already stepping away from Erin and passing her hand over to Remy.

"Erin." Well, this was awkward. "I don't mean to interrupt."

"Remy." Her cheeks were flushed from the dance, her whole demeanor softer and sweeter than he'd seen it before. Her smile seemed genuine, too, but her hand remained suspended in midair for a moment before she lowered it quickly.

Was there a better way to prove you'd been brought up in a barn with no manners than to leave a pretty girl hanging? Damn it, damn it.

Politeness got the better of him and he took her hand and stepped into the place of the man who'd held her a second ago.

"You don't need to—" she started.

"I still remember the steps." His words were gruffer than he'd intended. But how could she know what it was like for him to touch a woman's waist through a sheer silk dress? To hold her soft palm in his and see manicured fingernails resting along the back of his hand?

He liked that her nails were still painted jet black though she'd lightened up the inky strands of her hair. There was a toughness about her that he admired. It helped to think about that instead of the fact that she smelled like amber.

"I can see you know the steps." Erin spun with him under a yellow Chinese lantern, keeping pace with him so they didn't run into the couple ahead of them or slow down the couple behind. "If you weren't scowling so hard your eyes are crossed, I might almost think you liked to dance."

He shook his head and hoped his expression relaxed. He was tense.

"Sorry."

"Don't be." Erin moved with him easily, her body sleekly athletic and her steps unencumbered despite the boots she wore. "We can step off the floor over there." She pointed to a spot opposite the band where the crowd was a little thinner.

He felt so grateful for the offer, he could have kissed her, which was exactly *not* what he wanted to think about.

"Thanks. It's so crowded." He let her take the lead as they reached the far edge of the floor, at least until some big, drunk dude stood in her path.

Protectiveness surged.

Keeping his grip on her hand, Remy edged past her, politely staring the guy down, and kept them moving away from everyone else until they were almost in a pine tree thicket. He turned back to speak to her, but she gestured forward.

"Just through there is a walking trail, if you'd like to get some air. It's quieter." She kept her hand in his even now.

Or was he holding on to her?

Maybe he made her self-conscious about it, though, because as he stared at their entwined fingers, Erin let go.

"My turn to be sorry," she murmured, jamming her hands into the pockets of her denim jacket as they reached a wooden bridge over a small stream.

A sign with reflective letters glinted in the moonlight, reading Park Closed at Dusk. Up ahead, he

saw fenced baseball fields and a wooden pavilion. The bluegrass music floated through the trees, the lights of the dance still visible, but softer. He'd go back and look for Sarah in a minute, once he'd cleared his head.

"Don't be sorry." Remy leaned on one of the bridge's thick wooden handrails. "I'm the King of Awkward around you, Erin, and that's my fault, not yours."

She hoisted herself up onto the handrail to take a seat beside him, her cowboy boots dangling over the bridge.

"That's awesome because I'm usually the awkward one. I appreciate you letting me off the hook."

"Ever the gentleman," he remarked wryly, knowing he'd been anything but with her from the moment he'd barged into her store after hours and dripping wet, to the way he'd let his daughter have a meltdown in Erin's office. "You've been the unlucky beneficiary of the Weldon family craziness this week, that's for sure."

Out here, he seemed to relax a little bit. He didn't feel the same tension that he had experienced on the crowded dance floor. The sound of the rushing brook and the soft breeze rustling the leaves helped ease some of the resentment he felt at his attraction to Erin. Even better, he didn't need to be on guard to keep her safe from so many strangers.

"How'd your meeting go today?" she asked, tucking a strand of dark hair behind one ear.

The moonlight spilled over her in a way that made everything a shade of gray.

"It went well. Some of the guys on the crew think I ought to take over as the host for this segment, but I'm not sure." He shrugged. "How did you know I had a meeting?"

"Sarah came by the store today and mentioned you went without her." Erin traced the design on the skirt of her sundress and Remy realized it wasn't a floral pattern like he'd thought.

The design was a tropical beach scene. A girl balanced coconuts in a basket on one hip while a canoe rested at her feet, just out of the surf. It looked hand painted.

"Have you seen Sarah tonight?" He didn't want to get into another discussion about his daughter's problems, hating to be disloyal to her even though Erin's insights had helped him. "She sent me a text that she'd be here, but I haven't spotted her."

"I saw her when I first arrived. She's with my niece, Ally, and some of her friends." Erin didn't seem worried.

But then, she didn't know Sarah's history.

"I had hoped to speak to her tonight," he found himself confiding.

Ah hell. Talking to this woman was just too damned relaxing. Especially when he was over-

worked and overtired. What was it about Erin that made it so easy to be around her?

He hefted himself up onto the wooden rail beside her. They weren't touching, but the spot made for close quarters.

Erin shifted slightly. "The teenagers usually park their cars alongside the playground area. They kind of tailgate during the early part of the evening, and then they take over the dark end of the town square once it gets late. Ally said some of them were bringing stuff for laser tag tonight, but if you want, we can go back and check on them?"

He debated. Sometimes his daughter seemed upset he didn't pay more attention to her. But if he interrupted when she was making new friends… she might not thank him, either.

"In a few minutes maybe. Laser tag sounds fun." Maybe being here would be good for Sarah. She could be a kid and roam around town with more freedom than what he liked for her to have in Miami. "She just turned eighteen, so I'm trying not to be Joe Overprotective. But she's still in school and it's been a rough couple of— Crap." He shook his head. "I told myself I wasn't going to burden you with this stuff even if you are *way* too easy to talk to."

"I bet I'm only easy to talk to because I don't flirt with you." Erin quit tracing the pattern on her dress with her black-painted fingernail. Her pale eyes met his in the moonlight. "Women must hit on you constantly."

"You've seen my great dance moves." He didn't know how else to handle that one. Women did hit on him. "My wife used to say they only liked me for the accent."

Erin grinned. "Smart woman. There's something about a Cajun twang that is just an unfair advantage for a man."

He braced himself for more questions about Liv, but Erin continued speaking.

"Seriously, I don't blame you for wanting to talk about Sarah. It's got to be tough raising a teenager alone and not having anyone to—I don't know—bounce ideas around with. I don't like making decisions about the *store* without getting my sister's opinion. If I had kids?" She rolled her eyes. "I'd have to poll all my friends constantly to see if I was doing the right thing. It's a scary thing being responsible for a mini human."

"That doesn't mean I should unload my paternal worries on you just because you're a nice person." A nice person who'd felt way too good in his arms when they'd taken a few turns around the floor together.

"What worries? Sarah seems really great. She took the initiative to collect a bunch of stuff for my clothing drive today and brought it all over on one of the bicycles from the B and B. I was so impressed." Her voice was animated. Genuine.

And it relieved the hell out of him to think about Sarah jumping on the chance to do something worthwhile in town.

"Really? That is pretty cool." Good news about Sarah hadn't come around often in the past two years, but then, there hadn't been much to celebrate in their lives. "I'm trying my damnedest to raise her right, not just because I love her, but I owe it to her mom."

Erin was quiet for a long time. But then, he was used to people not knowing what to say when he talked about Liv.

"How unfair that she missed out on the chance to see Sarah now," Erin said finally. "Good parents work hard for the chance to be part of their kids' lives."

Remy studied her profile in the moonlight. She seemed a million miles away.

"Liv was definitely a good mom," he said carefully, not quite sure what was on Erin's mind.

She nodded slowly. "Sure sounds like it." Her expression seemed unguarded in a way he hadn't seen it before. "I was just thinking about other people I've known who sucked at parenting and still get chances to do it over again. I'm sorry your wife did her best and didn't get that second chance."

Something about the way she said the words

made him think he'd learned something personal about her. Yet, she'd already told him she didn't have children of her own.

"There's a hell of a lot of things in life that aren't fair." He looked at their hands propped next to each other on the railing. Her thin silver bracelets glinted next to his shirtsleeve. "But you sound like you've got someone in mind."

He didn't ask who since she'd been kind enough not to pin him down about Liv's death. He figured she'd talk about it when she was good and ready. Not that he was planning on…he *definitely* wasn't planning on sticking around beyond this week to get to know her better.

"A crappy ex-boyfriend who never told me he had kids." She shook her head. "I still can't believe there are people so shallow in this world that they'd rather cheat on their spouse and spend time with a lover than be with their family. I mean, why have a family if you're only going to ignore them?"

She turned to him with anguish in her eyes, which he'd been totally unprepared for. And that wasn't the only thing that surprised him.

"Your boyfriend was married?"

"Right." She nodded, her expression closing again. "Forgot to mention that part, as did he. But what killed me most is that he had *children* he was ignoring to be with me while I thought he was single and stupidly waiting around for a proposal."

Her laugh was sharp and humorless. "As if I'd ever want to be with someone who is a selfish, pathological liar." She clapped a hand over her mouth. "I had only one beer tonight. But I am going to use that as an excuse for my sudden bout of chattiness. I'm so sorry to—"

"Don't. Please don't apologize to me." He wrapped his fingers around her wrist, pulling her hand away from her face. "I told you I'm the King of Awkward around you, and I meant it. But I've been more awkward around the rest of the world for the last two years, and I've got to admit it's been—" he searched for the right word "—*refreshing* to talk to you and not feel like you're cringing for me with every word I say."

"All cringing is on my own behalf, I assure you." She untwined her wrist from his grip and jammed her fist into her pocket again. "I'm embarrassed over the choices I made this year, so I don't have a clue what possessed me to share any of that with you tonight while you've got something so traumatic of your own you're trying to deal with."

They sat together while the music played and the spring breeze turned cooler. Now and then, he could hear shouts from kids running through the woods, and he relaxed to think that Sarah was one of them. Maybe it was because Erin didn't ask about Liv the way so many other people did. Or maybe it was the bluegrass band sliding into an old zydeco tune that brought Remy back to another time and place. But something about the moment made him offer freely the truth he rarely ever spoke.

"My wife was murdered in a home invasion." He knew—no matter what family counselors and grief counselors and even Sarah's school guidance counselor liked to say—that admission would never get easier. It still ripped his chest raw to say it. To think about it. "That's the reason I'm still grappling with her death two years later. The reason I was freaked-out that first night we met when I couldn't get a cell signal. I needed to call Sarah to check on her because when I can't get in touch with her I can get—scared."

Erin's shocked expression was about what he'd come to expect, but there was an honesty about it. Unlike some people who already knew what had happened to Liv and asked him about it just to— he didn't know the reason—to pry? To search for more details than what had been in the papers? Erin obviously didn't have an inkling about what had happened.

"I'm—" Her voice cracked on a hoarse note. "I'm so sorry. And stunned. I had no idea."

He nodded. Accepted her words of sympathy. "Thank you. I'm telling you because I know what it's like to be drop-kicked by life and left sprawled on the floor." He'd had days he could hardly move let alone think, function, care for Sarah. "I'm still trying to find my way, for Sarah's sake more than my own."

"And yet you lost so much, too." Erin hugged her arms around her tighter, making him realize how cool the evening had gotten since they'd been out here.

"I should have been there." He knew where the blame rested for Liv's death. He could have made a thousand different choices that would have ensured she was still alive. For six months straight after her death, he'd run through them all in a litany of regrets most nights before he fell asleep. "The break-in happened while I was traveling for work."

Liv had insisted he keep the job even after her perfumes had started attracting international attention. She liked the quiet, she said.

Unwilling to dwell in the past, he dropped to his feet, sliding off the rail. He held a hand out for Erin to do the same. "We should head back so I can find Sarah."

It made him uneasy that—even as they were talking about Liv—he thought about what it would be like to step closer and slide his hands around Erin's waist. To lift her up and off until she stood in the circle of his arms again.

"You couldn't have possibly known." Erin took his hand briefly, just long enough to find her footing on the wooden bridge.

She turned to head back to the village square, but Remy's feet remained rooted to the spot.

"I did, though." It had to be the darkness that made the confessions easier. Or maybe two years had simply been long enough for him to choke on that truth by himself. "I knew that Sarah's felon father was resentful of the home I built for Liv and the life I tried to provide for her. It was only a matter of time before one of his convict friends got out and targeted a wealthy woman on a remote piece of property."

This time, Erin didn't try arguing with him. No doubt because she understood why he blamed himself.

She laid a hand on his forearm and drew him forward.

"You couldn't have known," she repeated. "Thank God Sarah wasn't hurt." She squeezed his arm hard. Once. Twice. "I'll help you find her."

Remy let her tug him along, her swift strides all business as they headed back to the party. No tearful nodding and patting him on the back that only made him feel pathetic. Every day that passed made him like Erin more.

And maybe that was the real reason he'd revealed the truth about his dead wife tonight. It didn't have anything to do with Erin being easy to talk to, or wanting to put them back on even footing after she'd shared something personal with him.

No. He'd told her the truth to push her away. To

clue her in to how much baggage he carried around and how ill equipped he was for a relationship. His head and his heart were still in the past. This way, Erin would know that he was a mental and emotional mess before they shared any more dances or long looks or accidental brushing of hands. Remy had figured out how to laugh again since his wife had died. How to do his job without the crippling sense of loss stealing hours of time and productivity.

But there was a certain kind of happiness that he would never feel in life again, and Erin Finley deserved to know that up front.

CHAPTER SIX

SARAH HAD LUCAS in her sights.

Heart pounding hard in her ears, she peered from her hiding spot beneath the slide. She lined up six feet two inches of delectable boy through the scope on the hot-pink plastic M4 assault rifle. Tipsy from the beer she'd pounded down twenty minutes before, she savored her soon-to-be triumph. She felt good. Happy. She was in a new town where no one knew her past. A cute boy had been flirting with her ever since she had arrived, and now she was about to make the ultimate kill in laser tag.

Except something about seeing Lucas through the scope sent a creepy-crawly sensation over her skin. Her mother hadn't been killed with a rifle. She'd been shot with a handgun at close range while working late in her studio. The police report mentioned the paint on her brush was still wet when they had arrived. She'd been working on artwork for a new fragrance bottle…

Don't think about it.

Sarah shuffled her feet, a few wood chips slipping into her sandals and biting into her toes.

Maybe it was the alcohol that messed with her reflexes and put the world in slow motion for a second. Normally, she never thought about the night her mom died.

Her eyes burned and she tried to refocus on Lucas through the scope, but she couldn't find him—

Beep! Beeeep! Beep!

The plastic disk strapped to her chest by a mini Velcro vest blinked and chimed, startling her. Dropping the gun, she slipped sideways, landing on her butt in the wood chips.

"Got you!" a guy shouted nearby. "You're out of the game, New Girl!"

She'd been hit. Not with a bullet, like her mom had. Just with a laser in a dumb game. Still, her eyes scorched with angry tears she would *not* let fall.

Her chest ached so badly she slid a hand beneath the screaming tagger device to press her fingers into the place above her heart. Her brain told her body to pull itself together, but she seemed locked in a personal freak-out all because she'd played a glorified version of cops and robbers on a playground.

"Hey, Sarah." The boy skidded to a stop, spraying a few wood chips against her calf.

At first, she could see only denim-covered legs,

but then his knees bent until a red T-shirt and lean, muscular arms came into view.

Lucas.

Get it together! the voice inside her screamed.

He grinned, his laser gun—a black M4, which she identified thanks to the weapon tirade given by the kid who'd lent his arsenal for the massive game of tag—slung around his chest by a strap.

She wasn't Miss Gun Control or anything. Her father had grown up in the freaking swamp deep in bayou country, so he had guns and knew how to use them. But something about a piece-of-crap plastic laser tag rifle was causing her to lose it in front of the cutest boy ever. She could tell he knew she was flipping out, too, because his grin turned upside down. Forehead wrinkled.

"Wow. You okay?" he asked finally after she'd sat there like a giant dumbass saying nothing for several long moments.

If that six-pack of beer had been close by, she would have chased away the sensation of phantom spiders crawling over her skin by downing a full one. Failing that, she reached for the next best thing.

"Better than okay." Her hand landed on his knee, the warmth of his body through the denim affecting her faster than alcohol. "I've been waiting for you to find me."

Her heart pounded faster as Lucas lifted a hand

toward her. For a second, she thought he'd touch her. Kiss her, maybe. But he simply stabbed the off button on her electronic tagger to stop the beeping sound. He didn't touch her, but his knuckle brushed close enough to her breast that she could feel the heat of his hand as he tugged the Velcro strap open and pulled off the device. He set it aside.

The quiet helped settle her racing heart until, slowly, the evening came back into focus. She could hear other kids' footsteps thumping past as they chased one another to the home base under the monkey bars. Girls were laughing. Someone blasted a car radio that still wasn't loud enough to drown out the bluegrass band performing at the other end of the town park.

"I guess you got your wish, New Girl." Lucas ducked his head and edged closer to her. "'Cause here I am."

"It's Sarah," she reminded him, brushing her hand a little higher on his thigh to make sure he understood what she wanted.

His eyes hooded as he shifted beside her. He understood all right.

"You like making trouble, don't you, Sarah?" His voice hummed, warm and soft in her ear.

Excitement vibrated along her skin, chasing away the sickening feeling in the pit of her gut. Lucas might be better than alcohol for forgetting her problems. She leaned forward, her lips just inches away from his. She'd never been so bold before, but she didn't care.

She needed this.

"I like you," she said simply, needing things to move faster. Now.

His gaze lowered from her eyes to her lips in a way that felt kind of significant. Green light, right?

Sarah tilted her head and closed the distance between them, taking the kiss he'd been thinking about. Her thoughts vanished like soap bubbles on the wind, drying up one by one until she could feel only the slide of his lips against hers, taste the play of beer and peppermint on his tongue. She breathed deeply, inhaling the spicy sent of his cologne and the hint of barbecue on the breeze from the outdoor grills at Lucky's.

He kissed her gently, taking his time. His fingers brushed along her cheek in a way that made her wish she was a different kind of girl. A girl who spent her Friday nights in a small Tennessee town where she sneaked kisses with cute boys while her parents danced under the stars. Instead, she was the New Girl from Miami who was a troublemaker with a dead mother, a biological father in jail and an adoptive father who believed she was better off with families like the Stedders, who could be more stable guardians for her than him.

Of course, her father just reached for any excuse not to hang out with her lately, even if it made no sense.

The pain under her rib cage returned and she soothed it by pressing her breasts to Lucas's chest. The hard feel of him beneath his tee was enough to warm her inside and out. He tensed all over, going still for a second before his kiss turned hungry. His tongue stroked between her lips and he put a hand on her waist.

Yes.

He tugged her closer, her legs scraping on the wood chips. Not that she cared. This was the kind of kiss that could make her forget things. Scraped calves were better than thinking about her mom's paintbrush still dripping with purple paint as she stared down a gunman's barrel.

Lucas stroked a palm up her spine, sealing their bodies together, and she pressed herself tighter to him as they fell to the ground. When his arms banded around her waist, no longer concerned with keeping her off the cold ground or going slow, she knew she'd gotten under his skin.

Ramped him up as much as she was.

She closed her eyes to focus on all the sensations. Hip to hip. Breast to chest. His thigh settling between her legs in a way that felt so very good. Her lightweight skirt was a girlie bit of froufrou that let her feel the play of his taut thigh muscles right where it counted.

He dragged a hand through her hair, his fingers scraping over her scalp and making her skin tingle. He swept down the back of her neck to pause at the shoulder of her sweater. And in that little patch of bare skin between her neck and the fabric, he circled the pad of his thumb lightly. For such a small touch—in a spot so far removed from the usual goodies that boys liked—the soft stroke was damn potent.

She couldn't concentrate on the kissing. Her head rolled back, giving him lots of room to maneuver.

"You like that?" he asked softly in her ear, the words barely breathed they were so close.

"Mmm," she managed, humming pleasure, her eyes remaining closed so she could enjoy every moment of this. The more physical things got, the less she had to live in her head and listen to her thoughts.

Bring it, Lucas.

Just as she thought it, he laid his lips against that tender place along her neck, his tongue taking over where his fingers had just been. The jolt of sexy bliss was better than anything she'd ever done with a guy in bed, and this definitely wasn't the first time she'd sought out pleasure to get rid of morbid thoughts of death and guns.

Sarah squeezed his shoulders tight, wanting the moment to go on and on. Crazy. But then, she might be crazy. She hadn't confided half her real feelings or fears to her counselor.

Lucas stopped suddenly, his head coming up. His eyes met hers in the darkness.

"Someone's coming." He sat up and pulled her with him. Tossed the tagger in her lap and pulled his rifle into his while she struggled to remember her name and why he needed to stop doing deliciously sweet things to her.

"Lucas?" Her fingers trembled a little as she tucked a loose strand of hair behind her ear.

"Sarah!" a man's voice shouted nearby.

"Ohmigod, it's my dad," she said, scrambling to straighten her sweater and skirt. Pull herself together. "Go," she urged Lucas.

"In a sec," he muttered, taking deep breaths.

She brushed off her skirt and slid out from under the slide. It didn't matter that she was eighteen and technically an adult. She'd die if her dad caught her fooling around in the dirt under a piece of playground equipment. If he knew half the stuff she'd done…

Her throat went dry just thinking about it.

"I'm here!" She waved to call his attention since he was on the other side of the playground near the monkey bars. She stumbled a little from the lingering effects of the beer, but mostly from the kiss.

He walked with Erin Finley, the lady from Last Chance Vintage with the killer clothes and funky hair. What was up with that? Sarah's father did not hang out with other women. Ever. They might flirt with him and bat their lashes, but he brushed them aside. It was weird to see him with Erin at night—not in a work situation.

"Sarah." He picked up the pace as he caught sight of her. "Did your phone battery die?" He held up his for emphasis. "I've been texting you."

"Sorry." She pulled her phone out of her skirt pocket and hoped the dark would hide the fact that Lucas was sneaking out from under the slide to skulk away. "We were just playing a game of laser tag and we all turned off our phones so they wouldn't give away our positions, you know? A ringtone sort of defeats the purpose of sneaking around the woods with your trusty M4 by your side."

She waved her pink weapon to prove her innocence and hoped Lucas had made it to the parking lot without anyone seeing. She thought she'd noticed Erin looking in that direction.

Had she seen something? Could she smell beer on Sarah's clothes? Sarah hadn't been the only one to bring a six-pack to the Friday night outdoor dance.

"You ready to head back to the B and B?" her dad asked, focused only on her.

And for the moment, she had to appreciate how

oblivious he could be even if it meant he didn't always pay much attention to her.

"Sure, Daddy." That was half the reason she'd come to this little town, after all. Lucas had been a fun side benefit. It wasn't all about running away from Brandon's letters. She wanted to hang out with her dad. "I've got my car parked over there."

She pointed behind the playground to the spots along the street.

"I'm this way." He gestured in the opposite direction. "You're leaving now, though, right?"

"Yes," she lied, hoping she'd have time for a real good night with Lucas first. She wanted to go to sleep with a fantastic memory in her head. Or maybe she would ask him if he could sneak out later in case she had trouble sleeping.

"I'm parked where Sarah is, too," Erin chimed in, stepping away from her father. "I'll walk with you."

Sarah hoped her disappointment didn't show. It took her a second to think how to respond. "Sure!" she finally replied way too brightly. She sounded like a giant doofus. "That'd be great. See you, Dad!"

Turning, she headed for her car. She wished she hadn't been so hasty, though, because she heard their low voices behind her, and realized Erin was saying something to her father for his ears only. And it looked really…private. Something squeezed in Sarah's chest. She'd been bitching at him to move on with life, right?

Why the hell did it hurt to see the way he looked at a consignment shop owner they'd never see again after the Tennessee episodes were filmed? Folding her arms, she stared at Erin as the woman walked toward her. She'd had Goth hair just a few days ago. How old did that make her? Young.

"Are you okay, Sarah?" Erin reached her and looked her up and down. Even in the dark, her pale eyes seemed to see everything. "You've got wood chips in your hair." She pulled out a few and paused as she pushed Sarah's hair behind her shoulder. "And a love bite on your neck."

"What?" Sarah's hand went to the spot, recalling how good it had felt when Lucas had kissed her there. "What are you talking about?"

Her face burned. But she hadn't done a damn thing wrong!

Erin's eyes narrowed. "I think I'm talking about the boy who I saw sneaking out from under the slide a minute after you came out of there."

Sarah prepped her defense—wounded innocence was a good one—except Erin was no longer there to see her expression of shocked disbelief. She was already heading for the row of cars where they'd both parked. Hurrying to catch up, Sarah waved goodbye to a few new friends from earlier that evening. She couldn't remember their names.

"We were just fooling around. Nothing major," Sarah explained when she reached Erin's side, matching her stride for stride. Now that they stood so close, she realized she was actually a little taller than Erin. Which was funny because Erin seemed bigger. "But that doesn't mean I want to throw it in my dad's face that I'm making out with some dude I only just met."

"Perfectly understandable." Erin reached the street and turned to face her as they stood under a big iron lamppost. "But I thought I'd heard something about that kid not having the best reputation. Have you been drinking?"

Resentment flared. Where did she get off asking her that?

"No," Sarah lied, hoping she didn't sound as pissed off as she felt. "We were kissing, not drinking."

Erin nodded slowly. "Fine. Just making sure you're okay to drive."

She wasn't sure if she was grateful to be let off the hook or disappointed that she'd fooled yet another grown-up into thinking she was fine. Capable. Strong.

"Perfectly." She pulled her car key out of her skirt pocket. "And I'll be careful around Lucas. People can change, you know. Maybe he's grown out of his bad stage."

Erin's smile lifted one side of her mouth and not

the other. "Some guys never do. But for his sake and yours, I hope you're right about him."

The kind words touched her and some of the resentment she'd felt earlier melted away as they stood in the rapidly cooling spring night.

"Me, too. Let me know if you need any more help with the clothing drive." She didn't know why she offered. Hanging out with Erin was bound to be a bad idea. Except that she'd at least be able to monitor the developing situation between this woman and her father. "My dad isn't putting me to work as much I would have liked."

Or maybe she just wanted to stay on Erin's good side. Keep your friends close and enemies closer, and all that. Though she wasn't sure what category to put Erin in yet.

"Are you free next Wednesday?" Erin reached down to her boot and unzipped a side compartment in the leather. She pulled out a key. "I'm doing a drive in The Strand salon just down the street from my store. Customers get a free basic manicure if they donate three items."

Sarah turned on her phone. "Did you put it on Instagram?"

"You sound just like my sister," Erin muttered. "No, it's not on Instagram. I printed flyers."

Sarah laughed, quickly scrolling through Ally Finley's social media followers to search for Heartache locals. "I can hang flyers, but I'll do this first. What are the hours?"

Once she got the details and set up a simple event page online, Sarah promised to be at The Strand on Wednesday if she could convince her father to stay in town that long. She said good-night to Erin and hopped in her car. Before putting the key in the ignition, she finished up some tasks on her phone. She was in the middle of ap-proving a new follower on Twitter—thinking it was someone from Heartache—when she recog-nized the name of her mom's hometown in Loui-siana. Belle Chasse.

Coincidence?

That creepy sensation she'd experienced earlier crawled over her skin again. Looking closer, Sarah saw the woman's name was Becky, but her ac-tual Twitter handle was "lockeduplove47," which seemed icky. Feeling a bad vibe, Sarah deleted the request and clicked out of the app.

Tossing the cell phone on her passenger seat, she had all the more reason to work at the salon for a little while this week. She needed to see Ally Fin-ley again and quiz her about Lucas—the girlfriend, the reputation, all of it. Sarah was edgy, restless and ready to come out of her skin. And she'd run for miles earlier today! Sure, she could buy more alcohol and drink herself into happy oblivion, but it seemed more fun to give her body over to Lucas until she couldn't think, could only feel.

Who better to help her than the boy with the worst reputation in town?

CHAPTER SEVEN

ERIN WISHED SHE had her sledgehammer.

It was morning. She was at home hand painting a new sign for Last Chance Vintage in her backyard. It should be relaxing, but she was impatient with the careful detail work. What she really wanted to do was take a sledgehammer to something. She was frustrated with everything—herself most of all.

Jamming the paintbrush back into the mason jar of red paint, she stretched her aching back, taking deep breaths to try to relax. She worked at an old picnic table she'd asked her brother to drag into the field beyond her lawn. She could spill all the paint she wanted without worry. With a million things to prepare before the filming started at the store, Erin had taken a few days off from working the register so she could focus.

Too bad her thoughts were stuck on a producer from out of town and the stark pain she'd seen in his eyes the night before. Remy Weldon was in far worse shape than she was emotionally. Which meant he wanted to avoid romantic entanglements, too, which was helpful. But she was incredibly attracted to him. And now that she'd glimpsed the personal hell he was going through, she didn't know how she would stay away. She'd never been the nurturer type—that was more Heather's thing—yet every latent feminine and gentle instinct inside her wanted to wrap Remy in her arms. Hold him.

And yes, sex him until he couldn't see any woman but her. There had been moments last night when he'd touched her and the touch had turned so electric she was sure he must feel the same way. What if they'd been put in each other's paths to help heal one another? Maybe the chemistry between them could burn away some of his old guilt. For that matter, she'd be glad to torch some of hers, too. Talking to Remy about Patrick—and seeing the weight of all Remy's baggage—made her realize she needed to stop carrying around so much guilt about being with a cheating, no-good bastard.

Time to move on.

The idea wouldn't let her go.

"Anyone home?" A shout from the other end of the yard yanked her attention from her anger at Patrick. And the mix of new feelings she seemed to be developing for Remy.

Bethany and their soon-to-be sister-in-law, Nina Spencer, stood on the back patio of Erin's house, carrying a bright blue cooler between them. Bethany wore a straw sun hat as big as an umbrella. Nina carried a basket with a towel peeping out of the top, and Erin would bet her last nickel it contained some kind of amazing baked good. After working for years in a specialty cupcake shop in Manhattan, Nina had moved back to Heartache and reunited with her high school sweetheart, Erin's brother Mack. Today she wore a T-shirt with the Finleys' logo on it for the bar Mack owned in Nashville. They divided their time between his home there and a converted barn apartment on the Finley family property.

"You come bearing gifts?" Erin asked, drawn by the promise of food, help and the welcome camaraderie of sisterhood. After keeping a low profile in town for the past six months, she was ready to start enjoying herself again.

Forgiving herself. Maybe seeing how much Remy was beating himself up over something he'd had no control over had made her ease up on the guilt.

"We brought a little of everything," Bethany announced, setting the cooler on the deck between the grill and the seating area. "Do you want to work first and eat later, or are you ready for a break?"

"So ready for a break." Capping her paint jar, Erin took off her apron and left it on the picnic table.

Her sisters-in-law exchanged a look.

"What?" Erin joined them on the patio, kicking off her shoes as her feet hit the outdoor carpet.

"We made bets on how much hard labor we'd

have to do before we got to try Nina's cupcakes," Bethany admitted. "Show her, Nina."

"They're lemon-berry." Nina lifted the tea towel on the basket to show off neat rows of yellow-frosted dreaminess. "I frosted them a little too soon after they came out of the oven, but I was dying to try them."

Erin inhaled the sweet-tangy scent. "Oh, wow. It seems only right that we eat these before we do anything else. Let me just run inside to wash up and I'll bring us some drinks."

"No need." Bethany was already digging in the cooler. "Nina spent time in catering, so she thought of everything."

Five minutes later, ensconced in a dark wicker patio chair with cream-colored cushions, Erin sipped her peach Bellini and took the smallest bites of her cupcake imaginable to make it last longer.

"This is so delicious. I can't begin to tell you."

"I think the frosting works with it," Nina observed, swiping her finger over the top of the cupcake to take a frosting-only bite. "It doesn't seem like overkill to me."

"No." Bethany shook her head. "But I love lemon. Sometimes you need the sour with the sweet to make you appreciate the taste of each." She gestured to the patio. "Like this little haven of Erin's back here. Who would guess she would create such a romantic and glamorous spot based on the rest of her decorating, which is so modern and kind of edgy? But back here, it's like a pasha's palace."

Erin had to smile at that. "Pasha's palace? Someone's been hitting the romance novels again."

Although she could appreciate the comparison. She had hung pendant lamps under the shelter of a pergola with a canopy. She had fallen in love with the lamps' amethyst glass shades, which had the curvy appeal of a genie's lamp. Plus, they were *purple*.

"Honey, don't knock it until you've been ravished in the desert and fed figs from the pasha's hand." Bethany pointed an accusing finger at both of them and Nina laughed so hard she snorted.

"I'm not knocking romance," Erin defended herself. "I'm all for seeking a thrill somewhere since there aren't any sexy Arabian princes in my life right now."

"You never mentioned what happened with the guy you wanted to bring down here last year. Or is the ban on that topic still being enforced six months later?" Nina had a reputation for speaking before measuring her words, a habit none of the younger Finleys possessed. With a mother who was bipolar, they'd grown up under the shadow of tirades where she'd shared *way* more than was appropriate.

Nina's tendency was a lot more charming.

"Turned out he was married. With kids." Erin

had admitted it to Remy, so she sure didn't see the point in keeping it from her sisters.

They were both so still it was as if neither of them breathed for a minute.

"The *dog*," Nina said finally. "Are you kidding me? And that's rhetorical, so don't answer that. Unbelievable."

Bethany shook her head. "I have got to fix my marriage. I cannot go out into a dating world where men act like that."

"Yes, well, me neither. That's why I've been working with my head down for six months trying not to think about it. But I'm done feeling like the greatest of all sinners when he lied to me from start to finish." She frowned and reached for a chunk of Manchego from a bamboo board displaying three kinds of cheeses, star fruit and grapes. Nina had labeled the cheeses with mini gardening tags on toothpicks. "And I know you're going to fix the marriage, Bethany. Scott seems really committed to it."

Erin had seen them together at the Harvest Dance last fall and Scott had promised their mom to fight for his wife. Erin had believed him. Scott was one of those guys who did not fail. He was a conqueror.

Had Remy been like that before he lost his wife? The thought made her ache all the more for him.

Bethany shook her head. "He's just going through

the motions. Like if he clocks enough hours seated in a counselor's chair we'll be given some kind of certificate that says we've magically been healed. He doesn't understand it's not enough just to show up."

"I did that for a long time," Nina volunteered, cutting a few slices of apple before drizzling honey on them. "Remember when I left Heartache after high school? Right after Mack's friend Vince died in a car crash because Vince and I had argued?"

"I didn't know you went into counseling." Although Erin recalled that time had been hell for both Mack and Nina. The hurt from that car crash had stolen eight years from them.

"I did. But it took a lot of sessions before I was ready to do more than just show up." Nina sliced more apple and passed around the plates. "And it's hard to spill your guts when you're not even sure that talking about what's wrong is going to change a thing."

Bethany's shoulders sagged. "So what turned things around for you? Do you remember what made you start working with the therapist?"

Setting her drink down, Erin waited for her answer, maybe as curious as Bethany. She'd never entered counseling even though Mack had taken her aside once and told her it had helped him resolve a lot of issues he'd had with their mother. Mack had thought all of his siblings should check in with a professional since bipolar disorder ran in families. But Erin never had. Maybe part of her was scared of what she could find out. And if she did learn that she had some of the same tendencies as her mother, what would she do about it? She had always feared that—since talking about their childhood wouldn't change it—no amount of therapy would really fix the broken parts of her.

Nina grinned. "I have a hard time staying quiet for long. Hard to believe, right? But I got fed up with not talking and figured what did I have to lose? I started telling the story about Vince's death and my role in it..." Her smile faded. "It was awful. And it didn't get better right away. It took months of feeling like I was scraping my insides out before I started to turn a corner."

"But it really helped?" Erin hadn't remained angry with her mother after a childhood that had been occasionally frightening. She just drew boundaries and figured that was healthy enough. Yet considering it had taken her months to shake loose the sense of failure about Patrick, she wondered again if she was missing out on a deeper understanding of herself by avoiding the counselor's office.

"So much." Nina took another sip of her Bellini. "I needed that outside perspective to help me see what was normal about what I was feeling and what... wasn't. I wouldn't have finished college without her help."

While Erin tried to imagine what it would be like to unlock all her family secrets and let a therapist wander around her thoughts, Bethany quizzed Nina more on the time frame for her experience and how she measured her results. She asked so many questions, in fact, that Erin got a much clearer idea of Bethany's commitment to the process.

When Bethany seemed to have exhausted her list of things to ask, silence fell over the group for a long moment.

"What will you do if Scott continues to just show up?" Erin asked. She'd hoped the couple had turned a corner last fall when they had agreed to see a counselor.

Bethany stared out over the fields toward the peach orchard while she thought about it.

"As long as there is still some love there, I'm going to keep trying." Her voice wobbled a little and Nina leaned over to sling an arm around her shoulders. "I will continue fighting for as long as there is a scrap of a chance that we still have a few seeds left of what we once shared."

Erin's eyes burned at her sister-in-law's heartfelt words. "Cheers to that." She lifted her glass in a toast. "Love is worth fighting for."

Or so she hoped. These days she wasn't sure she really believed she'd ever experience it herself.

"Cheers." Nina clinked her glass to both of theirs and Bethany smiled crookedly as she drank, too.

"No one said marriage would be easy." Bethany dug into her apples and Erin was glad to see her eating. She'd lost a lot of weight last summer, but she seemed to be holding steady now.

"Um. Right." Nina nodded. "But it took me eight years to get Mack even thinking in that matrimonial direction after he went and married someone else first. So let's go gently on the hopeful future newlywed, ladies."

Erin laughed, lifting her fingers to run them over a wind chime that hung near her chair. "Mack adores you. He only got divorced because he married the wrong woman the first time. I can tell you both—" she stared hard at the two women "—that you are the *right* choices for my brothers, assuming you can handle them. I hope you do because I love you guys, big-time."

"Aw!" Nina, who had no siblings and whose parents had abandoned her to her grandmother when she was in elementary school, rushed over to give her a hug. "Right back at you, chica."

"And it's not just because you make great cupcakes," Erin assured her, winking at Bethany over Nina's shoulder.

"Hey, my cupcakes got me a few marriage proposals back when I worked in New York, I kid you not. That's how I knew I was onto something." Nina plunked down in the chair close to Erin on the opposite side of the table where she'd started.

"You let me know when you need to turn up the heat for your next boyfriend and I'll make a batch guaranteed to have him thinking about a ring."

She couldn't possibly have guessed how the ring remark would affect her because, of course, Erin hadn't shared that particular detail about Patrick with them.

"I don't think we'll know who Erin has her eye on until the ring is already on her finger," Bethany remarked, eyeing Erin across the table. "She's always played it close to the vest."

"With my mother ready to turn the slightest comment into major drama, wouldn't you do the same?" Erin had her reasons.

Nina snorted.

"Well, sure." Bethany added a few cheese slices to her plate, carefully avoiding Erin's gaze. "That doesn't mean you should hold out on us."

Was there a trace of hurt in her voice? Erin had never been the kind to share much of her private life with anyone, but she was hoping days like today would become more common. She enjoyed these women, and she trusted them. Heather might be her sister by blood, but Bethany and Nina were part of the fabric of her family. Their presence at Finley events made things less strained as far as she was concerned.

"You're right." Erin sat up straighter. "So I'm turning over a new leaf, and you're going to be the first to hear my new decision about my nonexistent love life."

Bethany's eyebrows shot up.

"There's nothing as delectable as a good secret," Nina declared.

"I'm thinking about making a pass at the producer." It was probably crazy. But she couldn't stop thinking about the possibility.

"What?" Bethany exclaimed at the same time Nina said, "No way!"

"I know, Bethany, I told you I wasn't interested in a man in my life."

"Right. *Yesterday*," Bethany reminded her.

"I stand by that." Erin stirred the ice cubes in her drink, watching them swirl around the peaches floating on top. "I had my heart broken not that long ago, so I'm not ready to jump back into a relationship. But I realized the producer and I are both…in a transition period."

"He's your gap guy?" Nina clutched her arm, her silver rings flashing in the sunlight.

"Maybe he could be." And Remy needed a rebound woman, even if he didn't know it yet. "He's from Miami, so there won't be those awkward moments where you see each other around town. We can just…" She finished the sentence with a shrug. "You know. Enjoy each other and then go our separate ways."

The other women exchanged a look.

"Okay, stop with the telepathy," Erin complained. "What's wrong with that?"

"Sex complicates things," Nina started at the same time Bethany said, "It's not easy to keep emotions out of the equation."

"Right." Erin hadn't thought that far yet. Maybe the attraction was stronger than she'd realized if she was already making plans to follow the chemistry where it led before she'd considered all the possible consequences. "Normally, I'd agree with you. But I think Remy and I—"

"His name is Remy?" Nina sighed.

"He has a Cajun accent," Bethany offered.

"Anyway, I think we've both had our emotions trampled recently, so they're not really going to *be* involved."

"And there's a river in Africa called De-Nial." Nina adjusted her big straw hat to keep her face covered from the sun. "Although I support you in your quest for a good time."

"I'll drink to that," Bethany added. "Good for you, Erin."

They spent the rest of the afternoon working on signs for the new store space in Last Chance Vintage. Her sisters-in-law, Bethany and Nina, didn't mention Erin's plan again, which she appreciated. She wasn't sure why she'd confided in them when— as Bethany had pointed out—she usually kept her personal life very personal. Maybe it was because she was starting over, committing to her new life in Heartache rather than hoping she'd find happiness somewhere else. Or maybe it was because she felt like a bad friend for not sharing more about herself in the past.

Yet as the sun sank lower and the other women headed home, Erin realized it wasn't for either of those reasons. The simple truth was, she was nervous about acting on what she felt for Remy, especially in light of the things he'd shared with her.

There was a very real chance he'd say no. She knew he was trying to avoid the attraction. But she recognized his pain, and it called to her on a deeper level than the surface chemistry. She knew what it felt like to be hurt. Lost. Struggling to stay afloat. And if they had the kind of chemistry that could distract him from all of that for even a few hours at a time? She would at least propose it.

Telling Nina and Bethany about it was just Erin's way of making sure she didn't lose her nerve. Now that she'd shared the plan with her friends? She'd damn well follow through on it if only for the sake of her pride.

Dumb or brilliant, she wasn't sure. But she picked up the phone to call the Heartache B and B and invite Remy Weldon for dinner.

REMY WAS IN the middle of laying out a digital storyboard with his director in a teleconference session when his cell phone rang. Sarah had gone out earlier. They'd had a good talk the night before about making better choices to stay in touch with him frequently. They had adjoining rooms at the B and B for the next few days while Remy finished scouting the area for locations. Remy had touched base with Sarah's counselor, who had told him she was encouraged that Sarah had reached out to him and that spending more time together could be a good thing for both of them.

Her comments had lifted some of the pressure off Remy to rush through this job and get back to Miami. Now he sat alone in his room working on the cramped desk overrun by knickknacks, staring down at the caller ID to see who was interrupting his meeting.

It wasn't Sarah.

It was Erin Finley. He'd entered her contact information into his phone for reference's sake. He never expected her to call him for any reason. Unless, maybe she had a question about the coverage for her Dress for Success event. Curious, he told his director they'd finish up later and Remy took the call.

"Hello?" He had no reason to feel uneasy, yet his senses hummed with a kind of wariness he didn't normally experience around anyone, let alone a woman.

It must be the conversation they'd had last night

that was messing with his head now. He'd let her get too close. Shared too much.

"Hi, Remy. It's Erin."

Her voice worked on him like a good song on the radio. He wanted to turn it up. Listen to more. And damn, that wasn't a good thing.

"Hey." He fought to keep things more professional this time. "I was just working on some ideas for shooting the episode with Last Chance Vintage. It'd be nice if we could work on some kind of preliminary event for your clothing drive so that we're filming customers bringing in donations and you prepping the racks for the clients as you get ready for the show."

"That would be great." She spoke fast. "And we can talk about it more. But I called to invite you for dinner. At my house."

His brain blanked.

"You are welcome to bring Sarah, of course. I know she wants to spend more time with you—"

"I don't understand." He jabbed the button to turn off his computer screen, needing to focus on this call. On Erin and what she was suggesting.

"It's dinner," she repeated. "You know—a standard meal people eat every day. I'll prepare food I hope you like. We'll have some awkward conversation, but it could be a nice change from eating alone."

He had to smile, which probably counted as a

miracle given how much the invitation had rattled him.

"Right. I remember the meal."

"I'm a passable cook. Nothing to write home about, but I keep an excellent wine stash, so there's a chance you'll enjoy the cabernet too much to notice if I overcook the steak."

"Erin." He closed his eyes, thinking about having a meal in her home. That she cooked for him. "I thought last night, when I told you...the things I did... I thought we were agreeing that the whole undercurrent between us was a bad idea."

"Maybe I did agree at first." She was quiet for a moment, and he tried to picture her. Where she was. What she was thinking. Damn, but what *was* she thinking? "But I think that's a mistake," she continued finally. "I mean, putting the whole undercurrent between us aside, how long has it been since you had a dinner at a friend's house? How long since someone cooked for you and you held a real conversation over a meal?"

He didn't need to think about it. He could recall a date and time easily, but he tried like hell not to live in the past.

"I don't know..."

"What are you doing tomorrow?" she pressed. "Is Sarah around?"

"Sarah wants to go to the drive-in with a bunch

of her new friends tomorrow. Do you believe they have a drive-in theater in Heartache?"

"You're talking to one of its most vocal supporters when it nearly got shut down ten years ago."

Remy edged around the edge of the bed to peer out the small window overlooking the gardens behind the B and B. Another couple who were staying in the hotel were taking tea out under an awning while the hostess hurried to bring out another silver-covered platter.

"That's right. I forgot I was talking to the former mayor's daughter."

"I'm an activist at heart."

"I'm not a project for you." He said it more sharply than he'd intended, but he got the impression that Erin was a fix-it kind of woman, and not just because she renovated her own shop with power tools. Sometimes caring people could offer too much help.

"No," she agreed. "You're not my project. But you'll be glad for a steak with me tomorrow since Sarah already has plans."

He closed his eyes for a heartbeat. He liked this woman and all her capable, no-nonsense attitude. There was no denying it.

"I'll bring dessert," he said finally. "I found a restaurant up the street that brings in locally made cupcakes."

Remy told himself he was agreeing only for the meal and not for the way Erin Finley got under his skin. She was too damn easy to talk to, yes. But maybe she had a point about him not getting out more.

"I love cupcakes." She smiled when she said it, he could tell. "Get the lemon-berry, if you see them. They're fantastic."

CHAPTER EIGHT

WHEN ERIN HAD bad ideas, apparently they happened in threes.

Shoving the charred foil packet of potatoes away from the flames on the grill, she cursed herself for all three of those ideas. First, for deciding to start something with a guy who had made it clear he wanted nothing to do with her. Second, for confiding to Bethany and Nina that she was going to act on that decision. And third, for inviting him to this dumb dinner. She'd asked him in a fit of optimism, thinking they could enjoy each other's company while forgetting their pasts.

But while she was just trying to scrub the memory of a loser who had lied to her, Remy was still grappling with the traumatic loss of his wife. A loss he unreasonably blamed himself for.

How the hell had she ever thought sex and steak could fix that?

Burned potatoes sure wouldn't.

By the time her doorbell rang—the classic chime echoing through her sparsely furnished house and bouncing off the ceramic tile floors all the way to the back patio—she was close to tears. She had not shed a single tear for her loser ex-boyfriend since the day she'd found out he was married, and here she was sniffling hard. Erin slammed the grill shut and turned off the heat.

Marching through the house, she flung open the front door. Only to find Remy on her porch looking as lost and miserable as she felt.

To his credit, he held a bakery box in one hand and a bag from the liquor store in the other. His hazel gaze flicked over her, taking in her vintage pink sundress and skinny white patent-leather belt paired with gray argyle tennis shoes. As she stared right back, she couldn't help but think how they were a mismatch on so many levels. Remy was classically handsome in dark jeans and a white tee with a camel-colored linen jacket.

His dark hair was neatly combed, the ends curling at his collar, still damp. Her heartbeat jumped at the thought of him showering for this…for her. And that, right there, was why she'd been so pushy with him. She was crushing on him like a teenager no matter how much she wanted to deny it.

"Hi." He awkwardly held up the goods. "I may have overbought since I was hungry and everything looked good."

"You show grace under pressure when I practically twisted your arm into dinner." She took the bag and the box. "Come on in and let me apologize for being so bossy. It's a bad habit of mine."

"No apology necessary." He followed her through the living area, where white leather couches and bright blue glass lamps made the room look like a Wedgwood dish. A rattan coffee table and accent furniture kept it from being too fussy looking. "Nice place you have."

"Thank you." She took a left into the kitchen. "I like decorating and I find plenty of cool stuff when I go on buying trips for the store. It's a constant battle not to cram the house full of things I think are neat."

She felt nervous and tempted to call off the whole thing. Send him back to the B and B. But after he'd showered, shopped and shown up she also didn't want to be rude.

"Erin—"

"Remy—" She started at the same time, so they talked on top of each other. "You go first."

"I just wanted to thank you for inviting me over." He took her hand to turn her toward him. Then he let it go quickly, almost as if he wanted to make sure not to touch her. "I know I may not be the best company, but it was a good idea to have a place to go while Sarah is out. You were right about that."

Relieved she'd had good instincts about *something*, she relaxed a little, though her hand still tingled warm where he'd touched her.

"You may rescind those words once you see how badly I burned the potatoes." She set the wine on the wooden kitchen island and searched for a corkscrew. "I've been nervous all day, feeling like I twisted your arm into coming here."

"You didn't."

"Kind of I did." She passed the corkscrew to him to let him open the Chianti, then pulled down some glasses from an overhead cabinet. "My brother calls it Type B Bossiness because I tend to wear people down quietly."

He slid the cork free and poured two glasses, his head a hairbreadth from the pans that hung over the countertop. "I can see that. You don't have the traditional entrepreneur's mind-set."

"I work as hard as anyone else." She tipped her chin, defying him to say otherwise.

"That's easy to see." He leaned back on the counter and folded his arms, an amused smile on his lips. "But most of the shop owners I meet for this show are idea people. They have a big vision, but not always the day-to-day organization to make the dream work. You have both. Or at least, you have the follow-through."

"I can't afford to fail." She pointed at the glasses. "If you carry those outside, I'll start the steaks."

They moved to the back deck, where the sun was already casting a purple glow. In the distance, she could see the converted barn where Mack and

Nina had an apartment, but the lights were off and Erin guessed Nina must be staying at her grandmother's for the weekend.

"Everyone fails sometimes," Remy pointed out, his eye roaming the "pasha's palace" furnishings. "Want me to light the lamps?"

He picked up the igniter she kept near the hurricane lamp on one end table.

"Sure." She turned up the grill's heat to sear the meat, keeping half an eye on Remy as he moved to each of the purple glass shades to burn a candle inside the hanging fixtures.

The fading sun caught a mix of gold and brown in the scruff of hair around his jaw as he concentrated on his task. She hadn't lit the candles earlier, fearing the atmosphere would look too romantic— as if she was expecting more from the night than just dinner. Seeing the space lit up now seemed to turn up the heat on the night. Or was that just on her part?

He turned just in time to catch her staring. More warmth rushed to her cheeks.

"I need to time these," she blurted. "Do you have a watch?"

"Yours not working?" He set the igniter down and strode closer.

Of course she was wearing a watch herself. She was just way too nervous.

"You wouldn't need to ask that if you saw what

happened to the potatoes." She pointed to the two sad packets of foil charred to a crisp that she'd left on an upper shelf of the grill. "Can you tell me when two minutes are up?"

"Done." He kept her company while she waited for the sear to finish. "Until then, how about a toast?" He passed her one glass of wine and picked up the other.

"To Type B Bossiness." His gaze locked on hers and her heart rate cranked up speed. Thankfully, he turned away before she made an idiot of herself and swooned on him. "And springtime in Heartache."

Seizing the chance to focus on something besides him, she lifted her glass and admired the flowering dogwood trees and rogue honeysuckle patches that climbed up the potting shed in the backyard.

"Hope springs eternal. Cheers."

When she faced him and clinked her glass to his, she noticed his expression had changed. His face was totally blank. Skin pale. Eyes focused somewhere else entirely.

She put a hand on his arm. "Remy? You okay?"

He set his glass down unsteadily, a little Chianti splashing over the rim, but he didn't notice.

"Sorry." His voice was hoarse as he lowered himself to a seat. "It's been two years. Two. Years. And stuff still grabs me by the throat sometimes and takes me right back there…"

He shook his head. Shoved a weary hand through his hair.

"People grieve at their own pace." She switched off the grill and sat next to him. "It takes time."

She hated to spout lame platitudes, which he had probably heard too often, but she didn't know what more to do. She'd caught hints of the old pain in his eyes when she had first met him—before she'd known about his wife. And now, understanding where it came from, she felt even more helpless to do anything about it.

It was foolish for thinking anything could happen between them tonight. Remy wasn't anywhere near ready for a rebound fling. It sure put what she'd gone through with Patrick into perspective.

"You want to talk about it?" She debated the wisdom of taking his hand for about a nanosecond. Then, acting on basic human kindness, she took it and squeezed. "I don't claim to have any answers, but Type Bs make really great listeners."

He stared at the open fields beyond the lawn. "You remember, when we made the toast, you said 'hope springs eternal'? Liv had the words stenciled in her studio above the windows that looked out on her gardens. I helped paint it. In fact, it was one of the few things she didn't paint by hand in there." He shrugged. "She was a talented artist. But even I can handle filling in a stencil."

"It sounds beautiful."

"It was." His voice went rough again. His eyes focused on some point she couldn't see. "So beautiful, in fact, that she told Sarah's biological father all about it in a letter one of the many times she wrote to that bastard, trying to get Brandon to acknowledge their daughter." His gaze returned to Erin again. "I told you he's been in jail since before I met Liv? He's some kind of computer genius who, as Liv said, never 'lived up to his potential.'"

"Liv sounds like an amazing person."

"Yeah. But some days, it's hard to forgive her for talking to the waste-of-space felon. He's the reason she's dead. He told his cell mate all about our house." Remy squeezed her hand hard. Not in a bad way. But she wondered if he realized it. Her heart hurt for him. "The cell mate targeted our home for a robbery after he got out of prison two months later. He shot her in the studio where she was working. I kept that place until the trial was done and knew he was in jail for life. Then I burned the studio to the ground before I sold the main house."

She gasped. "Were you living there all that time?"

"Hell no. I moved Sarah to Miami to start over right afterward. I only went back for the trial to make sure the guy and his accomplice went to jail. Then I torched the place where they ended her life and ruined mine."

The image of this caring, charming man setting fire to the building where his wife was murdered tore at her.

"It's no wonder you're still grieving." What a horrible, horrible loss for him. "Her death was a shock and you probably couldn't begin mourning her until after the trial."

"All I thought about was revenge for a while. I wanted to kill him myself." He let go of her hand and found his wineglass. Taking a long swallow, he glanced over at her, waiting to see her reaction.

"I'm sure you did." Who wouldn't in his position?

"But I had Sarah to think about." He nodded slowly. "And the last thing I wanted was for my girl to have two fathers in jail."

"You're a good man." She watched the fireflies come out as the sun sank lower on the horizon. "Sarah is lucky to have you."

"I don't know about that. I became all kinds of overprotective. Sarah's counselor had to step in and tell me to cool it." He balanced the wineglass on his knee. "I'm finding it tough to figure out how to parent in a scary world."

"So whatever happened to Sarah's dad? Was he accountable in any way for sharing that information with another felon?"

"Of course not. I wanted Brandon in solitary confinement for the rest of his life, but I couldn't even get his cable television stations taken away." He set aside the wine and turned to face her on the love seat. "But in the months where I was consumed with justice, my career started to go south, the host of my top show quit, and Sarah began sneaking out at night since I hardly let her out of my sight during the day. I had to let go of some of the anger to move on. So here I am, ruining your nice dinner and repaying your kindness with maudlin stories that I normally never share."

"Maybe it's easier to talk to people who weren't involved." She found herself fidgeting and forced herself to stop. What was it about him that had her so on edge?

Her foremost feelings right now should be empathy and compassion. It bugged her that compassion and attraction were tied for first place, especially after all he'd told her.

"That's no excuse for being a bad guest."

"You brought lemon-berry cupcakes and wine, so you actually rate pretty well on my guest meter."

"Clearly, you've kept some questionable company."

No kidding.

"I'm much better at fixing other people's lives than figuring out my own."

He searched her eyes for a long moment, the candles he'd lit flickering overhead.

"How about you let me salvage the steaks to make it up to you?"

She appreciated him steering them back to less personal terrain.

"I'd never say no to having a man cook for me." She rose to her feet and forced herself to think about dinner instead of flirting. She'd been all wrong to consider acting on what she felt for him. Remy was still in the early stages of grieving. "Besides, if you can handle the steaks, I'll finish up the salad."

Deal struck—and some much-needed distance gained—Erin retreated into the house and pulled the veggies out of the refrigerator. Rinsing and chopping, she could only imagine what Remy must think of her for inviting him here tonight when he was still dealing with so many feelings for his wife. He hadn't moved on. Who knew when he would be ready to think about taking that step?

The best she could salvage from this tense date was the satisfaction of having reached out to a friend in a way she hadn't been able to for the past six months. If nothing else, meeting Remy had proved to her she *could* forget about Patrick and maybe even fall for someone again. But that someone wouldn't be Remy. For that matter, caring about a man like him could be hazardous to her heart. She'd been able to put Patrick behind her because he was innately an unworthy man.

Remy, on the other hand, was as worthy as they came. A good father and devoted husband.

Six months ago, she had been afraid men like him didn't exist. How ironic that now—when she was finally ready to move on—she met a loyal guy still very much in love with his wife.

THREE DAYS LATER, Sarah knocked on the partially closed door separating her father's room from hers at the Heartache B and B.

"Dad?" She shuffled her bare feet against the floral area rug that looked as though it belonged in a grandmother's room. Everything about the B and B was slightly worn and kitschy, but Sarah liked it here, far from Miami and the worries that dogged her constantly there.

"Come on in," he called.

She pushed the door open the rest of the way. A suitcase lay open on his bed, a couple of shirts already folded in a stack beside it. An iron steamed on the folding board nearby, his blue dress shirt freshly pressed. "What's going on?" She hesitated, a ball of cold dread knotting in her stomach. "We can't leave yet. The clothing drive is today at The Strand. I told Erin I'd help."

"We'll be here for the drive." He held up a big video camera, the kind she hadn't seen him use in a long time. "I'm going to take some footage, in fact. But I did find a red-eye flight tonight so we can get back home and sort things out with school."

"I thought you liked it here," she blurted, folding her arms across her sleep tank top. She swished her ponytail, crushed and lopsided from bed. "Plus, we were going to do some work together so you could show me what being a producer is all about."

"You can try out the video camera today." He passed her the big Nikon and resumed packing. "And I like Heartache just fine, Sarah, but we can't hide out from whatever is going on back home. You can't sacrifice your senior year. You've already missed a week of school."

Her heart thudded hard in her chest and she weighed her approach carefully. She didn't want to say the wrong thing. She took the camera and pretended to study it, not wanting her father to know how much it killed her inside to think about returning to Miami.

"But next week is spring break and we'll be off anyway. And what about my car? How will I get it home if I take the flight with you?" She pressed a few buttons and saw some raw footage of other towns and antiques shops that he'd recorded in the past.

"I'll pay to have it transported. I can drive you to school until then or you can ride with Mathilda." He emptied out the top drawer of the bureau and put the socks into the suitcase.

How could they leave? She hadn't seen Lucas since Friday night. He hadn't gone to the drive-in with the rest of his friends on Sunday. She'd texted him despite Mathilda warning her that would be giving him the upper hand in their new relationship. Lucas replied he needed to "take care of some other things" before they spent more time together.

Decoding that particular piece of Boy Speak had resulted in a three-hour phone call to Mathilda Monday night and they'd brainstormed a list of possibilities. At the top of her list was the wishful thought that he was breaking up with his girlfriend. But how long did that take? Surely, he would have had enough time between Friday night when they'd kissed and Sunday when she'd hoped to see him at the drive-in.

"Second semester of senior year doesn't really matter." Sarah set the camera on the bed, preparing her argument in her head. "Even the best students slack off near graduation, Dad. The colleges already have our grades on file. At this point, we're either accepted or we're not."

He studied her for a long moment.

"Do you have acceptance letters you haven't told me about?"

She could hear the cautious hopefulness in his voice, and it made her feel like total crap. And all the more committed not to go back home.

"Not yet." Tough to be accepted when she hadn't

applied anywhere except UF, an application Mathilda had forced her to fill out.

The clock on the wall ticked off the seconds in the silence.

"You haven't said much about where you applied." He strapped on his watch, a gift her mother had helped Sarah choose for him as a wedding present.

He'd worn it every day since, even when his wedding band had finally stopped appearing on his ring finger last fall.

"Those months were mega-stressful." She reached for the iron to turn it back on. "I'm going to use this since it's all set up, okay?"

Darting out of the room, she rummaged in her closet through the few items of clothing.

"Sarah," he called through the door. "If we can't have productive conversations about your future, we're going to end up back in the counselor's office."

Yanking a halter dress off the hanger, she marched back into his room.

"I'm going to have to talk to her anyway after I ditched the field trip." Why couldn't he just pull her out of school for the last eight weeks? What if Brandon—she refused to think of him as her father—knew where she attended classes?

Would he keep trying to send letters if she didn't respond to the one in her purse?

"Wouldn't it be simpler just to tell me what's going on?" Dad moved his dress shirt off the ironing board so she'd have room to work.

His arm skimmed the top of her head as he pulled on the shirt.

"Close quarters," she mumbled, sidestepping him enough to work at the ironing board shoved between the desk and the bed. "Remember when you first moved into that apartment where Mom and I lived?"

"It was small, but not this small."

"Right. And we were perfectly happy there." She slammed the iron onto the dress and started ramming it to all corners of the green cotton.

"You don't like the place in Miami?" He sat on the bed and she sensed his eyes on her. Finally paying attention.

"The apartment is okay. The city—" She shrugged, ironing too fast to do a good job. "Mathilda makes it bearable, I guess."

"When you start college, you can go wherever you want." He stood, taking the iron out of her hands and smoothing the wrinkles that she'd pressed into her dress. "We talked about applying to a wide range of places because you weren't sure where you wanted to live. Is there anywhere in particular you think you'd like?"

"Here."

"There are no colleges in Heartache."

"I meant to live and finish high school, not go to college."

He turned off the iron and set it aside. "Do you have a list on your computer of places you applied?"

"University of Florida." She had that, anyway. Sliding the dress off the ironing board, she wished she could go back to her room and forget this whole conversation.

"Where else?" He was a patient father, but she could see the frustration behind the calm facade.

"Just there." The words fell out. They were too hard to hold in anymore.

His arms stretched over his head as if he was waiting for the sky to fall. Then he laid his hands on his head. He walked around the room like that for a second, dodging the chair and the bed to pace in the half foot of space.

She swallowed. "I'm sorry. The applications were confusing. I haven't done well in school since we moved."

"I'm not mad at you. I'm mad at myself for not working on it with you or hiring someone to help you."

"Lots of kids apply on their own, Dad. It's not your fault. It's mine. I knew I was supposed to do more. I just…didn't."

She felt relieved to get that off her chest, but worried because the weight of it looked as if it fell on her father. He already carried so much.

She wanted his attention, but not the kind that made him resent her.

"That doesn't fix the larger problem."

She scrambled for something to keep the peace—and keep her here. "I can do community college for a year or two while I figure out where I want to go." Sarah clutched her dress tighter. "Or work."

He got that "dad scowl," which almost always meant no. "I'm not sure those are the best options."

She hit the lever to break down the ironing board and shoved it against one wall.

"Well, I'm tired of living in a city where I don't know anyone but Mathilda. I don't want to go to a big anonymous university." That was the problem with UF, she realized. Fine for Mathilda, but wrong for her. "I'm tired of not having family around me."

"You have family." He put his heavy hands on her shoulders, his voice so certain. "I'm here for you."

"For now." She didn't want to think about next year and how things would unfold once high school was done. "And only because I drove nine hundred miles to be with you."

His expression froze as his body stilled. A slight wrinkle between his eyebrows was the sole sign that told her she'd hurt him. But didn't he know how much he'd hurt her, too?

She didn't know what else to say, and—thankfully—he didn't stop her when she walked out to dress for the clothing drive. Erin needed her, and something about that felt damn good.

Not as good as a kiss from Lucas, of course. Something she was still determined to get even if—she checked her watch—she had only sixteen hours left to make that happen.

Sixteen hours. She swallowed down the panic at the thought of returning home, back where Brandon could find her. She couldn't leave. She grabbed her cell phone off the dresser. She needed to make a call to the only person who might make him listen to reason.

With shaking fingers, she dialed her counselor's number and hoped she would pick up.

CHAPTER NINE

TAKING REFUGE BEHIND his old camera—something he didn't do as much since he'd been moved to producing multiple shows—Remy had too much time to think about all the ways his life was crumbling beneath his feet.

He adjusted the lighting for an interior shot of Erin at The Strand as she spoke with a customer who'd brought in a clothing donation. Remy wished he'd been the one to put the smile on her face. Instead, he'd screwed up Erin's nice dinner by unloading details from his personal nightmares that he hadn't shared with anyone else. Who the hell would have guessed she'd come out with "hope springs eternal" for a toast?

Strangely, he hadn't experienced the same guilt he usually did when he thought about Liv. Instead, it'd felt like a ghostly slap in the face to get his act together and move on. Then, today, Sarah's bombshell had pulled the rug out from under him completely. He'd called the family counselor—someone he hadn't seen for months—and left a message, but the guy hadn't called back yet. Sarah's personal therapist was out today.

And yeah, he freely admitted he needed professional help to run his own life. Despite the paid experts on the payroll, he was screwing everything up. What would Liv have said if she knew Remy hadn't helped Sarah with those application forms?

His daughter had been at the salon longer than him. She'd ridden her bike over as soon as she'd changed while he had hung back to check out of the B and B. And pull his head together after her suggestion that he wasn't much of a family. After all the time he'd taken off to be there for her? Or at least to be around the house? True, they hadn't spent much time together in those months, but they'd both been in mourning, and, honest to Pete, most days he could barely keep his head above water.

"Remy?" Erin approached while he sent a few segments of the new video from his mini Sony camcorder to his laptop.

He'd given Sarah the big Nikon to interview some of the customers coming into the store. He tried not to take up too much room with his equipment—he had set up in a corner of the nail salon— but Erin still had to step over cords to get to him.

"Does the camera distract you?" He studied her face, wishing he'd been a better guest or a better friend when she'd been kind enough to invite him to dinner Sunday. "I'd hoped that by filming some preliminary shots of your work today, we'd have more cutaways available for the final episode. That means the full production crew won't have to spend as much time in Last Chance Vintage."

"That would be great." She had seemed at ease enough when she'd been talking to customers, but she regarded the equipment with wariness. "I wanted to mention that the salon will be giving away a hair-cut and makeover to one of the women who is in the Dress for Success program. If she'll talk about her experience, it would be inspiring for others to hear."

"Definitely point her out to me when she arrives." He turned the laptop so Erin could see some of his footage. "You look great, by the way."

"I tried to tone it down a little with the blouse." She tugged on the hem of her white poet's shirt with lace cuffs. "But it's like my hand was calibrated to land on this leather piece." She pantomimed the irresistible draw of it, her fingers landing on the studded collar of the black biker jacket she wore over the white blouse and black leggings.

"You've got a rocker vibe." He grinned. "In my dreams, I'll always see you with an air compressor in one hand."

The words were laced with a flirtation he hadn't intended to share but definitely felt. Despite the hum of hair dryers and salon chatter all around them, the rest of the room disappeared for the space of a few charged heartbeats.

Erin quirked her eyebrow. "Dreaming about me? Maybe it's your subconscious telling you a walk on the wild side would be good for you." She hadn't looked at him, keeping her eyes on his laptop, watching the live feed from Sarah's outdoor shots on half the screen and the footage Remy had taken of her on the other half.

His hands were drawn to her in the same way she'd described being drawn to the leather jacket. But he resisted. Did not move near her. But the pull was undeniable.

"Believe me, I'm getting the messages loud and clear from my subconscious, my regular conscious and every other sentient part of my being." He kept his voice low as he stood beside her, her ear at the level of his mouth and making quiet confidences easy. "But I've been leaving a path of destruction in my wake this year and I like you way too much to risk…hurting you."

There it was. The bald truth he hadn't been able to speak out loud the other night at her place when they'd been alone. When he could have acted on it. He wanted Erin. No question. He knew it for certain as he stood beside her, the amber scent of her in his nose.

He wanted her with a fierceness he hadn't been ready to acknowledge until today. Now he was too raw to keep his feelings to himself when he had a flight booked for tonight that could take him away from her forever. Nothing had happened between them, but he wanted her to know he'd thought about it.

A lot.

"That should have been my choice, not yours." Erin's blue eyes found his with a laser intensity that drove straight through him. "My heart. My risk."

Their gazes locked, the tension between them crackling to life.

She broke the connection and walked away from him, the studs on her jacket glinting in the overhead lights.

He didn't realize he'd been holding his breath until it rushed out in a gust. He thought he'd been doing the right thing putting the brakes on what he felt for her, when he still hadn't come to terms with the past let alone mapped out any kind of path for the future. Apparently, Erin disagreed.

How would he leave town tonight with that knowledge hanging over his head? Grinding his teeth in frustration, he picked up his camera and approached the woman she'd asked him to interview. He might have disappointed Erin in other ways, but he planned to make the best damn episode of *Interstate Antiquer* the show had ever produced. It wouldn't be enough to make it up to her for leaving town so suddenly, especially after how kind she'd been to him and Sarah.

For now, however, it was all he had to offer.

"THANKS TO ERIN and Dress for Success, I got an outfit for that interview." Jamie Raybourn smiled for the camera, her eyes closed while a makeup artist worked on one of her eyelids with a dove-gray shadow. "Now I'm going back to work and I have a real chance of keeping my apartment, too. I'm so much happier out from under the shadow of a man who didn't think I could do anything on my own. One day, I might even get my son back, too."

Erin's heart tightened at the thought of all this woman had endured. She hadn't told Bethany about Jamie's circumstances, letting the woman's skills win or lose her the job in the interview. She'd wrestled with what to do. Bethany might have been swayed to hire Jamie if she knew what the woman had faced: an ex-boyfriend who wasn't just a cheating bastard, but also liked to shove her around when he drank.

Unfortunately, Jamie had never pressed charges after those incidents, so it was his word against hers when she could have used all the ammunition possible to maintain custody of their son. Now that she had a job, however, her chances of holding steady and keeping her child with her full-time were much improved.

"I'm so happy for you, Jamie." Erin squeezed the woman's arm as Jamie opened her eyes and saw herself in the mirror.

Jamie squeezed back. "You don't know how close I was to losing everything."

Her voice broke, and the makeup artist stepped away, looking unsure what to do. Erin gestured to Remy to stop filming the interview segment, but Jamie held up a hand.

"No. It's okay." She reached for a tissue box on the small counter in front of the mirror and pulled free a blue swath to dab under her eyes without smudging the makeup. "He asked me if I wanted to share my story and I said yes. I stand by that. Not all the parts are pretty."

Inwardly, Erin cheered her bravery and decision. But left in the camera spotlight alone with Jamie, she had no idea what to say.

Help came from an unexpected source. Sarah rushed up behind Jamie's chair and met the woman's tearful gaze in the mirror.

"You look amazing," she said with the earnest honesty of a child, bending close so her face was beside Jamie's in the mirror. "Concentrate on that part because that *is* really pretty."

Of course Sarah's words made the tears Jamie had been holding back spill down her cheeks, but she was smiling again.

"You sweet thing." She patted Sarah's cheek. "I

do feel better now that I look better. I just hope I can do the 'new me' justice when I try to reproduce it in the mirror Monday, my first day at my new job."

Erin glanced at Remy while Sarah and the makeup artist chatted about the specifics of Jamie's hair and makeup. Erin wondered if she should be doing something differently or if she should just back out of the camera shot now that her part was sort of done. But although Remy didn't look through the camera lens, he wasn't looking at Erin. His eyes were on Sarah as if seeing her for the first time.

Was he surprised at her ease in front of the camera? Or maybe just struck by how grown-up she seemed? Erin didn't know and didn't pretend to understand their relationship, but it had to be a good thing that Remy was giving his daughter the chance she'd driven all the way from Miami to take. She wanted his attention, sure.

Sarah also wanted to be a part of his television world.

Maybe now that he'd seen her in action, he would give it to her.

All around Erin, happy things were going on. Jamie had a job. The Dress for Success clothing drive was accumulating more and more career wear for women who needed it. Remy and his daughter were communicating better. Yet, if everything was so flipping great, why did she still feel as though her life was falling apart?

By the time Remy shut off the camera and Jamie's makeover had been captured on film, Erin applauded the transformation along with the rest of the people in the salon. The change on the outside paled in comparison to how much this strong woman had turned her life around with grit and determination. Their clapping praised both aspects.

Afterward, Erin noticed Sarah scuttle off into a corner of the salon to text on her phone while Remy packed up his equipment.

Was this goodbye?

He'd strode into her life only just a week and a half ago, dripping wet and too damn polite for his own good. He hadn't wanted to get her floor wet, but now that she knew the circumstances of his wife's death, she understood that night all the more. He hadn't wanted Erin to be alone in the store with a stranger—even when the stranger was him. He was still trying to protect her now, keeping her at arm's length.

Damning the consequences, she strode over and unplugged the equipment he was trying to untangle from a knot of hair dryer and flat iron electrical cords. She untwisted from her end until they met in the middle, crouched together behind an unused manicure table.

Their hands brushed, his touch making her whole body hum with awareness. His aftershave smelled spicy and masculine, enticing her closer. She paid attention to that rush of heat and attraction now, allowing herself to enjoy it. No more ignoring it.

"Have you got plans for the rest of the day before your flight?" She had the store covered until closing since she hadn't been sure what time the event at The Strand would wrap up.

"I'm going to return some calls and then I need to spend time with Sarah to try and figure out what's got her so upset lately." He shook his head. "I know she wants to spend more time here, more time with me, but it seems like there's something I'm missing about this sudden need to drive all the way out here."

"I think it's a good idea to be there for her." Even if it meant that right here, right now might be the last time Erin ever got to be with Remy. "Let me know if you need a wingman. I took the day off for the filming."

She told herself to stand up. Shake his hand. Find some way to say goodbye to this man who intrigued her far more than was wise for either of them at this point in their lives. He leaned closer, his steady gaze missing nothing.

"Don't let yourself get comfortable behind the scenes, Erin." His fingers stroked her cheek, a featherlight touch that made her eyelids flutter. "You belong front and center, running the show."

What did that even mean? She couldn't concentrate on his words when his touch reminded her of what they might have had—if only briefly. She would regret it for the rest of her life if she didn't get to have one night with this man. They'd both known so much pain. They deserved something happy. They didn't need to worry about the risk of getting too attached as he was leaving anyway.

"Dad?" Sarah's voice, pitched at maximum teen excitability, brought Erin back down to reality.

Remy's touch vanished as he edged away from her.

"There you are!" Sarah held her phone in one hand and a small floral backpack in the other. "I got invited to a party after the girls' soccer game. Can I go?"

"What girls' game?" Remy stood, his well-tailored clothes emphasizing his narrow waist and hips. He'd taken off his jacket hours ago, his blue shirtsleeves folded to reveal strong, tanned forearms.

"The local high school girls' team. Ally Finley plays and so do some other kids I met the other night. It'd be a nice chance to say goodbye to everyone before I have to go back to Miami." She held up the backpack to show it to him. "I have everything I need in my bag, and you already have my suitcase packed in the rental car. We can meet at the airport before takeoff."

"Whoa." He held up both hands. "It's a school night. They can't stay out that late on a Wednesday, and I don't want you driving around town alone late at night. I'll pick you up at the field and we'll figure out where to leave your car until I can have it transported."

Erin was in the process of backing away from the conversation, remembering how Remy had not appreciated her input with his daughter in the past. But before she was out of earshot, she discreetly whispered to him, "You can leave the car at my house, if you want."

Just in case that bit of information helped.

It wasn't as if she was trying to lure him to her place to back him up against a wall and kiss the hell out of him. Although, if she had him alone for two minutes, she'd find a way.

Giving Remy privacy, Erin took the time to thank Trish for all her help coordinating the drive and then sent two volunteers to the tent behind Last Chance Vintage to store the day's donations.

At the sound of a girlish squeal, Erin turned to see Sarah fling her arms around Remy's neck and squeeze him. Clearly, she was happy with the outcome of the day.

"Thank you!" She practically danced from foot to foot. "I'll text you every hour, okay? I promise I will be safe." She kissed his cheek. "Thank you for letting me find friends."

Erin could almost see Remy flinch at the last comment, but she didn't understand their relationship well enough to know why. But she did know that Remy had the rest of the afternoon and evening free of commitments other than those calls he had to make.

A thrill tripped through her even as she told herself that didn't necessarily mean he would spend it with her.

Sarah bolted from the store with a shouted goodbye, waving and texting.

Erin didn't dare make eye contact with Remy for fear of spontaneously combusting. Now that she'd allowed herself to think in terms of the attraction and the chemistry that he felt, too, she could think of little else.

Following Sarah out the door, Erin headed to the parking lot behind the store and slid into the front seat of her car. She had to wait only about five minutes before Remy came out with his equipment and loaded it into the trunk of his rental.

Her heart beat fast as she rolled down her window.

She was a grown-up. She could handle the fallout no matter what happened between them. They deserved some happiness—a brief window of time to forget about the past.

"The invitation is still open if you need a place to hang out before your flight." She squinted up at him in the sunlight. His gray tie lifted in a sudden breeze.

His gaze damn near scorched her as his eyes wandered over her.

"I'll follow you."

Her heart did a little backflip and she allowed herself a smile.

"If you can keep up." Winking, she put her car in Drive and headed home.

She wasn't thinking past the next five minutes, let alone the next five hours. All she knew was that Remy Weldon wasn't going home until she got her hands on him.

CHAPTER TEN

KEEP UP?

Remy would have floored the gas if he'd been leading the way to Erin's house. He'd been willing to sacrifice what he wanted to make sure she didn't get hurt in the fallout when he left town, but Erin had made her stance clear. She wanted to take the risk.

She wanted him.

He followed her old Thunderbird away from Heartache's main street past peach orchards in full pink bloom. The car had a custom paint job in royal blue with metallic flecks, but underneath, the pimped-out ride was basically an antique. Erin had a way of rescuing worn-out things and giving them new appeal.

When she turned down the long driveway, he was right behind her. Thinking about her. As much as he'd wanted to be there for his daughter today, Sarah didn't want to leave Heartache, and he was in danger of alienating her more if he refused to let her spend time with her friends before he took her back to Miami. There'd be plenty of time to figure out what was going on with her once they left Tennessee.

Until then, Sarah had her friends and Remy—unbelievably—had Erin. One night to pretend the past didn't exist. One night where they wouldn't worry about the future or the complications of being together. After all, he'd be on a flight home before dawn.

He was out of his car and opening her door for her before she'd even collected her belongings off the passenger seat.

"I kept checking the rearview mirror on the drive here," she admitted as she took his hand and let him help her out.

He didn't let go of her. Lacing their fingers together, he held tight to the only woman who had been more than just a blip on his male radar in the past two years. Erin Finley fascinated him.

"You didn't seriously think you were going to lose me?" He climbed the front porch steps beside her, the mild breeze of a Tennessee spring stirring the scent of flowering trees and the barest hint of Erin's amber fragrance.

"Maybe not with my driving." She dug in her bag for keys and opened the door while he held the screen. "But I worried you'd have second thoughts."

His brain stalled when he noticed how fast she'd gotten inside her house.

"You don't have an alarm system out here?" He

realized there were homes within sight of hers—
her sister-in-law's house even. Still, Erin was a
single woman living by herself.

"I haven't spent that much time here since it was
built. I traveled a lot up until last fall." She dropped
her things on the rattan coffee table in the living
area and kicked off her black-heeled boots.

She reached into a bowl of cherries on the stand
and ate one, handing him one by the stem.

"All the more reason." He knew it troubled him
unreasonably, but he needed to say something.

He took the cherry and ate it mostly to be polite, though the burst of flavor on his tongue was
a pleasant surprise.

"You're right. I'll get an alarm for sure." Her
eyes were full of understanding as she reached to
swipe the juice from his lips.

He swallowed hard, shoving aside the worry
about the locks and anything else except for this
amazing woman.

"I'm glad you asked me over." His temperature
spiked at her nearness just knowing where this
would lead. Knowing there was no turning back.

"I'm glad to have a second chance to make my
interest known." She laid her palm flat against his
chest. Warm. Direct.

Sexy and sweet at the same time.

"I like it that you don't play games. That I don't
have to guess what you're thinking." He didn't

have the emotional fortitude for that kind of stuff these days.

She walked her fingers up the buttons of his shirt and landed at the knot of his tie.

"Are you suggesting you know what I'm thinking?" She inserted a finger between his collar and the tie, easing the knot down until the cotton silk released and the whole thing unwound.

His body roared with fresh heat.

"I've got a good idea." He cradled her face in his hands and studied her dilated pupils. Her flushed cheeks. "A very good idea."

Trailing a hand down her neck, he watched her eyelids flutter and close, her head tip back. Beneath his palm, her pulse went wild, a rapid tattoo against his hand that spurred his own heartbeat.

She opened her eyes to meet his gaze.

"Prove it," she dared him, lifting another cherry to her lips for a bite. "Show me."

Twenty different scenarios ran through his head in an instant as he envisioned everything from having her against the door to lowering her to the nearest couch. She had a hot tub out back. A kitchen island that he could seat her on and make himself comfortable between her thighs.

But he nixed all of those to sweep her off her feet.

A gasp that sounded like part surprise and part delight escaped her lips as he hoisted her high against his chest, savoring the armful of feminine curves.

"What way?" He strode toward the stairs as she pointed her answer.

"I'm not entirely sure this is what I was thinking, but I have to admit, I like your imagination." She popped the top button of his shirt collar as he carried her upstairs.

Her touch felt cool along his hot skin. He couldn't wait to feel all of her.

"I haven't gotten to the part you were thinking about yet." He spoke into her ear, close enough to feel her shiver at his words. "I merely needed the right place to show you."

She unfastened another button, her fingers diving into his shirt to graze along his shoulder and up his neck. He studied the lay of the land at the top of the staircase. Which way to go? She wasn't giving directions now. She wasn't paying attention to where they were going.

Good.

He wanted her distracted and thinking about him. Following where his instincts led, he found a room with a purple sweater hooked over the doorknob and toed the door the rest of the way open. The scent of amber increased ever so subtly and he knew his guess had been correct. Everything was white except for a few anime paintings in bright colors and a red lacquer headboard painted with small birds along one edge. Sunlight filtered in the bottom half of wooden blinds, which had been left partially slatted.

All of which he processed just enough to know where to lay her down.

Except she wouldn't let go of him when he tried to stand so he could undress. She twined her hands around his neck and pulled him down with her, sealing soft lips to his. Any plan he'd had after that disintegrated on impact. She tasted like lip gloss and cherries, a combination he'd never known was apparently his personal erotic trigger. Need for her pounded inside him and he'd only just taken his first taste of her.

"Erin." He pulled back, levering himself over her so he didn't crush her. "I could take all night to kiss you."

"You *could*. But I hope you won't." She slid her hand around his waist to palm the small of his back. She tugged at his shirt, freeing the hem from his pants in slow, teasing increments. "I'm going to need you to touch me everywhere at once. Maximize your efforts until I can't think anymore."

Arching her back, she brought her hips close to his.

There was no misunderstanding her. And while the tiniest sliver of his brain warned him that she deserved to be romanced, the rest of him got on board with her approach. Especially since her fingers worked the buttons on the rest of his shirt, flicking them open until she could push the fabric off his shoulders.

He shrugged out of his shirt and then applied himself to giving her what she wanted. Kissing his way down her neck, he licked the hollow at the base of her throat where her skin was impossibly soft. He skimmed the hem of her shirt up with one hand, palming her waist and tracing a teasing pattern with his thumb. They lay side by side on her bed now, so he stroked her hair with his other hand.

He watched her face as her eyes slid closed to focus on what he was doing. Pale freckles he'd never noticed stood out in the slanting rays of afternoon sun, her lashes a dark auburn as they fanned her cheeks.

Her lips were still stained a darker red from the cherry juice, inspiring him to revisit them. Sucking and nipping, he pulled her lower lip into his mouth. He wanted to taste more of her.

Lifting himself off her, he stood. As he started to remove his belt, it occurred to him he was not prepared for this. Condoms hadn't crossed his mind since…a long damn time.

"I didn't bring anything with me. That is, I didn't even think about—"

She arched an eyebrow before flipping over and crawling up the bed. Digging in a nightstand drawer, she produced the kind of box he was looking for, the shrink-wrap still on.

"I bought them for Sunday, because…you know. I was thinking about seducing you that night."

Sunday. When she'd invited him to dinner.

He didn't bother thinking about how things had gone once they'd taken their drinks out onto her patio. He might not have been ready for this then, but he sure as hell was now.

Not hesitating another second, he stepped out of his shoes. Ditched his pants and the boxers, too.

"My, my." Erin rose to a sitting position, scooting to the edge of the bed. "I like how you don't waste time."

Before he could help her, she tugged her white blouse up and off, tossing it into the growing pile of clothes on the floor. Full, beautiful breasts rose above the cups of a white lace bra with a tiny red ribbon in the center. One strap had already slid off her shoulder as she reached for him, her hand circling his erection and gently stroking.

"You're playing with fire." He gripped her wrist, keeping her hand still for a second until he found his breath and got himself under control. "I haven't been with anyone since—"

And then she was on her knees on the bed, covering his mouth with a kiss to quiet that thought. Tenderness for her hit him square in the chest, a gut check reminding him to treat her well. To do this right.

Willing down all his heat for her, Remy kissed her, taking his time to find the places that made her sigh or gasp or just wriggle closer. Behind her ear made her hold him tighter. The soft place just above her shoulder had her melting all over him. Only then, when she was too distracted to tease him, did he unhook the front clasp of her bra to reveal the rest of her full breasts.

They more than filled his hands, and he urged her back on the bed so he could take his time with each one, licking and nipping until the tips were tight, sensitive peaks. Erin's fingers ran through his hair until he pulled one nipple deep into his mouth.

While she murmured softly, moving against him in a restless dance, he peeled her leggings and panties off in a long sweep, baring the rest of her. His mouth never left her breast as he cupped her sex in his palm, barely grazing the silken folds, already damp for him. Then her nails curved gently into his shoulder and held, a pleasant, grounding pain to balance out the unbelievable pleasure of having her underneath him.

"Remy." She smoothed her fingers over the place where she'd held him tight a moment ago. "I want you inside me."

Not until that moment did he make the connection—one of the many reasons he liked Erin was for her bluntness. He cleaned up well, but his roots were as bayou earthy as they came.

"Yes, ma'am." He reached for the box and attacked the shrink-wrap.

She had to help him, a smile creeping over her lips.

"Open boxes much?" She brushed her fingers along the rough edge of his jaw.

"Not with a hot woman urging me to go faster." He freed a packet and ripped it open with his teeth.

Her light laughter felt like a stroke along his spine, a touch that tingled all the way down.

"You like that, *chère*?" he whispered in her ear, enjoying the feel of her silky hair against his lips. "I'll give you more to like in a minute."

Her breath caught in her throat as he eased a finger inside her. A small gasp echoed in the quiet room as he added a second. He had to close his eyes to dull some of the sensation threatening to catapult him over the edge. Everything about her made him want her more. Seeing her, tasting her, the amber scent along her neck…

"Remy." She wrapped her arms around his neck and he opened his eyes again. "Stay with me, okay? Right here, in this moment with me."

He nodded, his throat closing up tight.

Withdrawing his fingers, he positioned himself between her thighs. Sweat popped along the base of his neck from the effort to go slow, and he wasn't even inside her yet.

And then, slowly, he was.

Heat blasted up his spine, the sensations rocking him. He needed to stay still, holding himself right there, deep inside her until he could rein himself in. Erin's legs circled his hips, her ankles locking to keep him there.

"You feel incredible." He traced the curve of her hip. The indent of her waist.

"You're telling me?" She arched closer, her breasts pressing into his chest. "I've never felt this good in my life."

Taking a deep breath, he began to move inside her. Slowly at first, letting the pleasure build again. He thought about her lips. Her shoulders. Her sleek fall of bronze hair. Any small detail of the moment to keep his full focus away from the slick hold of her body on his.

So when her breathing shifted, he heard it. He was so dialed into her every movement he knew just where to touch her to take her higher. He could feel how close she was to finding her release and it pushed him nearer to his.

"I'm not going alone," she warned, her hips rising up to meet his, shifting the rhythm in a way he couldn't ignore.

Then it was just a matter of time. Control slipped. Desire flamed red hot. Release pounded through him in wave after wave. Vaguely, in the middle of it all, he knew that Erin found hers, too, her body arched and taut for long moments until she writhed with him in a tangle of limbs.

When he finished, he collapsed beside her. He might as well have passed out, unconscious, his brain a blank to the world while the rest of his body tried to recalibrate. Pleasure fed every nerve ending for long moments.

Eyes still closed, he stroked her hair. He became aware of a ceiling fan clicking overhead, stirring the faintest breeze. The longer he could soak in this peaceful ease, the better. He didn't want to think. Didn't want to remember the last time he'd lain naked beside a woman and breathed the same air.

"Maybe if we don't talk anymore tonight, we can end on this good note." Erin shifted beside him.

He forced open an eye to gauge her expression. She propped her elbow beneath her head as she watched him.

"A vow of silence to combat first-time awkwardness." He stroked his jaw, pretending to think it over. "Unorthodox, but it just might work. It would be nice to take home all these happy endorphins without ever tackling a big, meaningful conversation."

She bit her lip and twisted a strand of hair around her finger. "It would have to be a vow of sex *and* silence, though."

"Does that mean we have sex quietly?" He brushed a silky strand of dark hair away from her face. Tucked it behind her ear.

"Well, no. I meant we could have more sex despite the sworn oath of silence."

"Now we're getting somewhere." He reached for her just as his cell phone buzzed.

"I'll try and find us something to eat while you take that." Erin slid off the bed and shrugged into a pale green silk robe decorated with big pink flowers.

Sifting through the pile of clothes on her floor, he found his phone. The number belonged to Sarah's counselor and it wasn't her office phone. It was her cell, something she'd only given out for emergency contact in the past.

"Thanks for returning my call, Theresa." He sat on the edge of Erin's bed, his shoulders tense.

"Actually, I'm calling on Sarah's behalf."

The counselor had been with them since she'd been introduced to Sarah at a grief support group at the hospital after Liv's death. Theresa had been with his daughter through a lot, and while there had been ups and downs in Sarah's behavior, Remy trusted the woman's opinion.

"Didn't you get my message?" He'd called to ask her what she thought about Sarah not applying to colleges. "I'm worried that Sarah's keeping secrets. She isn't following through on important things and—"

"Remy, Sarah has confided some things to me that are troubling, but she has invoked her doctor-patient privilege at a time when I would have really preferred to bring you in on the discussion."

Her words delivered a solid punch to his gut.

"What kind of things?" He pulled on his boxers and pants, feeling he'd better be dressed for this.

He wished he hadn't let Sarah go to that party tonight.

Had he been in too much of a hurry to be with Erin?

"I can't discuss it with you, but I can promise I'm encouraging her to talk to you about it."

Fear and frustration rattled him from his toes. He paced Erin's bedroom, barely seeing where he was going. He wanted to be on that plane now so he could sort this out in Theresa's office face-to-face with Sarah.

"You can't be serious. If she's in trouble or making bad choices, you can't just let her get hurt."

"Of course not. Please. Remy, I've been with Sarah a long time. She's scared and trying to do the right thing."

"What's she scared of?" he half shouted, on edge at the thought of his daughter afraid when he couldn't do a damn thing about it. "Is it me? Was she scared to tell me about the colleges?"

"No. Listen. I need for you to calm down."

"I defy you to be calm if someone told you your kid was scared and wouldn't come to you about it." He stopped just in front of Erin's door and leaned his forehead against it. His temples had started to ache and the pressure felt good.

"I understand. Believe me, I do." Theresa paused. "Remy, is there any way you can delay your trip back to Miami?"

His head shot up.

"Excuse me?" On alert, he wondered for a second if Sarah had concocted something to stay in Heartache longer, then felt guilty for thinking it.

"I wondered if you could extend your work trip so that Sarah could take a little breather from home."

"She has school. She's already missed a week."

"Next week is her spring break. I'd be happy to contact the school myself."

"I have a career. A life." He pounded his fist against a bureau, making the miniature female superhero action figures adorning it jump. "I could lose my job."

He'd already pushed it, taking so much time off after Liv's death. He needed to increase the ratings on all three of his shows, but *Interstate Antiquer* especially.

"It's only for a little while until we deal with an important issue."

"An issue I can't know about." Closing his eyes, he squeezed his temples and wondered what the hell the studio executives would have to say about this.

"Unfortunately, I have reason to believe that Sarah isn't safe in Miami." The counselor's words took his knees out from under him.

He was standing one second. The next, sitting on the floor.

"What are you taking about?" The blood drained from his face, his extremities. The room spun.

"I'm talking about being very vigilant where Sarah's safety is concerned. This is just a precaution until I talk to her school counselor and get a better handle on the situation, but until then, she will be safer with you in Tennessee or wherever else you need to travel."

"If you have endangered her in any way by not telling me what's going on—" He couldn't finish the sentence since there was no reasonable retribution he could name.

"Sarah is a strong girl. You should be proud of her for confiding her fears to someone." She emphasized the last word ever so subtly, as if to remind him that Sarah didn't trust him enough to talk to him.

Then again, he could just be listening to Theresa with a lot of guilt on his conscience.

"I would do anything to keep her safe."

"I know. And when you tell Sarah of the change in plans, you might not want to mention the specifics of our conversation. I haven't said anything that would break confidentiality, of course, but it might help her open up to you sooner if she didn't feel pressured."

"I'll do my best." Thanking her, he disconnected the call and wondered what the hell to do for the next few days.

Stay in Heartache? He was sure that would be Sarah's preference, although he could move on and scout other locations in northern Tennessee or Kentucky for future episodes.

One thing was certain: he needed to figure out what was going on with her. Because whatever it was must be serious. It would take all his willpower to stay here and wait for Sarah to confide in him when what he really wanted to do was catch that plane to Miami by himself and interrogate every last kid in her school until he found out what had her spooked.

For now, he needed to leave Erin's and put tonight out of his mind. It had been welcome. Incredible, even. But this wasn't the right time in his life to make choices for himself.

CHAPTER ELEVEN

SARAH THOUGHT ABOUT checking her phone for the tenth time in an hour. But the last time she'd looked she'd gotten a Twitter direct message from "lockeduplove47." It totally creeped her out that someone from her mom's hometown wanted to connect with her. For her last night in Heartache, she didn't want to think about the past. The soccer game had ended. Everyone was leaving the bleachers to climb up a nearby hill so they could have a party in the middle of nowhere. It sounded fun, and Lucas had told Ally he'd be there even though he hadn't put in an appearance at the game.

Sarah really, really needed to have fun tonight. Stressed about leaving Heartache, she had called her counselor on her "for emergencies only" private line to confide about the letter from Brandon. She'd regretted the confidence as soon as the words were out. Sure, it had felt good for a nanosecond to share the truth with someone, but what if her counselor told her dad? Theresa had said Sarah needed to think hard about going to her father with the information or else they'd need to "revisit" the issue. Did that mean Theresa would tell him any-how? He'd lose it.

Plus, what if he made her open the letter? The thing felt like a bomb in her purse that she had to handle carefully. What if there was some weird detail in there about her mom or her mom's death? She couldn't stand for the whole nightmare to come back just when they'd finally, finally put some space between them and that awful night. She couldn't go backward. Refused to return to the days when she woke from nightmares five times before dawn and cried through the hours she didn't sleep.

"Hey, New Girl," a guy's voice called from be-hind the bleachers. "Are you coming down or do I have to go up there and get you?"

Her heart raced.

She turned on the cold metal seat to see Lucas standing on the grass while kids flooded out of the stands to head either toward the parking lot or up the hill for the party.

"It depends," she shouted back, a tingly excite-ment taking hold and chasing away the worries about everything else. "If you keep calling me New Girl, you're going to have a tough time getting me to go anywhere with you."

He folded his arms.

"Is that how it is?"

"Definitely." She had no idea where this boldness had come from. She'd been taking other kinds of risks this year, but not with boys.

Especially not ones she genuinely liked.

"Then I guess I didn't make the same impression on you that you did on me." He didn't seem to care that other kids noticed them talking.

A few even pointed and whispered.

Would he really make a scene like this unless he'd broken up with the girlfriend?

"Is that so?" She edged closer to the bars where she peeped through to watch him.

The lights had gone out right after the soccer game and the sun was setting, but her eyes had adjusted to the growing dimness. Hints of purple edged the sky.

"You're really not coming down here, are you?" he asked.

"Not unless you remember my name." She was pretty sure he remembered her name.

Although she worried just a little that he hadn't given in and said it yet.

He nodded slowly. Watching her. Then he walked toward the bleachers.

A thrill shot through her. He was coming for her. By the time he rounded the corner of the bleachers, the seats were empty except for her. He didn't bother finding the stairs. He stepped up onto the first level and took big steps diagonally to her.

The shortest distance between two points…

Her breath caught in her throat when he reached her. He stood a step below and leaned over her. One hand landed on the metal seat on either side of her butt.

"Hey, *Sarah*." He drew out her name in a way that made her shiver.

"Hey." She felt nervous inside, not like the night at the playground where she'd been on edge. "You did know my name."

"Of course." His dark eyes wandered over her face as if he was going to memorize her. "I just wanted to wait to use it until I was nice and close to you."

His voice became softer as he loomed nearer. Sarah's heart ricocheted in her chest.

"Oh?" She was just full of eloquence tonight. She bit her lip to stop herself from kissing him.

He smelled like soap and something spicy. Her mom would have known what it was.

"Yeah. Like this." His lips closed over hers with a tenderness that had been missing the first time.

He didn't kiss her so much as he savored her like something sweet and delicious. She didn't bother trying to make things happen faster. To do anything else besides sit still and enjoy it would take away from the incredible kiss.

When he pulled back, it took her a moment to open her eyes.

He watched her and she wondered what he saw.

A girl who was falling for him? He'd be surprised when she told him she had to leave town tonight.

"I heard you had a girlfriend," she blurted out with zero forethought.

"I did. But since I knew you were more of a troublemaker than me, I thought I'd better break up with her before I saw you again." His breath was warm and minty against her lips.

"You're blaming me for your breakup?" She wanted to kiss him more, not talk about some other girl, so why had she brought it up?

But it bugged her that he'd avoided her the past few days.

"I'm saying I couldn't stay away from you and I'm too much of a nice guy to hurt her." He straightened and held out a hand to help her up.

"I don't know about the nice-guy part. Rumor has it you've got a reputation around town." Wrapping her fingers around his, she tucked her phone in her purse.

"One mistake shouldn't be a black mark against me forever," he muttered darkly.

"Sorry—"

"No. It's not your fault. People talk." He kept her hand in his as they walked down the steps and onto the cool, damp grass. "I'm trying to do better. Be better."

"So what are you hanging around a troublemaker for if you've reformed?" She pulled on his hand enough to stop him. The hillside was quiet, the last car pulling out of the parking lot in a disappearing trail of red taillights.

In the distance, country music played and kids laughed, but it seemed so far away.

Lucas, on the other hand, felt very real.

"I told you. I couldn't stay away. I remember what it's like to feel like you're teetering on the edge of running wild all the time." His words were surprisingly serious after how much they'd teased each other. "Maybe I know what it's like to need someone to—hold you steady."

Sarah's chest squeezed.

"What if we just end up making each other wilder?" She shouldn't have let him break up with some nice girl for her, especially when her father was forcing her to go home.

How upset would Lucas be—rightfully so—when she disappeared after this?

"You let me worry about that." He slid his hands along her hips, his touch leaving a path of warmth wherever they went. "Maybe *I'll* reform *you*."

She knew he was teasing again. Kind of.

But part of her worried. It wasn't Lucas's job to change her—to make her into the kind of person she wished she could be. Her counselor had told her that was Sarah's job.

Right. Easy for her to say.

She squeezed Lucas's hand tighter as they quickly

climbed up the hill to the party. Sometimes, if you ran fast enough, trouble couldn't catch up.

"I'M GOING WITH YOU."

Erin pulled a sweatshirt off a hook near the back door and threw it on after Remy's terse explanation. He planned to go looking for Sarah at her party since she wasn't answering her phone. He was worried.

Erin wasn't clear on the details of what Sarah was dealing with. However, she couldn't be sure if it was because Remy wanted to keep their personal lives private or because he didn't understand himself. All Erin knew was that she'd gotten a reprieve from his inevitable departure from Heartache and she couldn't help but be a little grateful for that.

"No." He shook his head. "I can find her. I need to focus on Sarah and figure out what's going on with her."

"So I'll leave once you locate her." She zipped up the sweatshirt and opened the folding doors to the laundry room off the kitchen, certain she'd find some shorts to throw on. "But at least you'll have some help. I know where that field is and it's not going to be on your GPS."

She found a jean skirt and stepped into it, pulling it over the skimpy silk robe she'd worn into the kitchen to make them something to eat after the most incredible, world-rocking sex. That seemed like forever ago.

"There's a bonfire in a small town. I think I'll find it." His jaw was tight, his shoulders tense.

She read the rejection in every taut line of his body.

"You really don't want me to go." She wrapped her arms around herself, finally getting the message. "Okay." She took a step back. "I've never been a clingy woman, and I'm not going to start now. I only wanted to help."

"I grew up on a bayou. I punted around in a pirogue, fished off a dock I shared with water moccasins and—on occasion—a three-hundred-pound gator." He scrubbed a hand through his hair. "So some days I take exception to the implication that I can't find my own daughter at a neighborhood party."

She'd touched a raw nerve. No surprise really. Intimacy exposed those raw spots. Intellectually, she knew this.

It still hurt to have him push her away with both hands. How many times had she tried to help her mother as a kid, only to have her mom yell at her, belittle her or ignore her?

"Right." She stuffed her hands in the pocket of the sweatshirt and headed for the refrigerator, taking deep breaths to stay level. Not engage. "Want a drink for the road?"

She pulled a soda out of the fridge and popped the top.

"I'm good." His jaw jutted. "Sorry to leave in a rush."

"Good luck." She didn't know what else to say.

"Erin—"

"Don't." She didn't want to hear him blame the situation with his daughter, or his past, or anything else for why he needed to leave on such a sour note. "We knew all along you'd be leaving after this and I went into it with my eyes wide-open. I'm not sorry about what we did. But if you say any more about why this was a bad idea...I might be."

He took a deep breath and, for a second, she thought he might argue with her. So she wasn't sure if she was disappointed or relieved when he turned and walked out her door.

Maybe she was a little of both.

She set aside the soda she hadn't really wanted and sat at her kitchen table. With her sister on the road, she didn't have anyone to talk to. Her mother could be a helpful ear every now and then, but other times she didn't come to the door when Erin knocked. Some days, she could deal with that, knowing her mom was bipolar. But today? She wouldn't do well if she discovered she was locked out of her mom's house.

Nina had gone back to Nashville to be with Mack. Bethany might be around, and would surely be sympathetic to the frustrations of complicated men. But it was hard to open that door with her sister-in-law since it also invited commentary about Scott, which was hard for Erin to hear.

When her phone chimed with a text, she was surprised.

That it was from Remy surprised her even more.

Did he want help after all?

Don't forget to install an alarm system.

Shoving the phone aside, Erin locked the doors and went upstairs. Bypassing her bedroom—now full of too many memories—she lay down in the guest room and tried not to think about the fact she'd given herself so completely to a man she'd met only a week or so ago.

No, she didn't regret it. One of the reasons she'd let herself think about being with him was that he'd be leaving Heartache. While she might not like what that said about her, she couldn't deny that him being on a plane back to Miami right now would be easier on her heart than him staying in town and not wanting anything to do with her.

Any hope she'd had of him being her rebound guy had disintegrated when he'd gotten the phone call about Sarah. Like it or not, Erin would have to face the consequences of taking things to the next level with a man who'd told her—more than once—that his life was too complicated to get involved with anyone right now.

That made her a) too stubborn for her own good; b) attracted to the wrong sort of men; or c) following patterns of trying to help people who were impossible to comfort.

Closing her eyes, Erin feared all of the above were true. When was she going to stop trying to be the strong shoulder for people who didn't want one? She'd wasted months with Patrick trying to help him find joy in a life mired in work—introducing him to the arts and encouraging his painting. She'd started the whole Dress for Success program because it rubbed her raw to see Jamie struggling through life when Erin knew a way to help. She was a helper by nature, but she knew that wasn't what Remy needed from her.

Tonight, she couldn't think her way through it because she was emotionally raw herself.

When her phone rang again, this time with an incoming call, she bolted upright.

"Hello?" She vowed she was not running out to help Remy find that damn field.

"Erin?"

Her nerve endings tingled. Not in a good way.

"Who is this?" Her voice scratched on an uncertain note.

"Don't hang up. It's Patrick."

She damn well wanted to hang up. But shock

glued her fingers to the phone as the past reached through the airwaves. No words came.

"Please, Erin. We need to talk."

CHAPTER TWELVE

"How did you get this number?"

Anger made her voice shake. After six months, she thought she was done worrying about a call like this from the piece of slime who'd betrayed her trust. She'd changed her house phone and her cell phone so that he'd get the message in no uncertain terms that she didn't want to speak to him again. Ever.

"I found it through an online search. It wasn't easy, but you're too important to me. Erin—"

"Can you put your wife on the phone, please?" She cut him off short. She didn't want even a shadow of him in her life. "I'd like to let her know you're harassing me."

Too wound up to sit through this call, she flipped on the bedside lamp and paced the guest room.

"One call in six months is harassment? I've been separated from Kristen for months anyhow, so my soon-to-be ex-wife is not home and not a factor for us any longer."

Too little, too late. If he was even telling the truth.

"Ah." Erin stepped over a basket of wood-block

letters that belonged at the store, tense with old frustration she'd managed to stuff down for so long. "How original."

"Erin, come on, baby," he pleaded. "She and I were having problems long before I met you."

She stopped pacing. As much as she did not want to talk to him, she had always wondered how he justified this omission in her mind. "Did it ever occur to you I might want to know you were married and had children? All that time we were together it never came up?"

"At first, I didn't say anything because I knew I'd never have a chance with you if you found out."

Sitting on the edge of a pale blue wingback, she stared at a silver-framed photo of herself with her family at the Grand Canyon when she was nine years old.

"Obviously. Common social convention is to take yourself off the market once you're married. This should not be news to you." She told herself the only reason she stayed on the phone was to fantasize about reaching across the airwaves and strangling him. Although she couldn't ignore the fact that a part of her wanted to understand how she could have been so gullible, to find something in what he said to help her see how this man had managed to turn her into a cliché.

"But then, once we started to spend more time with each other, I knew we were meant to be together." He spoke with a passion that defied logic after all the time they'd spent apart and how very clearly she'd dumped him on his cheating ass.

Surely, he had something better to offer than the same arguments as before?

"And this is what you called to tell me? That we were 'meant to be together'?" She shook her head, wishing he'd come up with something better. She'd encouraged him to follow his dreams. He had taken up guitar when they'd been together. She thought she was special to him.

First in his heart.

Of course, there was no scenario that would have made what he'd done okay. Still, she'd spent a lot of time imagining his reasons. The romantic drivel he'd just spouted was about as disappointing an effort as she could envision.

"I know. I know." His voice broke. "I just couldn't let you think you'd ever come in second place to her. You were always important to me. I always planned to leave her."

She might have bought that line five months ago when she'd still nursed a small hope in her heart. But not now. She'd done a lot of growing up since screwing up her life.

"You're wrong, Patrick. If I was ever important to you, you would have been up front with me." She didn't think he could keep on hurting her, but right now, with the memory of Remy's touches still simmering along her skin, she felt the sting of betrayal all over again.

Patrick wasn't the first man to put her second, and now—after Remy—he wasn't the last. Remy was more loyal to his dead wife than Patrick had ever been to the mother of his children.

At least Remy was honest about it. How ironic that his honorability made her hurt all the more. And made her realize how very little Patrick had honored her.

Patrick started to argue. "You *are* important—"

"Please don't call me again." She spoke on top of him, blurting the words in a rush before disconnecting the call.

Stuffing her phone in the pocket of her sweatshirt, she hoped it was the last she heard from him. She'd gotten the answer she was curious about and it provided zero comfort.

She shuffled down the stairs knowing she was now too keyed up to sleep. She grabbed a folded blanket from an ottoman in the living room and brought it outside on the patio with her. Stars winked in the cool night air as she dropped into the love seat. It was funny how she'd fought so hard to avoid romantic entanglements these past months only to find herself incredibly tangled.

Patrick didn't count except that she felt five times the guilt now, knowing he'd left his wife. His kids.

That broke her heart, even if he had been planning to leave his family all along.

But Remy… She closed her eyes as the night air whispered over her skin like a lover's sigh. Things were only going to get more complicated where he was concerned. As much as that worried her, she was already in too deep to walk away.

THE BONFIRE WHIPPED from a sudden gust of breeze, flames arcing sideways while Remy climbed the hill toward the sounds of music and laughter.

Erin had been correct. He wouldn't have located this spot on his own. He had ended up stopping at a gas station to ask where to find the soccer field, and that had gotten him here well enough. His head was too twisted with worries about Sarah for him to make sense of what had happened with Erin, so he'd used it as an excuse to run. He hadn't thought far enough ahead to the aftermath of his first time being with another woman, figuring he and Erin would both be back to their own lives with some good memories to take with them.

Now? He trudged faster up the hill and tried not to think about how long he might be stuck in Heartache. How long he'd have to pretend he had it all together when even his eighteen-year-old daughter didn't trust him enough to confide in him.

Clearing the last ridge above the soccer field, Remy saw the shadowy outline of a tailgate party.

He didn't know how the trucks had gotten up here—certainly not via the path he'd taken—but there were five pickups parked in a way that the vehicles made a half circle around the bonfire. There were probably twenty-five or thirty kids either watching the flames, dancing in truck beds or chasing each other around the cottonwood trees. A country tune crooned from a stereo system.

For a moment, he wished he'd brought Erin. Maybe she would have been able to find Sarah more discreetly than he could since she probably knew some of these kids. Because, however he approached this on his own, Sarah was going to accuse him of embarrassing her.

With no help for it now, he marched into the fray, flattening the tall grass with every step.

"Excuse me." He approached a couple of teenage boys who fought the wind to light a cigarette. "I'm trying to find my daughter. Have you seen Sarah Weldon?"

"The new girl?" one of them asked, tucking the unlit cigarette behind his ear before pocketing his lighter.

"She was over there," the other boy answered, pointing to a spot beyond the ring of trucks, near a sprawling red oak. "With Lucas."

"Thanks." Remy moved away from the fire just as a log slipped and sent sparks flying.

A few girls squealed as bits of red-hot cinders

blew everywhere. The bad feeling in the pit of his stomach grew. What if she'd concocted a story for Theresa about being scared to return home when she really just wanted to hang out with some guy she'd met? She hadn't said anything about Lucas to him, but that didn't mean much these days. There was a lot she didn't tell him.

Losing patience with wandering around in the dark, he shouted for her.

"Sarah!"

The group quieted, heads swiveling in his direction.

Damage done, he shouted again, "Sarah, I've come to take you home."

Nearby, a girl seated on the front fender of one of the trucks scooted closer to her boyfriend, whispering. No doubt the presence of a strange man among the group was scary. Damn it. He stalked away from the kids around the fire and headed toward the woods where the boys had said they saw her earlier.

With someone named Lucas.

"Dad?"

A shadow broke free from the tree line nearby. The figure hurried forward.

"Sarah." He marched toward her, seeing no sign of anyone else with her, although it was hard to see into the dark cluster of red oaks and cottonwoods. "What are you doing out here?"

White fluff from the cottonwood seeds rained down as another wind gusted. They stood halfway between the bonfire and the trees in a no-man's-land between the two. It was quieter even moving twenty yards from the stereo system.

"I'm at a party." Her tone wavered somewhere between exasperated and deeply offended. She picked a piece of the cottony fluff off her sleeve. "You told me I could go, remember?"

Remy continued to study the thicket behind her, wanting to know whom she was hanging out with back there.

"Of course. What I mean is, what are you doing back here when the party is obviously over there?" He jerked a thumb in the direction of the trucks and music.

"Clearing my head," she snapped as she checked her watch. "It isn't time to go home yet. What are you doing here?"

"Informing you that I've postponed the trip to Miami." He didn't appreciate her attempt to distract him. "But now that I'm here, I'd like to know what you're doing in the woods with some kid I've never heard of until tonight. Who is this Lucas?"

"A friend. Amazingly, I've managed to make a few in the short time I've been here." Folding her arms, she stared him down.

For a moment, she reminded him of her mother, that quiet strength emerging to calm down a situation. Remy's throat burned. Was this why he'd avoided spending too much time with Sarah this year—other than in a guardian/protector role? Because she could raise old ghosts with just a look?

Regret flowed through him and he clapped a hand on her shoulder.

"I only want to make sure you're not drinking again."

"I'm not." She met his gaze, a hard glint in the reflected firelight. "But I was having fun with my new friends."

"Is that why you haven't answered my texts? Because I wouldn't have needed to track you down, Sarah, if I could have gotten ahold of you."

"Oh." She swallowed, guilt clear on her face before she started digging in her bag for her phone. "I haven't been checking it."

Her dad frowned. "That thing is usually superglued to your hand."

A few things spilled out from her purse in her rush. He bent to help her.

"I've got it!" she snapped, swiping up some stuff and jamming it back in the bag. "Can we just go now?"

Phone in one hand, she tucked the leather satchel under the other arm, her movements jerky.

"Okay." He pointed at the path down the hill. "I'm parked down here."

"Me, too." She hurried away from the bonfire.

"You don't need to tell anyone you're leaving?" He looked back over his shoulder where the music had gotten slower and a few couples were dancing close together.

He thought he recognized Ally Finley—Erin's niece—who whispered something in Sarah's ear as she walked past.

"No. I'm sure the party is breaking up soon anyway." She walked faster.

She seemed annoyed. Agitated. That made two of them. He waited until they'd cleared the party and were safely back down to the parking area for the soccer field before he spoke again.

"I got a call from Theresa earlier."

"She *told* you?" She twisted the strap of her purse around one finger, her voice pitched at a frightened whisper.

"No, Sarah. She's waiting for you to talk to me."

"Can we get in the car at least?"

"Fine." He unlocked the doors on the rental. "Get in and we'll pick up your vehicle tomorrow."

He could see the light on her phone as she hopped in the passenger side. Was she checking the messages that she'd missed from him earlier? Or saying good-night to this Lucas person?

"Oh, God." Sarah's eyes were wide in the reflected electronic light of the screen.

"What?" He struggled to hold on to his patience,

but it felt as though every time they needed to talk something else came up.

She tensed. Bit her lip as she stared at him. Finally, she sighed and blurted, "I've been getting messages online from someone who lives in Mom's hometown. Belle Chasse."

His stomach twisted, old fear churning in his gut.

"Is this why you don't want to go back to Miami? Is this guy harassing you?"

Tense with the need to act, he was already thinking through their legal options for an injunction.

"Just listen," she pleaded, sounding close to tears. "I was ignoring this person's notes in social media when I saw where she was from." She turned the phone toward him so he could see a social media profile for "lockeduplove47," also known as Becky from Belle Chasse.

The woman appeared around his age, with frizzy blond hair and a neck tattoo of a fleur-de-lis.

"I've never heard of her. Maybe she was someone who went to school with your mother?"

"Right. That's the kind of thing that I was thinking, so I ignored her." She shrugged. "I didn't want to worry you. And you know I try not to dwell on that stuff so…"

"I know." He covered her shaking hand with his. "You've been stronger than any teenager should have to be."

"Not really. Theresa says I just ignore stuff, which kind of isn't the same." She slid away her hand and used it to change screens on the phone. "But anyhow, the woman just messaged me with this."

She flipped the device so he could read it.

Your dad regrets the hurt he's caused you. If you give him a chance, you'll see what a kind, warm-hearted man he really is!

Heat burned his chest, as if he'd swallowed sparks from the bonfire. He gripped the phone so hard he accidentally shut the screen off.

"What the hell is she talking about?" He'd never met the woman, so he could only assume that when she referred to Sarah's "dad" she must mean Brandon.

"That's what I've been scared about." Sarah took her phone back and put it inside her bag, chewing her bottom lip raw. Then she withdrew a folded piece of paper. No, an envelope. It shook in her hand as she held it up. "I got this two weeks ago."

Fear crushed his chest in a dark forewarning. He wasn't going to like this.

"What is it?" His voice was scratchy, the sound barely there. He reached overhead to turn on the dome light.

Sarah handed him a crumbled and dirt-smudged

letter sent to her from a federal penitentiary in Pollock, Louisiana.

"It's from my father. My real father."

"AND YOU DIDN'T open it?" Erin asked, propping a pillow under her head as she adjusted her phone on her other ear.

She had almost been scared to answer the call when it had come in half an hour ago, worried it might be Patrick again. She'd been so relieved to see Remy's number—on more than one level—too much so to analyze now. Later, she would sift through the flutter of excitement.

Or at least, she'd been relieved until she'd heard about what had happened to Sarah. He didn't sound like himself, the stress of the night threading through every word.

"I wasn't sure of the best protocol from a legal standpoint. I don't know what kind of laws protect us from Sarah's father, but if there's any chance that he broke one when he contacted her, I want to be certain they've got the best evidence to prosecute him or the woman who is contacting Sarah online."

If it really was a woman.

Erin didn't say it aloud, not wanting to upset Remy more, but who could trust a profile name and photo? Anyone could pose behind a fake identity online.

"So you'll talk to the police tomorrow?" She clicked off the ceiling fan, using a remote beside her bed, so she could hear better.

She'd fallen into a fitful sleep thinking about what approach to take with Remy the next time she saw him. Pretend their night together never happened? Well, now she knew they hadn't destroyed their friendship by sleeping together. Maybe they could still salvage some kind of relationship for the rest of his time in Heartache.

"Yes. And Sarah's counselor, too. I didn't think it would be fair to Sarah after all she's been through to drag her into the station at midnight. Plus, her therapist might want to talk to her before the letter is opened."

"I'm glad she confided in you." She sat up, hugging her knees as she watched the moonlight filter in through the wooden slats of her blinds.

"Finally." He didn't sound happy about it. Was he upset that a felon was contacting Sarah? Or did he still resent that she'd kept it a secret that whole time?

"Is there anything I can do?" She had to at least offer. "I know you want to be there for her. But if I can help in any way—"

"I've been thinking about that." He spoke softly, his voice a little more relaxed than when they'd first started this conversation. "I know you deserved more from me after we were together. I left with a chip on my shoulder, but it didn't have anything to do with you."

She wondered how true that was but didn't question him on it for now.

"You had good reason to be concerned for your daughter."

"I could kill Brandon for doing this to her. She's only eighteen. He's the reason she lost her mother." Quiet anger rumbled through the phone. "What kind of father treats his kid this way? He could be putting her at risk, and he damn well doesn't have the excuse that he didn't realize the danger."

"Having children doesn't make a person a good parent." She'd been reminded of that tonight after the call from Patrick. How could he have walked out on his kids?

Remy was quiet for a minute. "You asked before if you could do anything for Sarah."

"I meant it." And she was touched that he trusted her enough to ask.

"I thought I'd let her assist the crew during the filming at Last Chance Vintage. We're going to be in town anyway and she's been lobbying to take a more active role in learning about production."

"I think that's a great idea."

"Since I won't be on the set all the time, I'd be grateful if you could, you know, look out for her. With all this distraction of the letter from prison, I haven't gotten to speak with her about her college options or her frustration with living in Miami. And tonight I think she was hanging around with some local kid she has never mentioned or brought around—Lucas."

"Lucas Maynard?" She remembered Sarah saying he'd changed. Not that she knew much about the trouble he'd gotten into in the past, but in a small town you heard rumors even if you didn't want to.

He hesitated for a moment, and she could hear the late news playing in the background on his television. He must be in his room at the B and B.

"Is that a bad thing?" he finally asked.

"I don't know, actually." She didn't want to spread idle gossip, especially when she wasn't positive she was thinking of the right teen. "I'll ask my sister-in-law. I think he's in Ally's grade at school."

"I'd appreciate that."

"And Remy, of course I'll do my best to keep an eye out for Sarah anytime you're not around." She didn't know if it was wise to tangle their lives up more, but she couldn't possibly say no if it meant supporting a family who'd been through so much.

She was doing the Dress for Success event for the same basic reason—to give single parents the tools they needed to care for their families.

"Thank you." He cleared his throat. "I know last night didn't turn out exactly the way we thought it would."

"Some parts turned out better," she teased, hoping to lighten the mood.

"Definitely. But other aspects got a whole lot more complicated."

She closed her eyes, remembering the way he'd made her feel. The urgency underlying every touch.

"They don't have to be." She didn't need her hand held. Didn't have to be a part of his life just because they'd slept together.

"I just don't want you to feel obligated—"

"I won't."

"Or give you a false impression—"

"You can't." She cut him off sharply, unwilling to hear him spell out all the reasons they couldn't be together. "I'm not going to fall for another guy who is…unavailable."

"Okay, then," he said carefully, making her wish she hadn't been so abrupt.

"So will you be at the store tomorrow when the filming starts?" She changed the subject, not sure what else to say about where they stood.

He was right—they hadn't meant to be in this position afterward. But now that they would have to be around each other in the aftermath, she would try to make the best of it.

"Briefly. I'll stick around long enough to introduce the crew and get you started."

She was curious about how he'd spend the rest of the day, but maybe he would be looking into the legalities of Sarah's father sending her mail. Remy didn't offer anything more, however.

"Great." She forced a smile, hoping it brought an easiness to her voice she didn't feel. "I'll see you in the morning, then."

Disconnecting the call, she held the phone for a long time afterward. She'd meant what she'd said about not falling for him. She couldn't afford that kind of hit to her heart—not so close on the heels of what had happened with Patrick.

It was a shame, her heart whispered just before she fell asleep. Because if ever there would have been an amazing guy to take another chance with, it would have been Remy. A caring father, a generous lover, a talented professional… He possessed so many qualities she wanted in a man. But his wife's death might very well have robbed him of the ability to love another woman the same way. Finding that out would be enough to break a woman's heart—not just for six months, but possibly for the rest of time.

CHAPTER THIRTEEN

SARAH STARED THROUGH the lens of camera number three, a stationary angle that would record the cash register and front counter of Last Chance Vintage on a continuous basis.

Finally, she was working behind a camera and learning something about how a television show came together. Who needed a college education when she could assist a super-successful producer like her dad? She'd waited too long to learn more about her mother's career and talent. Now she'd never have the chance to see her working in her studio again. But there was no reason she couldn't learn more about her father's world and experience it for herself. The day would be perfect, if not for a trip to the police station hanging over her head.

Shoving thoughts of the letter aside, she played with the focus on the camera, seeing what all the buttons did.

The morning sun shone bright through the front windows of the store crowded with her dad's production crew and—it seemed like—half the population of Heartache, Tennessee. Twenty people milled around the front of the building, waiting for the store to open so they could be a part of *Interstate Antiquer*.

At least, that was her dad's perspective. She happened to know that all those people on the street were there for Erin because Erin had tons of friends.

Sarah sharpened the focus on the camera, bringing Erin into clear view at the front counter. Erin laughed at something Ally said a second before Mrs. Finley brought out a makeup brush to dust powder over Erin's face.

"Aunt Erin looks great." Ally rushed over to gush at Sarah's side. She glanced down at the viewing window for the camera to see what the scene would look like once it was recorded.

Ally had taken the day off school to be present for the first day of filming. Of course, Ally had already gotten into Vanderbilt in Nashville, so she didn't need to worry about her grades or her attendance record. Lucky.

"That outfit is killer," Sarah agreed, admiring the tribal-patterned shorts Erin wore with dark lace leggings and knee boots. A creamy linen blouse topped it off and she wore her hair up in a messy clip. "I'm glad she didn't go too conservative like she was talking about with Trish at the clothing drive."

"Although this *is* kind of conservative for her," Ally pointed out. "She'd been wearing a lot of Goth stuff up until last week. Even her hair is lighter now."

Sarah wondered if the recent changes had anything to do with her father. The two of them had definitely spent a lot of time together in the past week and a half. And Sarah had noticed her dad smiled at Erin more than he smiled at most people. Which was still hardly ever considering he'd turned a lot more serious in the past two years. But she had noticed.

Even now, her dad strolled over to Erin and Bethany to introduce the crew's gofer who'd brought coffees for everyone. Erin smiled at the gofer kid as she thanked him. For the most part, though, Erin's eyes seemed stuck to Dad.

"Ally, do you think your aunt likes my father?" She wasn't sure how she felt about that. For so long, she'd been hoping he would stop grieving and living in the past.

Then again, she couldn't picture him with anyone else but her mom.

"I don't know, but it sounds like your dad is kind of a rock star with the mom crowd." Ally raised her cell phone and snapped photos of the store and all the cameras.

"It's weird. I have a teacher who practically drools when he comes into school for a meeting." Sarah shuddered.

"You don't live with your mom?" Ally asked while texting, not even looking up.

"No." Sarah didn't get asked the question very often. Back at school, everyone had known what had happened to her mother thanks to the papers. The internet. The TV news every night for months during the trial. "She died a couple of years ago."

Ally's eyes flashed up to hers, her phone forgotten.

"I'm so sorry. I didn't know." Her hand covered Sarah's wrist in automatic sympathy.

Or was it empathy?

If she'd studied for her SATs, maybe she'd know. Either way, it felt nice.

"Thanks." She didn't mention that her biological father had been the reason that her mother was dead now. Or that Sarah was on her way to the police station to let them know what a twisted creep her DNA donor was.

Ally might not feel so sympathetic then. Swallowing back her nervousness about the police station visit, Sarah set the camcorder on Auto-record and shuffled out of the way of one of the production guys carrying in an extra spotlight.

"I'm glad you're staying in Heartache for a little while," Ally said. "I'm going to school tomorrow, but then we're off all next week if you want to do anything."

"That'd be nice." Idly, she flipped through a

rack of blouses organized by color and size, stopping when she got to a tee with a bunch of female superheroes on the front. "Will there be any more parties? I had fun last night."

She and Lucas had been making out in the woods before her father's arrival. Total buzzkill.

"Did you? I wondered if everything was okay since your dad came to get you."

"Right. Well, that part was a major downer, but I was having fun until then." Why did he try to pry confidences out of her that were supposed to be private between her and Theresa?

"Is he worried about you being with Lucas?" Ally passed her a bright blue miniskirt. "This would be cute with the superheroes tee, by the way."

"Why would he worry about Lucas?" She couldn't focus on the skirt. She moved out of the way of a rolling camera as it followed another customer through the store.

"Oh." Ally shook her head. "No reason. I just wondered why your dad wanted you to leave."

Ally sounded sincere, yet her cheeks turned pink as she leafed through the clothing racks faster.

"Why does everyone think Lucas is trouble?" Sarah kept her voice low, since the cameras were probably picking up audio now. There weren't any close to them, but she knew the microphones on her dad's equipment were much better than anything she had on her phone.

"I'm not sure, honestly." Ally shrugged. "I don't want to spread rumors anyway."

"Ally—"

"Sarah?" Her dad interrupted—as always—just when things were getting interesting. "Are you ready to go?"

He must have ESP in addition to all his other protector-father instincts.

"Okay." It wasn't as if she'd have this conversation with her new friend in front of him anyhow. "Text me later," she told Ally as she brought the shirt and skirt to the front of the store. Turning to her dad, she asked, "We'll stop by the shop afterward, right?"

"I can drop you off here if you like, but I'm probably going to get some work done at the hotel."

"Or you can just drop me off at the soccer field and I'll pick up my car." She handed the clothes to Ally's mom, who still stood by the front counter while Erin helped a customer. "Can I hold these until later, Mrs. Finley?"

"Of course," she said, smiling, though Sarah was pretty sure she had a tear in her eye. "I'll let Erin know."

If there hadn't been other people around, Sarah would have asked her if she was okay. She didn't want to put Mrs. Finley on the spot, though, so she simply thanked her and followed her father out the front door.

"Dad?" She hurried to catch up to his long steps. *He's mad at me.* She kept thinking it even though Theresa always told her that he wasn't mad just because he didn't have much to say.

Pausing outside the rental car, he waited for her to speak.

"I'm sorry I didn't tell you about the letter sooner." She hated it when he became quiet. It reminded her too much of those months right after her mom's death where he'd barely spoken.

She slid into the passenger side of the big four-door Lincoln and buckled up. Then she locked the door, too, knowing how much he appreciated it when she took extra safety precautions.

He didn't speak for a long moment as he got in and started the car. He looked tired. Sad. She remembered days when he'd been so full of energy even after he came home from a business trip. He'd race into the house with surprise concert tickets for her mom or a new phone with a shiny pink case for her. She missed that—not for the phones or tickets—but just seeing him full of life and happiness. Finally, he looked at her.

"Why didn't you tell me?"

A million answers came to mind. Any of which would have been true since there were—literally—

a million reasons why. But she went with one she hoped he might understand.

"I keep thinking we're finally done with the nightmare, and then something new happens to make it come back." She couldn't look at him when she said it or she would cry and that would hurt him worse. "I just couldn't stand for this letter to undo all the hard work we've done to put it behind us."

"That's the problem." Exhaling a long breath, he pounded the steering wheel lightly with his fist. "The past isn't really behind us, is it?" He picked up the stupid envelope with the postmark from Pollock, Louisiana.

"Maybe if we tried harder to move forward, it would be." She'd never said it in so many words to him. But that was what she wanted more than anything.

She held her breath waiting for his verdict, her chest really tight.

"I think we have different ideas of what it means to try hard, Sarah." He set the letter down in the console between them. "For you, it means forgetting. For me, it means making sure nothing like that can ever touch us again."

His expression seemed so distant, his words a reminder they were moving apart in every way possible. She'd already lost her mom. Soon she'd lose the only man she'd ever really thought of as a father, and not just because she'd need to take more responsibility for herself after high school ended. Also because the man she used to know was fading a little more every day, his happy spirit smudged by grief and worry.

Without another word, he backed out of the parking spot onto the street and headed in the direction of the cop shop.

She'd have to tell her story all over again to strangers. She would read the letter that Brandon had sent and maybe find out why he'd contacted her. Already the knot in her stomach tightened and grew cold. She needed Lucas here with her.

It didn't matter to her what he'd done in the past. Didn't matter that people like Ally thought he'd done something wrong. Sarah had plenty of experience putting the past behind her. She just wished she could do this together with Lucas instead of sitting beside her quiet, brooding father, who always seemed a moment away from being mad.

She was happy they were staying in Heartache. She'd have time to seek out Lucas and find out why everyone thought he was trouble. As for her father? Maybe he could spend more time with Erin Finley. He might not realize he needed a woman around, and compared to the drooling teacher or the random flirty women he worked with, Erin seemed really cool. She did compassionate things like organize clothing drives, plus she was kind of artsy.

Sarah liked that. And deep down, she knew her dad must like that, too. He'd been an artist once, before he'd set that aside to be some kind of super-provider for her and her mom.

Besides, Sarah was tired of dishing out all the wise life advice to her dad and having it fall on deaf ears. She needed help with him. She also needed a distraction for when she wanted to hang out with Lucas. Maybe if her father was busy dating, he wouldn't have time to chase her down at every party.

After this police station visit was over, she was going to commence Operation Return to Dating.

THE HITS JUST kept coming.

Tipping his chair back on two legs, Remy rested his head on the waiting room wall at the police station while he sat outside a conference room where a female investigator had taken Sarah for a private discussion.

The lady investigator had spoken to him first, assuring Remy that she needed to ask Sarah questions privately about whether or not she felt safe at home. They were a fairly standard list and Theresa had warned him that the local cops might speak to her without him being present since she was eighteen. But it was making him nuts to think about her having to undergo some kind of police quiz alone.

Hadn't the poor kid been through enough in the

past two years without her idiot of a biological father bringing this down on her head?

Uninspiring gray walls surrounded him as did a few other people in uncomfortable wooden chairs. A man and his son had arrived to fill out a report about a stolen bike. A young woman waited for information about becoming a police officer. Another woman waited for her husband—the cop at the front desk—to finish his shift so she could take him out to dinner for his birthday.

The birthday couple exchanged looks every other minute. And the "I want to get you naked" vibe seemed inappropriate at best. Then again, maybe Remy just envied that certainty of going home with someone. Of celebrating a birthday with someone. He missed the normal ebb and flow of an everyday, average life.

Damn, but he wished his daughter would be done soon.

His phone chimed and he almost ignored it in case it was work related. But what if it was Sarah's counselor?

Are you OK? How is Sarah?

The text from Erin eased some of the tension in his chest. In spite of everything, hearing from her felt good. Maybe even like a slice of normal in an otherwise upside-down day. He lowered his chair back to the floor to key in a reply.

Letter from her dad nonthreatening. Taking all day to document every facet of his stupidity.

Remy hit Send.

The return chime sounded in about two seconds, making him wonder how she could read that fast, let alone type.

Did he break a law in contacting her?

The answer was so convoluted he didn't know quite where to begin. The local police believed there was a responsibility on Sarah's part to file a new form with the Bureau of Prisons once she turned eighteen to stay on Brandon's "Do Not Contact" list. Remy would be sure the paperwork was filed immediately. He had already contacted his lawyer.

Gray area. I can explain over dinner if you don't mind surly company.

After he sent the message, he realized it didn't sound like much of an invitation. He was about to send something more politely worded when she responded.

Will there be cupcakes?

He grinned. That in itself was a miracle considering the day he'd had. Being back in a police station—just that alone—was tough. But thinking about Sarah and how scared she'd been with that letter in her possession for two weeks… That made him mad.

Definitely. I can take you out or bring food to you. Your choice.

The door to the conference room opened and Sarah walked out, the lady police officer behind her. They were both smiling. Relaxed. The woman was asking Sarah about the clothing drive at the store.

Remy's heart recovered a little more even as his phone chimed with one final message.

You had me at "bring food."

"PSST." BETHANY GAVE Erin a gentle poke in the shoulder as she typed another note. "You shouldn't be texting while being filmed on TV," she whispered through clenched teeth.

Erin looked up at her empty store. Half the town had filtered through in the morning hours, some of them eager to see what all the fuss was about with a film crew in town and the rest eager to *be* on film. But now things had quieted down so that her only shopper was an elderly woman from the next town over who'd driven in to look for clothes for her kids and grandkids. Ally had left for her part-time job at the hair salon. A few of the production guys had taken off for parts unknown so that only two people manned the equipment.

The customer was self-sufficient, picking through the racks with a practiced eye.

"Remy said I should behave naturally." Erin was excited about his unexpected dinner invitation. Probably far more than she should be.

She'd assumed after the way they'd parted the night before that he was ready to put that time behind him. Now she wondered. She'd been buzzing inside ever since she got his text. Would he stay for a while…after dinner? Her skin heated as she thought about what that might mean.

Was it foolish to wish for more from him? To hope that his texts were a sign there might be room in his heart for…something? She knew better than that. And yet she was going to meet him anyway.

"Yes, but don't you want to use the publicity as a chance to show people what a dynamic, exciting store you run?" Bethany lifted the small sign Erin had painted for the sale rack. It showed a picture of a rainbow, unicorn and a pot of gold all around the word *Sale*.

"Show off your stuff. You've got so many great visual elements here."

Erin set down her phone, not sure what to do while the cameras rolled. There were downtimes in retail and it wasn't as if she spent all day straightening the stacks of clothes or dusting off antiques.

"I'm barely surviving the cameras so far, Bethany. I can't suddenly start turning cartwheels for attention. It's just not my style."

"I know, but when you have an opportunity to really do something well—" Her breath hitched, her eyes filling with tears. "Oh, God."

She clapped her hands over her mouth, staring up at the ceiling without blinking until the tears dried without falling.

"Are you okay?" Erin hoped the cameras wouldn't notice the drama behind the counter. "What's wrong?"

"Nothing." Bethany sniffed and lowered her voice. "I can't talk about it here."

"Is it Scott?" Erin came around the front of the counter so her back would block the cameras from seeing her sister-in-law.

"I think he's giving up on us. For good." She had barely squeaked out the last word when she turned and darted through the break in the heavy plastic divider into the store's renovated area.

Erin debated what to do. Man the store and be

there for the cameras and one self-sufficient shopper or follow Bethany?

The debate was short since the Finley motto had always been Family First.

Edging between the sheets of protective plastic, she found Bethany sobbing against a counter.

"I'm sorry," she blurted between sniffles. "I'm so sorry. I just started thinking about how Scott always accuses me of being a perfectionist and trying to make everything better. I shouldn't tell you how to run your television spot and I shouldn't tell him how to run his life. I don't know. I just—" She raised her hands in the air, a gesture of helplessness. "I don't know what to do anymore. I feel like everything I say is wrong. Every conversation is a land mine."

Erin felt her sister-in-law's hurt sharply. She didn't want this for Bethany.

"First of all, I love your advice and you always have good ideas, so feel free to tell me how to run the store anytime." Erin dug under a cabinet where she kept building supplies and found a roll of clean paper towels. She passed it to Bethany. "If Heather was here, she would kiss you for telling me to stop texting on national television."

Bethany tore off some of the toweling and wiped her nose. "All my advice drives Scott crazy. But I feel like he doesn't have a plan to save our marriage. He sits in our therapy sessions and waits for them to be over. And if I ask him about it, he clams up."

"I'm sure it can be intimidating to be married to someone who is so incredibly competent, but he has to know how lucky he is to have you."

Her watery laugh didn't sound convinced.

"I mean it." Erin sat on one of the counters, the scent of lumber and wood stain heavy in the air. "The whole family earns money on our shares in Finleys' Building Supplies because you keep the place in the black year after year. Mack has you to thank for being able to invest in his own bar in Nashville. I have your business savvy to thank for having enough start-up cash to get Last Chance Vintage off the ground. Heather does, too, for that matter."

"But I think I chased him away from the business that he planned to make his life." Bethany swiped her eyes, smearing mascara. "Remember when I quit teaching, I just planned to help him. I was going to be like a second in command. Then I ended up taking it over. Things have never been the same since then."

"It's not your fault you had great ideas and really found a niche." She ripped off another paper towel and stepped closer to Bethany. "Here, let me fix your makeup."

She wiped away the excess and noticed her sister-in-law was shaking from the stress.

"You should go back out front," Bethany urged. "I shouldn't even be here if I can't hold it together in public anymore."

"I'm your family." Erin crumpled the paper and threw it away. "If we can't shed tears in front of each other, it's a lonely damn world."

That forced a crooked smile from her.

"I don't see *you* shedding too many tears during the hard times."

"The last man who upset me this badly didn't deserve my tears." Erin didn't know what she'd do if Patrick called her again. How could he think for a second she would want to hear from him? "I'm saving up mine for someone really worthy."

She knew there was a good chance she'd be the one crying when Remy left town. Especially since she wasn't being nearly cautious enough when he extended dinner invitations. But right now, all she could think about was the bright, shining moments that felt happy in the short term.

Didn't she deserve some of that in her life?

"I wouldn't wish this hurt on you." Bethany combed her fingers through her hair and smoothed the front of her blouse.

"I know." Erin's phone chimed in her hand and she wondered what Remy wanted. Funny how she knew it was him. "But maybe you can't have those beautiful highs without the hardship of the lows."

Bethany shook her head. "I'll tell you this much.

I'd really like to get off the roller coaster either way. And I'd sure feel better if he had a plan—if he offered any inkling of some strategy that might save us."

Erin hugged her goodbye, hard, and wished she could do more than just go back into the front of the store while her sister-in-law took time to gather her composure. Their one customer was still working her way through the racks, onto the boys' clothes now that she'd looked at all the toys and the girls' stuff.

Only then did she check her incoming text.

Is it okay if a cute, fairly well-mannered eighteen-year-old joins us? I will double the number of cupcakes.

They'd be dining as a family.

Erin couldn't help a wistful smile. No doubt about it, she was enjoying some beautiful highs this week. Typing her reply, she ignored the cameras completely.

Shoes, dresses and boys are some of my favorite conversational topics, actually. Your guest sounds fun.

Remy's note came right back.

Boy(s)? Plural?

Her heart flip-flopped as if she was the eighteen-year-old.

I will get back to you on these questions in person.

Then waited.

Can't. Wait.

She felt as though someone had turned a light on inside her. She wondered if she looked in a mirror right then if she'd see herself glowing.

"Ma'am?" she called out to her customer. "Looks like it's just ten minutes until closing."

The woman gave a terse nod and kept digging through the racks of clothes. No doubt Bethany wouldn't approve of that business practice, either. But while Remy was in town, Erin planned to squeeze every moment of joy out of her time with him even if it meant putting a piece of her fragile heart on the line again.

CHAPTER FOURTEEN

WHEN HER DOORBELL rang two hours later, Erin opened it to find Remy holding two grocery bags and Sarah beside him with a pastry box. A lightning strike lit up the sky behind them, brightly illuminating the father and daughter for a moment.

"Welcome! Come in before you get soaked." She held the door wide.

"Don't worry, Erin." Sarah hurried inside ahead of her dad. "I'm only here in a cooking capacity. I'm completely *not* elbowing my way into dinner."

Erin looked to Remy for guidance on what she meant, but he just shrugged.

"I'm really looking forward to visiting with you, too," Erin assured her. "Of course, you'll join us. If anything, *I'm* the one elbowing my way into your family dinner."

She gestured at the kitchen and Sarah moved toward it in a rush of ponytail and black poncho fringe. Outside, thunder rumbled in the distance.

"Your kitchen is so cute!" Sarah ran a hand over the rounded lines of a yellow Frigidaire refrigerator. "Everything is so clean and modern, but retro, too. Cool, isn't it, Dad?"

Remy nodded. "Cool and cute. Definitely."

He winked at Erin from behind Sarah's back.

"But to answer your question, I only offered to come so I could cook for you both," Sarah insisted. "I owe my dad a thank-you for being patient with me when I've been one headache after another for him this week."

"I tried telling her we wanted her to stay and enjoy the food she cooks," Remy explained, setting the bags on the pale yellow–tiled kitchen counter. "But she's on a mission."

"Wow." Erin checked out the pile of produce Sarah pulled from one of the grocery sacks. "Maybe we should let her run with this mission. Whatever dinner is in the works looks like it's going to be good."

"We stopped at a farmers' market and everything smelled so fresh." Sarah passed Erin a quart of strawberries. "See?"

Dutifully, Erin inhaled while Remy withdrew a bottle of wine. Father and daughter made an easy team together in this kitchen that Sarah had never set foot in before. It was nice to see them both in a moment where they were relaxed. Happy, even. Erin was curious about what had happened at the police station, but didn't want to risk breaking the mood.

"I know right where you got them." She found a colander and tried to wash some of the fruit, but Sarah shooed her away. "You must have stopped at the farm where Ally's boyfriend, Ethan, lives."

"Really?" Sarah's expressive green eyes grew wide. "Ally told me all about Ethan's family and how they take farming really serious. I guess they try to live like pioneers or something, doing everything themselves. I think it's neat to know you have the skills to, like—run away and live off the grid."

Remy stilled, but Sarah didn't notice as she moved around the kitchen, turning on the oven and pulling down a cutting board from an open shelf. Another lightning flash brightened the kitchen, making Erin reach into a cupboard for a flashlight, along with some candles and matches, just in case.

"Wouldn't you miss modern conveniences, though?" Erin asked carefully. "Like good shopping or restaurants?"

"Maybe." She looked over her shoulder at her father. "Dad, you grew up where it was so rural you were practically off the grid. Didn't you like it in the bayou?"

She drawled the last word with Cajun flair, making Erin realize they'd come from different walks of life in Louisiana. While Sarah had a Southern lilt to her voice that sounded different than the Heartache locals, it also didn't sound like Remy's thicker drawl.

"I wanted a better life than fishing could provide." He reached for the corkscrew and went about opening the wine.

His clipped answer made Erin realize how little she knew about him outside his history with his wife.

"Did you always know you wanted to go into TV production?" she asked, sneaking a peek at the recipe Sarah had open on the digital tablet she'd propped against the flour canister.

Grabbing the fruit while Sarah was busy putting together what looked like a quiche, Erin washed and sliced the berries for the strawberry salad recipe.

"No."

"Dad was a photographer." Sarah whisked eggs and chopped veggies as if she'd done it a hundred times before.

Remy helped a little, but it was clear he deferred to his daughter's cooking wisdom, tackling the jobs she assigned, like slicing tomatoes and grating fresh mozzarella cheese.

"What made you change fields?" Erin found a big bowl for the strawberries and added mandarin oranges.

"I just followed the opportunities that came up," he replied with a shrug.

"Mom always said it would have been hard to have two artists in the family, although I never understood why." Sarah slid the quiche into the oven. Then, noticing that Erin had assembled the salad, she beamed. "Erin! You didn't have to do all that."

"Happy to help. The recipe looks great." She tried to piece together Remy's creative roots while the teen cleaned up the kitchen. Had his wife really discouraged his photography career because there couldn't be two artists in a family?

Erin wondered why Liv had thought that. Did two similar temperaments clash? Or would two artists mean too little income?

But that was a cynical thought.

She tried to focus on Sarah's chatter as she worked. Erin didn't think most eighteen-year-olds—even if they knew how to cook—took the time to wash the prep dishes and wipe down the countertops, but Sarah worked with smooth efficiency. Because she was in a hurry to leave? Or was it simple practice from managing the household for her father?

"Okay, I'm out of here," she announced when she was done. She kissed Remy on the cheek. "Ally will be here to pick me up any second. I just texted her."

"You really can't stay and share the feast?" Erin asked, genuinely disappointed. She appreciated the insights she'd gotten about Remy and was enjoying getting to know his daughter better.

"Ally and I are going to do our fingernails with some manicure art stuff she got at The Strand." Sarah wriggled her bare digits for emphasis. "I guess her house is super nearby?"

She peered out the window into the dark.

"Right over there." Erin pointed. There were fields between her house and her mother's and Scott and Bethany's, but they were still close enough to see lights in one another's windows. "You could have jogged if it wasn't starting to pour."

"Oh, I see her taillights! She's backing out now." Sarah whirled around and gave Erin a hug, her hair silky smooth and apple scented. "Hope you like the quiche!"

"I'm going to love it. Thank you so much." Erin walked her to the front door. Rain spattered through the screen despite the deep overhang on the porch. "Want an umbrella?"

"No. I'll be fine. See you at the shoot tomorrow. And remind Dad that Ally's taking me back to the B and B after?"

"Of course." Erin waved at Ally as her niece pulled into the driveway. "Have fun."

When she closed the door behind her, the house seemed unusually quiet. Remy stood in the dim hallway between her and the kitchen, his shoulders backlit in a way that put him in shadow.

Even the outline of him was handsome with his square shoulders and narrow hips. He wore a blue dress shirt with the cuffs rolled up and the collar unbuttoned.

"She sure fills a house, doesn't she?" Erin accepted the glass of wine Remy held out to her, their fingers brushing briefly in the exchange.

"Always has." Remy lifted his glass in the direction of the front door. "And cheers to her for that or I would have lost my mind long before now."

Erin understood that now, having had the chance to see them together. While Remy obviously excelled at his job, Sarah had more than held her own on the home front. They seemed to have a good relationship, but when Erin thought about what they'd been through together, she ached for them both.

She nodded at the love seat in the front room and Remy followed her there, taking a seat beside her. She didn't bother turning on the lights. The lightning outside the window provided a spectacular show.

"Where did she learn to cook like that?" Erin settled deeper into the leather cushions, making her feet comfortable on the rattan coffee table while they waited for their dinner to bake.

"Self-taught, I guess. She's always had an interest in cuisine, but she truly started cooking with a vengeance once it was just her and me."

Erin's throat dried up as she pictured a grieving girl learning how to cook to feed herself and her father.

"She's been very good to you," she observed quietly before taking a sip of the pinot grigio Remy had brought. "I didn't want to ask in front of her, but I've been wondering how things went at the police station."

"They kept the letter. Initially, Sarah didn't want to see what it said, but after I read it and the police did, too, we encouraged her to take a look."

"You said it wasn't threatening." That was as much as he'd offered in his text.

"No." His jaw tensed. Even in the lightning flashes, she could see the hard set to his profile. "He apologized for sharing anything about her mother with—" his hand fisted on the sofa beside her "—others. He said he didn't expect her to ever forgive him, but he wanted her to know he was sorry for that and for not being a part of her life."

The words were halting as if each one stuck in his throat.

"It sounded sincere?" She tried to reconcile her vision of Liv Weldon—the artist for whom Remy had sacrificed his photography to provide her with more opportunities—with Sarah's felon biological father.

Surely, the man must have some redeeming qualities to have wooed a woman like Liv in the first place.

"I thought so. And, as you can imagine, I searched for any turn of phrase that could be construed as malicious or remotely insensitive."

"So does Sarah feel she'll be safe at home again now that the police are aware this guy has tried to contact her? And what about the social media messages from an unknown account?"

"The police are looking into it and they suggested she delete her account. As for how safe Sarah will feel back home...I didn't bring that up." He shook his head and set down his glass. "The past few days with her have just really knocked me on my butt. I figured I'd take a day or two of no drama and ask her counselor's advice. There's no rush to get home with Sarah's school on vacation next week anyhow." His eyes found hers. "Besides, this town has been damn good to me. I don't mind sticking around a little longer."

His words slid over her senses, inciting a shiver. Had he changed gears to distract her from talking about Sarah? Or to distract himself from thoughts of the past?

"I'm glad to hear it." She was relieved he'd given up trying to protect her from getting involved with him. Not that she expected him to let his guard down overnight. But maybe, with time, they could still have something together. "You haven't seen the best of Heartache yet."

"You're wrong about that." He reached for her, his fingers brushing her cheek in a soft caress.

It would be easy to get swept away by his touch. To kiss him until they forgot everything else. But she didn't want to lose this chance to get to know him better, to understand what made him tick.

"Can I ask you a question?" She peered out at the rainstorm again, grateful to be indoors with the scent of dinner cooking in the oven and the warmth of the man next to her.

"That sounds ominous." His touch fell away from her cheek.

"It's not. I promise." She scooted closer to him, letting her forehead fall on his shoulder.

Just that one small point of contact.

"Okay. Shoot."

"What was it like living in bayou country?" She'd traveled a lot scouring the Southeast for antiques and unique items for Last Chance Vintage, but she'd never been south of New Orleans.

More important, she wanted to hear him talk about another time in his life—before the trauma of his wife's death.

"Well…let's just say I wasn't lyin' 'bout growing up near gators." He let loose the full-fledged Cajun drawl, making her smile.

She relaxed, glad they could just be together and enjoy each other.

"Do you have family there?"

"A couple of brothers. And my mom." His cheek tipped to rest on the top of her head. "They'll never leave Terrebonne. My brothers drink too much and spend their Friday nights in the dance halls. One is a cop. The other is a net maker, if you can believe there still is such a thing."

"You're not close with them?" Why wouldn't he have moved back to that area after Liv's death?

God, it was so tough to consider sleeping with him again when every other second something circled back around to thoughts of his dead wife.

"I've always been the black sheep. They couldn't understand why I would ever want to live anywhere that didn't let me fish off my back porch." He hesitated. "I guess I had trouble watching a way of life erode right under my feet. Every day, more of the bayou sinks into the sea. Swamps I used to punt through are part of the Gulf now."

"Is that because the Mississippi doesn't flood the same way or something like that?" She tried to remember what she'd heard about the state's changing ecosystem.

"That's part of it. We don't get the silt from the floods the way we used to. Stopping the flooding introduced a lot of problems the engineers hadn't accounted for." He shook his head. "But there are other issues—the salt water kills the old oaks. There are oil spills and the general havoc wreaked by industry. It's sad to witness."

"You should produce a show on that." She lifted her head to meet his eyes. "Wouldn't you be in a good position now to help?"

"Television viewers aren't always receptive to causes. I'd get better ratings filming my brothers' fights in the dance halls than showing the sad remnants of a fading culture."

"So make a show called *Bayou Brothers* and sneak in your message between brawls and gator wrestling." She toyed with his shirt collar and traced the placket down his chest.

"That's not a bad idea except I was thinking about going back to photography once Sarah starts college." He lifted his wineglass. "*If* she goes to college."

"Really?" Erin saw him with new eyes. "I wasn't sure how serious Sarah was when she said you gave up photography because her mom wanted you to."

"Her version of events is overly simplified." Remy reached behind them to a sofa table where he'd laid his phone. He seemed to search through a few screens while he spoke. "I saw the promise in Liv's art and wanted to do whatever I could to get it into the right galleries. Plus, I wanted her to concentrate on making the most of her creativity because she'd gone through some rough years raising Sarah alone."

He turned the phone toward Erin to show her a bright painting of a cypress tree off center on a canvas. The pride on his face was obvious.

"Is that her work?" Erin took the phone to see it better, enjoying the peeks into his life in a way she'd never had with Patrick. She liked knowing what made Remy tick.

"Yes. She did a whole series based on some of my early photographs around Houma." He slid a finger across the phone screen for her. "You can see more of the paintings and the photos she worked from."

"Your photos?" she clarified, pausing on the twilight image of the skeleton cypress with no leaves. A casket floated in the water at its base. "This is really powerful."

She turned the phone so he could see which photo she meant.

"I can't take much credit for that. It's the draw of the place, not the art."

"What about the choice of composition? The timing for the best lighting?" She was surprised to hear him undersell himself. "That's the artistry."

He rubbed a hand through the light scruff of golden-brown hair along his jaw. "If I go back to photography, I'll improve. Until then, I hope to stockpile enough funds to pay off Sarah's education."

She flipped through more images—paintings and photos alike—one after the other and began to see the creative synergy between them.

"I can't believe you quit photography with such

a gift." She didn't mean it as a judgment, however, and worried he might take it that way. "What I mean is, you obviously inspired one another. It must have been hard to decide to do something else."

"I had an idea for a local television show about the art community. It was self-serving since I wanted to feature Liv first and foremost. But as I was pitching the guy I wanted to sponsor the project, we got talking about something else—a show about local singers. I ended up making that, *Voice of America*, instead."

"You produce *American Voice*?" She nearly dropped his phone.

American Voice was still on the air, still in the tabloids, and had been incredibly lucrative judging by the celebrity singers who coached young talent on each week's episode.

"Not the version you now see on television. But I owned the rights since I started it on a regional level, and I retained a share of the project after I sold off creative control." He grinned for a moment, a rogue dimple making its first appearance that she could remember. Then the smile faded. "The show paid for that big house I built in Lafayette. It put me in demand as a producer. I started traveling more."

She reached for his hand and held it. He was a success on multiple fronts and had achieved so many dreams at a young age, only to see them end in a horrific way. Leaning over, she kissed his shoulder and hoped it was okay to gently steer the conversation away from the dark sadness still dogging him.

"It's an amazing talent to bring artistic vision to the masses." She couldn't believe all he'd accomplished in a short time.

"I know. Liv had that talent in spades. She started a second business as a perfumer and that was going really well, too."

Erin shook her head. "I meant *you*, though. You've got a great talent, Remy. A lot of creative people don't get the satisfaction of seeing their work enjoyed by the public, but you found a way for people to view your earliest photos. You've created multiple television shows that give viewers something entertaining *and* substantive."

"It doesn't mean a lot, though, when I can't even get Sarah off to college successfully." He rested his elbows on his knees. "Maybe I've been away from my bayou roots too long. My mama would say that people count a whole lot more than things. And it's people that I keep failing."

She opened her mouth to argue the point, but the lights flickered. Once. Twice.

Then went out altogether.

"It's okay." Erin stood, grateful for the flashes

of lightning that lit her way. "I put some candles out earlier."

She made her way to the kitchen and patted around the counter until she found the box of matches.

"I should call Sarah." Light from Remy's phone illuminated the living room. "Or text, I guess. Kids don't use phones to talk."

Erin lit the two tapers, then moved around the living room with the box of matches to light a few candles she kept on the mantel and end tables.

By the time she was done, the house glowed with warm light. The house wouldn't cool off that much since a rainstorm in a Tennessee spring didn't bring the temperature down that much.

"I think the quiche is almost done anyhow." She pulled it out of the oven. "It smells amazing."

"Sarah is a great cook." Remy strode toward the kitchen, stopping to lean on the island. "She says they're fine, by the way. Ally invited her to sleep over."

"Good." Erin wondered how Bethany was doing after being so upset at the store. "Ally could use friends around her right now. Her mother and father are going through a tough year."

"Even the best marriages are tested."

Did he speak from experience? She had pictured his marriage as perfect.

Erin left the quiche on the counter. "We should probably wait a few minutes to let that cool."

His teeth flashed white in the glow of candle-light.

"Leaving one to wonder how we should fill the time?" His hands settled on her hips, drawing her near.

"I could always quiz you more about your art," she suggested, laying her hands on his chest. "Or your plans for the future."

He leaned closer to speak into her ear. "For every suggestion you make, I'll bet I have a better idea."

Her heartbeat sped faster.

"You think so?"

He traced a finger over the exposed skin along her collarbone. Goose bumps trailed in his wake, her mouth drying up with the memory of just how good he could make her feel.

"Just lead me into a room with real blinds." He didn't need to remind her the living room window looked out at the field between her house and her mother's.

"I like the implication you're going to do wicked deeds you don't want anyone else to see." No more wondering if this would happen again. No more waiting. Just living in the moment, with each other. Taking his hand, she drew him deeper into the house, grabbing one lit candle from the mantel.

Then she headed up the stairs. To her bedroom.

"I like any opportunity to be with you." He stopped her just outside the bedroom door. Turning her to face him, he removed the jar candle from her hand and set it on top of a small bookshelf in the hallway.

In the flickering light, she could see the serious set to his face. And while she appreciated all that male interest and intensity, she also wished she could make him smile more.

"What are you thinking?" he asked, his hand cupping her chin. "I can practically see your mind race."

"I'm thinking about how happy I'm about to make you." She nipped his ear, surprising a smile out of him after all.

With a quiet growl of approval, he angled her face and slanted his mouth over hers.

He was a kisser in a class by himself. Erin held on tight and savored each heated stroke of his tongue. A woman could lose herself in a kiss like that. In a man like this.

She couldn't afford to get lost in him that way.

Easing back, she undid a button on his shirt and placed her lips over the skin she exposed. His heart beat heavily, a dull vibration that zinged right through her. With trembling fingers, she unfastened another button. And another.

Then reaching behind him, she shoved open her bedroom door and nudged him backward into the darkness. The quiet of the power outage was a deep silence broken only by their breathing, which grew more ragged with every touch.

Erin shoved his shirt off his shoulders and smoothed both hands over the expanse of his chest. What an incredibly well-made man.

She kissed her way down his chest, lingering over the ridges between abdominal muscles while she unfastened his belt. Undid his pants.

Every now and then, a lightning flash filled the room in a slow strobe effect. Only then did she get to see the visual of him standing over her in all his strong, muscular glory while she kissed and stroked him through his boxer shorts and then—without them. But even when her greedy eyes couldn't see him, she savored the taste and texture of his skin, so hot where she kissed him. Her hands wrapped around his thighs, the muscles straining as she teased him closer and closer to fulfillment.

She would have brought him there, too, if he hadn't hauled her to her feet and started undressing her with fast, determined fingers. His harsh breathing filled her ears as he kissed her neck and stripped off her shirt, kissed the swell of her breasts and then swept aside her bra. Hungry swipes of his tongue along each nipple had her panting hard, too, her fingers twisting in his hair as he kissed lower to her hip and belly.

When he slid off her shorts, he wrestled for a moment with the lace tights she wore underneath, but once he got a hand beneath them, he helped her shimmy out of those, too. Soon she lay bare except for a pair of plain blue silk panties featuring a strategically placed cutout heart.

He spotted it in a blink of lightning. He sought it with his fingers in the dark afterward, then measured the place for a kiss right there in that small, bare place.

She nearly came off the bed when he licked her there, too.

The needy sound she made in the back of her throat filled the quiet room. In answer, he reached beneath her underwear and plucked gently at her swollen sex until she came apart in his arms.

Only then did he tug the silk from her hips. Retrieve the condom box from the nightstand where they'd left it the night before. And enter her with a slow stroke that nearly sent her over the edge for a second time.

"I wanted to be the one to make *you* happy," she protested halfheartedly as he pushed himself all the way inside her.

"That's exactly what you did." He thumbed a path along her lower lip and kissed her again. "I've never felt anything as beautiful as that."

Some of the boundaries she had put in place to protect her heart damn near melted under those words. She tucked her head against his chest and rode the pleasure with him, letting it take her higher and higher all over again.

When they came together, the moment drew out in a timeless way she knew she would never forget. She gripped his shoulders with both hands, holding on tight and allowing each delicious shudder to travel from her toes to her forehead, racking her body with lush waves of release.

They held each other quietly in the aftermath, not moving when the lights flicked on and the ceiling fan stirred overhead. It was only when her stomach growled for the second time that Erin suggested they go have dinner.

Only to realize he'd fallen asleep beside her.

Tenderness curled inside her at seeing him relax with her that way. She studied his face in sleep, the lines of loss around his eyes eased for a moment. He looked younger. She stroked his face and hair for a long time, until her eyes drifted shut.

Right up until the moment he twitched. Tensed.

"Where?" he snarled out, still sleeping.

His tone—both furious and terrified—made her breath catch. She recoiled to the edge of the mattress. Not sure if she should wake him or slip out of bed.

Was it kinder to let him sleep through a bad dream so he might forget it? She laid her hand on his arm carefully, and hoped her whisper-soft touch might soothe him.

His muscles tightened. His jaw flexed. No doubt about it, he was deep in a nightmare.

CHAPTER FIFTEEN

THE ROAD HOME was wet and rainy.

Remy navigated the curves along Vermillion River just before dawn after touching down at the local airport half an hour prior. He steered the Lexus sedan through Lafayette toward the new house, which became a little more elegant every time he left for a few days. Liv was like a magician that way. Everything she touched with those creative hands of hers turned more graceful and refined. Hell, he'd gone from being a backwoods photographer to a reality show producer with prospects.

She had that effect on people and places. So even though the cost of the travertine marble was putting the decorating costs way over budget, Liv was happy. Soon, her new perfume would go to market and that would help defray some of the extra expenses. When he'd talked to her on the phone before bed the night before, she said she was finalizing the package designs.

He couldn't wait to see what she'd come up with. Actually, he just couldn't wait to see her. The *production job sucked ass for the long hours and the travel, but it had given the woman he loved the opportunity to pursue her dreams in a way his photography never could have. Now Sarah was in private school. He had a new home on three acres along the river. Liv had gardens and a studio.*

If he could come up with another show like American Voice, *he'd be able to ease up on the travel. Spend more time helping Liv. His brothers had laughed until tears streamed down their ugly mugs when he told them he liked working in the hothouse with the flowers. But then, not even Liv could work magic on Armand and Landry.*

He slowed down as he turned the last corner before the new house, savoring the sight of the place he'd worked hard to build. An unnatural light shone ahead. The reflection of a streetlight distorted by the rainfall? Except there were no streetlights out here...

Police cars lined the front of his house. Three of them. Two with their headlights shining into the rain, each drop illuminated so clearly it could have been snow falling in front of the cars.

He noticed it every time he remembered this night. Every time he took those heavy, leaden steps toward the house. He might have been running, but each step was so slow it was as if he saw every detail. His own life flashing in front of his eyes, because he knew. He knew his happiness was too good to be true. His life too perfect.

He'd come too far, too fast. The boy from the bayou had gotten the princess, but then the dream had crumbled to ashes.

Yeah, he knew. Even before the lady cop tried her best to intercept him.

He started shouting at her to let him see his wife.

"Where's my wife?" he yelled at every single face that tried to get in his way. Tried to tell him gently...

"REMY."

A frightened voice pulled him out of the dream before he could see Liv.

He'd just sprinted from the house out to the studio in back, his feet sliding on wet grass. All the lights were on...

"Remy?"

Soft hands clutched his arm. Made him realize he wasn't out in the cold rain, but in a warm bed. In sheets that smelled like amber.

Ah damn.

"It's okay." He forced his eyes open and remained in two worlds at the same time. "I'm awake now."

"Sorry." Erin knelt beside him on the bed, her hold on his arm easing. "I was worried about you."

"Bad dream." He sat up, cradled his head in his hands. "I've had it a million times."

He didn't want to talk about it and he was grateful she didn't ask for specifics.

"Is it better if you sleep all the way through or wake up in the middle?" She hugged her pillow.

"I never wake up in the middle, so I'm not sure." It felt strange having her here when he still had one foot in Lafayette.

But it wasn't a bad thing. Erin's warmth and her scent helped chase away the cold, metallic fear that always filled him after the nightmare.

"Would it help to talk about it?" She rubbed his knee through the sheet, her touch pulling him out of the dream more and more.

"No." He didn't want to linger in that dream. "I'd rather talk about anything else."

He covered his face and waited for his heart rate to slow.

"If you're sure."

"God, yes."

She was quiet for a minute. "I used to have a recurring nightmare that my family forgot me during a summer vacation."

Absently, she threaded their fingers together. His and hers. He wondered if she could tell how grateful he was to change the subject. The ceiling fan ticked overhead, drying the cold sweat on his forehead.

The electricity must have come back on. Erin wore an oversize T-shirt and a loose pair of yellow cotton shorts.

"I pictured the Finley family as far too perfect to forget a kid." He wanted to lighten the dark mood still fogging his brain. "Your dad was mayor for a decade, right? And I know your family owns a hardware store and a construction business."

"I forgot how thoroughly you did your homework on the store."

"It pays to know who you're dealing with."

"Wish I'd learned that lesson sooner in life." She glanced at their clasped hands. "Anyway, the dream was based on a real Finley family vacation. We'd rented donkeys to view the Grand Canyon, and my mom had a mini-breakdown, which created a big drama, and everyone sort of flocked to help her."

Remy tried to recall what else she'd said about her family. He didn't know much about her other than the affair with the married guy that still tore at her conscience. How self-absorbed had he been to unload so many of his problems on her while she just listened.

"Your mom is scared of heights?"

"Mom is scared of lots of things. Being confined by a seat belt. Bridges. Avocados. I could list for a while. She's bipolar, but she has some other issues that she takes better care of these days. Back then, there wasn't the same awareness or care available, so we just walked on eggshells a lot and tried not to upset her."

"That sounds like an impossible balancing act." He remembered what she'd said about spending the whole day contemplating which candy to buy at the store. The story took on a darker cast as he imagined her and her siblings trying to stay away from their home. Avoid their mother.

"For her, too. I mean, she tried to keep herself together. I think that vacation was her idea so she could relax. But renting donkeys..." Erin shook her head. "Total disaster. I was trying to distance myself from her and the screaming because the sound rattled around the canyon and amplified a thousand times over. There was no escape."

She held the pillow tighter and he realized it hurt her to remember this. Remy sat up in bed and put a hand on her knee, rubbing lightly.

"That must have been scary."

"Yes. But it got twelve times scarier once the screaming ended and I had no idea where any of them went." She traced the red stitching on the pillowcase with her fingernail. "Logically, I figured they went up, right? But I'd strayed so far off the path, I couldn't tell what *was* the path anymore."

"How long before they found you?"

She forced a dark laugh. "That's the thing. I found *them* two hours later. They never noticed I was gone."

"How old were you?" He hadn't met all of her family yet, and right now, he wasn't sure he wanted to.

"Nine. Heather swears she told Scott I was missing, but he was either too scared to process what she said, or Heather remembers wrong." She shrugged and shifted positions so she sat cross-legged, leaning against the headboard. "So yeah, it was just two hours of scariness, but it's all nicely preserved in my dreams from seeing the rattlesnake to the donkey's refusal to move for about twenty minutes."

"You stayed on the donkey the whole time?" He pictured Sarah when he'd first met her and how worried he'd been that he'd do something wrong as a parent because he had zero experience.

And he would have never forgotten her. She would have been scared to death.

"Yes, thank God. He knew the route even though I didn't, apparently. And Dad explained later the tour probably took the same twenty-minute rest stop every time they made the trek, so the animal just followed the usual routine when he refused to budge all that time."

"You were gone for two whole hours at nine years old?" He traced the pale network of veins on her foot, wondering how a whole family could overlook this vibrant woman.

"That really speaks to how much drama my

mother is capable of creating." Her obvious attempt to brush it aside didn't come close to making him forget about it, but he sure as hell understood the need to ignore bad memories.

"You don't deserve to be overlooked. Ever." He squeezed her foot gently.

"It's weird, though, because being overlooked is sort of what I strove for my entire childhood. If my mom didn't notice me, I wouldn't be the target of her next fury. So in some ways it was a victory that no one noticed I'd gone missing."

He couldn't believe that was how she would rationalize it, although it certainly explained a lot about how independent she was. "Erin."

She must have heard the concern in his voice because she hurried to interrupt.

"I know. I mean, obviously I realize as an adult that wasn't cool. Maybe it was one of those 'be careful what you wish for' moments." She took a deep breath. "Anyway, it was a long time ago. I haven't dreamed about rattlesnakes for years, but I always hated the way I could practically taste the red dust of the desert on my teeth when I woke up afterward."

She'd only shared it to help him forget about his nightmare. He rubbed her arms and up to her shoulders, kneading away the tension there.

"You let me know if the rattlesnakes come back,"

he drawled in her ear to make her smile. "I'll show them what I used to do to the water moccasins."

"Ew. I don't think I want to know, but thanks just the same."

He slowed his soft massage of her shoulders. Skimmed a touch over her cheek.

"Thank *you*, Erin."

Her cheeks flushed a little, this beautiful woman who wasn't used to anyone paying enough attention to her. If he didn't come with so much damn baggage attached, he would have liked to be the man who showed her how captivating he found her.

"Should we go try the quiche?" she asked, quite possibly looking to distract him from focusing on her.

His stomach growled in an answer too obvious to ignore.

"I'm taking that as a yes." She darted from the bed, flipping some lights on in the house as she left the room.

Remy took his time finding his shorts and shirt. He was fairly level despite having the nightmare again. He'd thought he'd gotten a handle on them. But maybe being with Erin—getting involved with someone—was churning up the old feelings he'd tried to put a lid on.

He stepped into her bathroom to splash cold water on his face and pull himself together. A grief counselor had once warned him that two steps forward could also mean one step back as he tried to put the past behind him. Were the nightmares his step back?

Erin had woken him up this time—before things had turned really bad. He'd have to make sure he didn't fall asleep around her again.

"THAT LOOKS AMAZING." Sarah admired Ally's deft skill with a toothpick as she steered the butterfly sticker into the center of her pinkie nail.

"I love watching the manicurist work at the salon. She's so creative with nail designs. I can't make the cool freehand art she does, but I can do stickers. They just take patience." Ally sat cross-legged on a bright turquoise futon in one corner of her massive bedroom.

Her family owned a construction business, so her parents let her customize her room with a reading loft and a mini-fridge built into one wall. There was a curtain of feathers around the loft so you could read in privacy, and Sarah thought it was the prettiest thing ever. In the corner by the futon, Ally had a chest that turned into a game table and that was where all her nail art stuff sat. They'd been listening to a local band's new music on Ally's laptop. The computer was attached to a huge flat-screen TV that played the music videos on the wall next to them.

"Well, your artistic side shows in the room,"

Sarah announced. "Have I mentioned that it's totally sick?"

"Thanks." Ally laid a new design on the next nail. "I didn't get into it until recently, but my house has been kind of crazy this year while my parents go through—I don't know—like 'how to be married' classes. When I complained about the arguments, my mother said I should make my room a *sanctuary*."

"You really did, too." Sarah's gaze went to the birds and owls painted close to the ceiling like a border. "I think the little owls are my favorite up there."

"Yeah?" Ally stopped painting on the top coat for a minute to look up at them. "That's funny you say that because I did the owls and Aunt Erin did all the birds. Actually, the border was her idea because she said the feathers around the loft would look good if we made it a theme."

"I had a dream room once." Sarah didn't think about it. She just said it. Maybe because she'd talked about the past a few times today—at the cop station and again at Erin's house—and it hadn't been bad. The moments at Erin's had actually been pretty good because she'd shared some of the happy stuff.

"Did you move or something?" Ally went back to putting another butterfly on the next nail. Each nail was a different color with a contrasting set of wings.

"Yes." She had hated that move. "My dad was in a hurry to leave the house where my mom died, so he had our stuff from Louisiana packed and shipped to the new place in Florida. It was weird. The last time I walked out of that house I didn't even realize it would be the last time I was in it."

"So why was the old room a dream room?" Ally put a pink butterfly on the blue nail. An orange butterfly on the green nail. She reached for the TV remote and turned down the volume on the country music. "What did you like best about it?"

"One wall had ten tiny mirrors in gold frames. Every frame was different. One had angels carved in it, and another one had a dragon. But mostly they were just really swirly. I liked those little mirrors."

"But your dad didn't pack those up?" Ally lifted her hand and tilted it to see the side in the light.

"No. None of the decor came with us."

They were both quiet for a moment. Sarah was trying to figure out how she felt about that—her father leaving so much behind—when Ally spoke.

"I used to think that packing up and moving away would solve my problems."

"As in…run away?"

Ally pulled another butterfly out of the jar with a pair of tweezers. "Yeah. I used to think about it a lot last fall when nothing was going right. But the thing is, you can't run away from yourself."

"I don't get it." She shook her head. "What do you mean?"

"You can move to a new place where everything around you is different. But if *you're* no different, the problems are just going to come with you." Ally shrugged. "Well, that's how I worked it out in my head. I figured I'd wait and get a fresh start after I fixed *me* first."

Sarah's problems had definitely followed her to Heartache. Leaving Florida hadn't fixed anything, although it had given her some time with her dad. Staying in Heartache might not necessarily make anything better for her. Theresa kept telling her she needed to face her grief about her mom instead of ignoring it.

That answer seemed so painful, though.

"I don't think you need fixing, Ally. You seem pretty great to me." She looked around the gorgeous bedroom. "Great home. Cute guy. Fun job at the salon. And you got into a really good college."

"I put a lot of energy into making everything around me look perfect because I didn't feel perfect inside. I was like this walking stress nightmare." Ally slid a hand under hers and tilted it so she could see. "Look how pretty!"

"They're beautiful. I love how bright the colors are." But she couldn't get as excited about her nails thinking about Ally stressing herself out. "So you're better now?"

"Mostly. I mean, my parents are still walking a tightrope, and I'm scared they won't stay together, but Ethan tells me that's their issue, not mine." Ally capped the topcoat and turned on a little fan so their nails would dry faster.

"It's cool you can talk about it." She, on the other hand, was not comfortable with sharing a lot of personal stuff. In fact, she'd pushed herself to stay quiet about so many things that she kissed boys instead of talking to them. Before that, she'd have drinks with them instead of having conversations.

There was something pretty messed up about it.

"It kinda helps working in a salon. The women there dish all the time, but it's not mean and gossipy like at school. They give advice and try to help each other, or they just talk to…de-stress."

A pounding on a door nearby made Ally jump.

"I hope that's not my father," Sarah said. "Every time I go somewhere lately he shows up to bring me home." She followed her friend out of the bedroom and down to the living room, where Ally's mother was pulling open the door.

It wasn't her dad, though.

"Evening, Mrs. Finley." Three guys dressed in work overalls stood on the porch. Behind them, a truck with Finleys' Building Supplies painted on one side sat in the driveway. "We've got a delivery to make if you don't mind pointing us in the direction of the games room."

"But I didn't order anything." Ally's mom folded her arms. The woman was so thin Sarah had the urge to go cook her something to eat.

She might not know how to talk about her problems the way Ally had learned to, but she could cook comfort food like nobody's business.

"Mr. Finley did, ma'am. He asked for you to call him if there was any problem."

"No. No problem." Mrs. Finley shook her head, her hair slipping out of a ponytail. "Girls, will you show them where to go?"

"Sure. It's this way." Ally waved the main deliveryman forward while the other two went back to their truck.

Sarah followed, careful not to let her nails touch anything as Ally brought the man past an in-home theater to a big, empty room with hardwood floors and leaf-green walls. A few framed photos of Ally as a young girl hung on the walls, along with some cute paintings that looked like school art projects.

"Great." The dude turned in a slow circle and then knocked on walls in a few places. "We'll try to be in and out as quickly as we can, but I think it'll still take an hour or two to set things up. It might be a better surprise for your mom if she waits to come in until the end."

"I'll do my best, but Mom hates surprises." Ally smiled at the guy. "Can *we* know what you're doing?"

"Sorry, girls. It's your dad's orders." He shoved

some papers into his back pocket and hurried back into the hall. "We'll have to make several trips through the house."

"Ugh." Ally grumbled and took a seat on a built-in cabinet under one window. "Does your dad do weird stuff like this?"

"He used to." She hoisted herself up beside her friend. "I miss those days."

"I'm sorry. I forgot about your mom." Ally let the sentence hang for a long moment, maybe curious to hear more about how she'd died.

"It's okay. I'm just ready for my father to have a life again. He's spent so long being sad." Sometimes it made her feel guilty. As though she didn't love her mom enough and that was why she didn't spend all her time feeling down about her death.

It *was* heartbreaking. She'd have a hole in her heart her entire life because of it. But she also felt her mother would want her to go out and be happy whenever she could. Use her creative gifts. Give back to the world. That was how her mom was— selfless and kind.

She wanted so much to be like that and not like Brandon. Brandon, whose letter said he'd spend the rest of his life being sorry for what he'd done. As if that helped.

"My mom has been sad for a long time, too." Ally kept her voice low as footsteps came down the hall toward them. "I just hope whatever surprise this is, it makes things better and not worse."

The delivery guys appeared with two huge, long, flat boxes and started cracking them open with a crowbar. While Ally asked them questions they wouldn't answer, Sarah noticed Mrs. Finley dart past the door every now and then. She thought about going out there to keep her company—or offer to make mac and cheese for everyone—but her phone buzzed with a text.

Can I see you tomorrow?

Lucas.

She'd been thinking about him since they'd kissed in the woods during the tailgate party. She'd had to beg him not to come out and introduce himself to her father. She just wasn't ready for that complication yet. But she could tell he'd been frustrated with her.

"Ally." She showed her the message while the construction crew went to work hammering boards together for a large frame. "Are you going to Lucky's tomorrow?"

"If the weather is nice, for sure." Ally watched the guys work. "I'll bet half my class will be there."

Lucky's? she texted back.

Her phone buzzed again a few seconds later.

How about someplace quieter?

She didn't show that one to Ally. She still hadn't asked him about the rumors of his bad reputation, so she didn't know how serious they were. How smart would it be to meet him somewhere private when she didn't know that much about him?

Funny, she could practically hear Mathilda's voice in her head telling her it was a bad idea.

I kinda like the idea of a reunion under the slide.

She hit Send, hoping he'd be okay with that. She felt guilty for the mixed messages. She'd been trying to forget about the letter from jail last night, and she'd gladly indulged in kissing and a little more than that to put everything else out of her head.

No doubt about it, she regretted misleading him since she was thinking they'd better put the brakes on the physical side of things until they knew more about each other.

OK. But we need to talk.

She stared at his message while Ally texted her friends about the surprise construction crew in the basement. Sarah didn't want to be rude, but she wasn't sure she wanted to stay the whole time they put the mystery furniture—or whatever it was—together. Besides, Lucas's message made her a little uneasy. She needed time on her own to process it.

Would he give her a hard time about not introducing him to her father? She hadn't had a real boyfriend in two years. She'd had fast, hot hookups that had been sorta physical while maintaining her virginity. She liked Lucas too much for that kind of thing.

And in the past week and a half, she felt she'd outgrown it. She was eighteen now. She'd admitted the truth to her dad about the college application fiasco. She'd told him about the letter. For the first time in a long time, she felt as though she was in the driver's seat for her future. She wanted to do better than she had in the past. Then again, so did Lucas. Maybe they could reform together.

Finally, she typed, Me, too.

"Oh, my God. Sarah, are you looking at this?" Ally grabbed her arm.

Pocketing her phone, she looked at the project taking shape in the games room.

"He bought chalkboards?" She stared at the six-foot-high trifold panels that looked like something a professional sports team would use in the locker room to draw up plays.

"The backs are filled with writing," Ally whispered excitedly. "I peeked."

"I don't get it." She watched one of the other

guys fill a new bookcase with brand-new hard-cover titles. *"Fifty Most Romantic Dates,"* she read aloud. *"Best Weekend Trips: Southeast US."* What is all this stuff?"

"It's his plan." Mrs. Finley stood in the doorway, her hands covering her mouth as she stared at the strange assortment of things her husband had ordered for the room.

Sarah had thought she'd seen tears in the older woman's eyes earlier in the day at Last Chance Vintage, but now there was no doubt. Rivulets streamed down both cheeks.

She hurried over to stand on her one side while Ally stood on her other.

"It's okay, Mom, right?" Ally asked, brushing aside a strand of hair from her mom's face. "This is a good thing, isn't it?"

Mrs. Finley nodded, a sort of hysterical laugh breaking through the tears.

"I told your father he had no plan to save our marriage. That we'd never figure it out if we didn't do something different."

The delivery guys seemed to become aware of the developing drama and the oldest—the gray-haired man who'd told Ally it might be better to surprise her—quickly flipped over one of the chalkboards.

The other two men did the same, until the room was crammed full of words.

"'Take date nights. See reference shelf one.'" Ally read the first board and hugged Mrs. Finley. "There are footnotes, Mom."

Mrs. Finley laughed harder. And cried more.

Sarah felt a little as if she didn't belong in their private moment. But hey, no one told her to leave, and it was sort of awesome soaking in the happiness of a special day. A happy mom.

Actually, maybe it hurt a little inside, too. Ached some and felt good.

What pained her most wasn't missing her mom. It hurt more to think about her dad not having moments like this. She moved away from Ally and her mom to look out the window of the games room, back toward Erin's house.

Through the rain, she could see lights were on. Downstairs…and up.

Was her father still there?

She hoped Heartache would be good luck for him and bring him happiness. She wished it with all her might.

CHAPTER SIXTEEN

"IT WAS THE sweetest thing ever." Sarah sighed happily the next day as she finished telling Erin her version of Scott's gift to Bethany.

Erin had already heard from her sister-in-law that morning. Bethany had called the store early to say Scott had made a big step forward in committing to their marriage. But it was fun hearing Sarah's account as the production crew packed up their equipment for the day and Erin cleaned up the store. Remy had texted her from the road after he had found a good boutique to feature on *Interstate Antiquer*. It would solidify the show's comeback. He hoped to return to town by eight o'clock.

"But Scott wasn't there?" Now, at half-past six, she ran a mop along the skid marks on the hardwood floor from the camera dollies.

"I guess he was kind of keeping an eye on the house from your mom's. The other home that's kind of close, right?" Sarah dumped a bunch of matchbooks into the bin where Erin normally kept the small collection.

A customer had taken them all out one by one

to inspect each individually and hadn't bought a single one. That would make for really exciting television. She hoped Remy was right about this show being a good thing for the business.

"That would be Mom's." She should get over there again. She hadn't seen her mother since Remy came to town and *Interstate Antiquer* had started filming. "I think Scott's been there a lot the past few months to give Ally's mother some space while they figured things out."

"We saw him walking toward Ally's house when we pulled out of the driveway for her to take me back to the B and B." Sarah replaced a few vintage skeleton keys on a yellow-painted Peg-Board where they hung from ribbon scraps. "So romantic. Don't you think?"

Erin opened the back door to let some air in and dry the floors. A brass wind chime jingled in the fragrant spring breeze.

"Yes. And she deserves that big sweet gesture because it's been a hard year for her."

"My dad has had a hard year." Sarah lowered her voice, her head down as she moved an orange blouse from a rack full of kids' clothes to return the garment to its rightful place. "I wish he'd find some happiness."

And didn't that conversation feel as though it had the potential for land mines? She picked up a hammer that had been mislaid when she'd hung a new sign earlier and put it on a shelf near the register.

"I do, too," Erin said carefully, gathering up some donated items she planned to put into the storage area. "Would you mind opening that door for me?"

"Sure." Sarah hurried to help, turning on the overhead light with the pull chain. "Wow. Look at all this cool stuff. Want me to bring anything else in here?"

"There are two more stacks of things that were brought in today—"

"I know the ones." Sarah was already rushing away, only to return half a minute later with both stacks.

"You are incredibly efficient." Erin waved her down the narrow steps into the small unit that had been a root cellar at one time. She loaded the clothes into a moisture-proof chest for sorting another day. "I don't know what you plan to do for a career, but you'll be awesome at it."

Sarah stilled. "Did my dad tell you I didn't apply to colleges?"

"No." She had sidestepped one land mine only to land on another, apparently. And as much as she didn't want to step on Remy's toes with parenting, she also couldn't help thinking this young woman could use some more female influences in her life. It wasn't easy being eighteen. "That is, I know he worries about you, but I didn't know that. Don't you want to go to college?"

"Maybe." Sarah ran a hand over an old toboggan that Erin liked to use in Christmas window displays. "It's been hard to think about college with Dad so unhappy. It's like he's been stuck since Mom died, and if I'm not there to help out… I mean, I guess he'll be okay. But we haven't felt like a family lately. And he's, you know…all I have left."

The tender thoughtfulness behind the words just about took Erin's breath away. Her eyes burned.

"You will keep on being family no matter where you go." Erin wasn't a natural-born hugger, but she found herself draping an arm around the teen's shoulders and squeezing. "Your dad is lucky to have you. As more time passes, he'll see how much you've been there for him."

"Because it was sweet of him to adopt me and everything, but it's just a piece of paper. And my biological father sure did ruin Dad's life." Sarah swiped away a tear.

The bastard had ruined his daughter's life, as well. She noticed Sarah didn't mention that, her tender heart more concerned for Remy. Did she ever put her own needs first? Her own grief first?

"Sarah. You are not his daughter because of a piece of paper. He told me last night that he would have lost his mind a long time ago without you.

Another time, he told me you were a 'powerhouse personality' and he smiled with such pride when he said it."

"Really?" Sarah's lips quirked sideways, her green eyes hopeful.

"Yes. And that's how a father looks when he talks about his kids. At least—that's how good, devoted fathers should look when they talk about their kids. You might have gotten a bad hand from your biological father, but the father you chose? He's the best."

Sarah swiped more tears away and smiled. "I *totally* chose him, too. My mom had dated some real loser guys before Dad showed up. But Dad clapped for all my dances and ate all the terrible food I made and pretended it was great. I was determined to make that match happen."

Erin turned to dig in a supply closet and found the extra paper products. She pulled out a new box of tissues and handed Sarah a few, kept one for herself while she was at it.

"Well, you had good instincts. But I don't think you need to miss out on college to keep that relationship strong, Sarah. He will want to see you settled and happy somewhere."

"In the old days, kids learned their parents' trade and had apprenticeships." Sarah blew her nose and shoved the tissue in her pocket. "Aristotle didn't have a college education and he turned out okay."

"Aristotle?"

But Sarah was already in the supply closet, putting away the tissue box.

"Oh, my God. I can't believe you have this mirror." She came out of the storage shelves with a small gilt-framed piece. An angel head was centered over the top, with smaller cherubs on either side, the gilt frame taking up twice the square inches of the reflective glass.

"Isn't it beautiful? I got it last year when I was traveling, but I don't have a good Italianate or Victorian section of the store to showcase fancy pieces like that."

"Just yesterday I was telling Ally about my mirror collection on the wall of our old house. I had one so similar to this." Sarah cradled it in careful hands, tracing the angel face with the tip of her butterfly manicure.

"That's serendipitous. It must have been meant to find its way to you." She suspected it was left behind in Remy's haste to move them far from Louisiana.

Sarah looked up from the intricate gold scrollwork. "Oh, I couldn't keep it." She tried handing it back to Erin. "I think it's just another sign that I'm on the right track with the next match I'm making."

The girl's hopes were so obvious Erin worried.

As much as she wanted to spend more time with Remy, she knew he wasn't ready to take things faster.

"I don't know about any matches." That sounded like trouble to her ears. She tucked her hands behind her back so she couldn't take the mirror from Sarah. "This is my gift to you so you'll remember me when you're having an amazing first semester at a fun college. I know you'll be glad that you didn't follow in Aristotle's footsteps."

"Well, thank you." Sarah hugged the mirror. "It's a good omen and I could use some more of those. Thank you, Erin."

They smiled at each other as Sarah backed away, an undeniable new bond formed.

"You'd better get going if you want time to change before the dancing starts at Lucky's tonight." She headed up the stairs and back into the store.

Sarah switched off the light. "Are you and Dad going to be there?"

"If he gets done with work soon, I think so." She couldn't help but feel some of Sarah's enthusiasm.

Not that she wanted to rely on the relationship maneuverings of a teenager to land a guy…

Wait a minute.

Was she really rooting for this thing to work out between them on a more permanent basis?

Despite all her efforts to keep things simple—

yes. She couldn't deny she wanted more with Remy. She hadn't taken it slow. Her hopeful heart had gotten the better of her even though he worried he wasn't anywhere near ready for the same kinds of things she was. How could he look toward the future when he was still so rooted in the past? When so many of their conversations still circled around to his life with Liv and all he'd lost?

"Great. I want Ally to tell you how I was just talking about that mirror last night. She won't believe when I show her this." Sarah picked up her keys off the front counter. "Thank you!"

The store seemed to echo with her voice for moments afterward. Erin watched her jog out to her car and drive away with a wave.

What an amazing young woman, and to think Remy played a part in her upbringing. Sarah just needed to figure out a path in life and she'd be okay.

As Erin enjoyed that thought it occurred to her she was thinking like the girl's…mom? Her bout of nerves only increased. She had no idea how she was supposed to fit into this girl's life if things progressed between her and Remy. Sarah had been through so much, and Erin didn't want to disappoint her.

Sarah was in a fragile place. Erin would offer her whatever hand she could to get through this time. Although, it would be good to know more about that boy Remy asked her about—Lucas. She hadn't found a private time to quiz Bethany about him.

"Excuse me?" A man stood at her back step, near the potted rosebush. "You still open?"

He stepped inside on her just-mopped floor, his big work boots not staying on the mat. Had he been one of the film crew hands? She thought she knew just about everyone in town and she didn't recognize this florid-faced man. She didn't peg him for an antiques customer, but maybe he'd come in to check it out for a wife.

"No." She checked her watch. "We've been closed for almost an hour, but we reopen at ten tomorrow."

"I just had a quick question—"

Didn't they always? She sighed inwardly and straightened a display of yellow-hued carnival glass.

"Maybe you can tell me if you're the woman responsible for my girlfriend leaving me?" His tone turned hard. Angry.

Her hand slid behind the counter to find her cell phone. Her heart beat faster as she walked her fingers along the desktop, not finding the phone.

His face flushed red. Heavy eyebrows slashed inward as he glared at her.

"Excuse me?" Her eyes flicked to the open door behind him. If she needed to call out, someone might hear her.

But for now, the man stayed where he was. He

didn't approach her. She would not panic. She needed to get closer to the door. Or find the damn phone. Where was it?

"I heard from my sister that the woman running this store gave my Jamie all-new clothes and set her up with a fancy job. Now she doesn't need me anymore and she's acting like a single woman again." He clenched his big fists at his sides.

Erin's throat convulsed in a swallow-choke that wouldn't have allowed her to speak if she wanted to. Why hadn't she locked the door when Sarah left?

Although, thank God, Sarah wasn't here. She would never forgive herself if anything had happened to her after all that Remy had been through.

"Well?" he bellowed.

She swallowed again, forcing her voice to stay steady. "I'm sorry, sir. I sell clothes here, but I don't remember selling any to your girlfriend. And—" A panicky stab of fear cut off her words for a moment. "To be honest, you're making me nervous, so I'm going to have to ask you to leave."

Maybe he would go. Maybe he had simply needed to vent and complain. She prayed that was all.

Prayed...and tried to remember where she'd laid that hammer she'd used earlier.

"It's funny you say that, because I'm going to have to ask *you* to tell my Jamie that her place is with her man." He snarled the words, although he hadn't made an overt threat yet.

She remembered where she had put the hammer.

Sidling closer to the register, she felt for the shelf alongside it.

"Hey, sis," a friendly voice called from the doorway. "Is it too late for a donation?"

Her older brother Scott appeared next to the potted rosebush, a big box in his hands.

Relief nearly brought her to her knees.

Until the big, surly stranger pulled a knife.

REMY TURNED OFF the GPS as he neared the exit off I-65 for Heartache. It hadn't taken him long to learn his way around town. This small map-dot in central Tennessee had ended up feeling more like home in the course of almost two weeks than Miami had done in the years he'd lived there.

Then again, maybe he hadn't really wanted Miami to feel like home. Part of the reason he'd chosen the city after Liv's death was to be anonymous. The fewer people he connected with, the less he needed to talk about the past, but it sure as hell hadn't helped him move on. Whereas being in Heartache had hauled him back to the land of the living and it felt—nice.

With the pink and gold colors of sunset slanting across his windshield, Remy drank in the moment that seemed like coming home. He'd spoken to Theresa, Sarah's counselor, and they had a plan for helping her apply to some schools that used rolling admissions. However, he wanted Sarah to be on board with it. This week would give him that time to figure it out.

Now, after a quick stop at the B and B to change, he'd call Erin and find out where to meet her. He could take her out for dinner and then guide her around the dance floor under the stars. If the band playing at Lucky's tonight was half as good as the group he'd heard last week, they would have a fun night. Actually, he could have a good time with Erin by cranking up the radio on her deck and two-stepping through the damp grass in her backyard. He needed more of that in his life if he was going to make a real effort to move on.

Needed more of Erin.

Not quite sure what to do about that thought, he shoved it aside for now. He'd bought another week to be with her, and he planned to enjoy the time without worrying about what happened afterward.

Heading through the center of town to get to the Heartache B and B, Remy turned onto Main Street.

His heart stopped when he saw the cop cars in front of Erin's store. Blinking hard, he hoped for a second this was another nightmare—a new one that merged past and present. Cold sweat popped along the back of his shoulders. Clammy hands slid on the steering wheel as he slowed the sedan to a crawl.

Two county sheriff's cruisers flanked the shop doors. All the lights were on in Last Chance Vintage, while the other stores were dark and closed for the night.

Remy must have parked his vehicle in a blind fog because, in the next moment, he walked toward the front door. Voices emerged from inside, but not hers. Not Erin's. Where the hell was Erin?

Uniformed officers appeared in front of him.

One face after another. None of them the right one.

The hissing static of the past filled his ears. He couldn't hear what any of them were saying. He lumbered around the store like a wounded bear, bumping into racks and knocking over a display until an officer grabbed him by the elbow.

"Where is she?" he shouted, his words the only ones he could hear.

Except for hers.

"Remy?"

Erin burst into the store through the open back door.

Relief pierced his chest like a tranquilizer dart, stopping the fear. He reached for her, unsteady as hell, and she wrapped him in a hug so hard she might have kept him on his feet. Burying his nose in her hair, he inhaled the amber fragrance of her perfume, the clean smell of her shampoo.

Her heart pounded softly against his chest, making him realize he held her too tightly. With a kiss to her forehead, he loosened his hold. Stared into cornflower blue eyes.

"I wish I'd called you. I'm sorry I didn't think of it sooner. Maybe I hoped everything would be cleared up before you got here. Or maybe I'm not thinking clearly at all."

"You're okay." He needed to affirm it. To hear her say it.

His pulse still jittered too fast.

"I'm fine. Everything's fine." She stroked his arm. Kissed his shoulder. "I'm just a little…scattered. I had a disgruntled visitor earlier, but he's gone now. The police escorted him off the premises and I've already given my statement, so I think we're about done here."

It occurred to him the police were now worried about him. Four officers stood close by, their posture broadcasting a tense physical alertness that Remy recognized from his brother's friends. Another guy lurked behind Erin—but he seemed more relaxed as he spoke into his cell phone and paced around the back door. He recognized the man from a quick introduction the week before—Erin's brother Scott.

"You need an alarm." Remy didn't care about the tense cops or the pacing brother.

He cared about keeping her safe and making sure the police never had a reason to respond to a call from her again.

"I left the back door open," Erin admitted. "That's my fault for not being more careful."

"An alarm isn't a bad idea, Erin," the youngest-looking detective spoke up. "Now that you're helping women who are in difficult circumstances, your chances of running into bitter ex-husbands and boy-friends definitely increases."

Erin nodded as she threaded her fingers through Remy's and squeezed. "I'll take care of it. Thank you for coming."

"We're going to ask for a restraining order if you don't hold this guy," Remy informed the officers as they filed toward the door, his brain engaging now that the adrenaline flow had slowed down. "Keep that in mind if you're driving by the place."

"Will do," the youngest one assured him. "I assure you, the state of Tennessee does not look on aggravated assault lightly. We'll throw everything we've got at this guy."

Everything inside him stilled while the cop went on his way with a wave at Erin. Remy's chest squeezed painfully.

"Aggravated assault?" He'd spent enough time

in courtroom legalese to know when a weapon was involved.

"Thanks again!" Erin called to the departing officers. When she turned back to him, she appeared worried, her lip caught between her teeth. "It's okay. He's gone now."

"*Aggravated assault?* What happened?" he ground out, the remnants of old fear spiking. "This sounds like more than a 'disgruntled visitor.'"

"Erin, I'm taking off," her brother called from the back of the store. "I don't want to keep Bethany waiting. You sure you're okay?" The guy's eyes wandered to Remy and then back to his sister.

"I'm fine." Erin let go of his hand to hug Scott. "Thank you so much."

"I'm glad I was here." Her brother hugged her hard. "Call if you need anything."

"I will, I promise." She kissed his cheek. "Go enjoy your date."

Her words reminded him that this was the brother who'd been having problems with his wife. Remy wondered if the guy knew how lucky he was to be married long enough to bicker over chores and date nights.

Damn, but that sounded bitter.

"Erin." He didn't think that hearing what had happened tonight would improve his mood, but he needed to know. "What went on here?"

He dropped into a seat behind the front desk,

weary to his toes and scared for whatever she might say next.

"You remember Jamie Raybourn?" She switched off a few old-fashioned desk lamps that were operated by pull chains.

"She's the one we filmed for the extra segment." He steepled his fingers together as he listened, trying to hold on to his patience. "We got really good footage at the hair salon."

"Yes. And her ex-boyfriend lives in the next town over." Erin set aside her phone and leaned on the front desk across from him. "He heard that I helped Jamie get on her feet and make a fresh start. That ticked him off."

"So what good would it do to come over here?" He wished he'd been with her.

"He said I needed to tell Jamie that a woman's place was with her man."

"And?" He braced himself.

If the dirtbag had pulled a gun on her, Remy didn't think he'd be able to stay in his chair.

"Scott came in the back door then, thank goodness, because the guy drew a knife."

"A knife?" He swore even as his head swam with dark visions of what could have happened. He leaned forward in the chair to slap a stabilizing hand on the surface of the counter.

"I know." Erin shook her head. "It was tense for a minute."

"What happened?" He edged the words past the fear in his throat.

"I threw a hammer at him. Scott bowled him over with a box of used clothes." She gestured to a bunch of dresses and blouses on the floor in the far corner of the room.

He hadn't even noticed that before.

"You're kidding." He couldn't decide if that had been quick thinking on her part or if she'd seriously endangered herself by throwing a potentially lethal item at an armed intruder.

His head hurt for thinking about all the things that could have happened to her.

"No. It was over fast after that." She started picking the clothes up. "The knife came out of his hand when Scott knocked him over, so I kicked it under those shelves." She indicated a heavy piece of furniture against the wall. "The police took the weapon as evidence. They were here in about two minutes after I called since they patrol the park well on nights when Lucky's hosts the outdoor dining."

"Right." He couldn't absorb all the details, his chest aching from fears he might never be able to shake.

Sure, she was fine now. But how much worse would this make his nightmares? His panic attacks that still came back? More important, how much danger did it put Erin in to work on her Dress for Success campaign?

"Remy?" She dropped the skirt she held and left it on a braid rug near the pie safe. "Are you okay? I can finish straightening this mess tomorrow. Let's go get some food and try to put this behind us."

How many times had he heard that over the past two years? "Put the past behind us" was the refrain everyone else came back to, but, damn it, he wasn't budging when Erin's safety was at stake. Maybe Sarah's, too.

"I don't think food is going to help." This kind of queasiness wouldn't be chased away easily. "I should probably check in with Sarah." He was already texting.

"When she left here, she was going to change at the bed-and-breakfast, then go to the park to see her friends."

"When was that?" Cold dread coated his skin. He'd forgotten that Sarah had planned to help the camera crew today. "Was she here when that maniac came?"

"No, thank God." Erin hesitated.

"What is it?"

"Nothing. Just…we had a good visit before she left. She hoped we'd be at Lucky's tonight, but I'll warn you—I think she's trying to matchmake." She traced the pattern in a paisley handkerchief draped under a display of snuffboxes.

"Matchmake? Between who?"

Erin's eyes met his with disbelief shifting to something that looked like wariness.

Anger.

"Us, Remy. I think she likes the idea of you and me. And since she's a girl who—you said yourself—is 'all in' when she likes someone, I didn't know if you'd want to talk to her about that."

"Right." Did that mean he should warn Sarah there wasn't a chance in hell he'd ever be the right man for Erin? Or that he should try harder to make things work with her? "Remember me saying last night I wanted to enjoy a day or two of no drama?"

Erin tensed. "I do." She moved closer to him. Dropped a hand on his shoulder while he slouched in the chair. "I truly wish we could have had that."

For a moment, he closed his eyes and enjoyed her nearness. But he couldn't avoid the new realization that was becoming more and more apparent.

"I know you were ready to take a risk on us. To just enjoy the time we had. But I don't think I understood how much I'd be risking, too." Maybe he'd figured he was too numb after Liv's death to have his heart tromped on. He hadn't thought about the fact that Sarah could get hurt again. "However, now that I've seen my recurring nightmare come to life today, I understand the potential for fallout is damn high."

"We still have a whole week together." Her eyes were unnaturally bright and he regretted the fact that she'd already had enough crap to deal with today. "And you're giving up already?"

It tore him up to see her so upset.

"Erin, I know I should be comforting you right now, not raking through my own issues."

Her silence told him how much she agreed. Normally, she was quick to offer reassurance. Comfort. Smooth things over. But not about this.

"Right." He forged ahead, unwilling to hide from the truth. "Of course that's what a good man would do right now. So what more proof do we need that I can't do this yet? That I don't have my life in order enough to offer you the kind of relationship you deserve?"

She was quiet for so long he wondered if she would answer at all. But when she met his gaze, her voice was steady.

"I do deserve better. You're right about that much." She bit her lip, as if weighing how much to say, but then she pressed on. "I thought after what we'd shared, you might start to see you deserve better, too. But you have to reach for that happiness and look forward to find it. Maybe you need to start seeing me for what I have to offer and not just as another vulnerable woman in your life who might get hurt."

Her words peppered his chest like a series of arrows, stinging even after she became quiet again. Rubbed raw inside, he didn't have a clue what to say to make things better. She was 100 percent accurate about him not being able to look forward.

Yet, as she collected her things and moved toward the door, he found himself going with her. The searching look she gave him over one shoulder told him what she was thinking. Was he walking her to the car because he wanted to be with her? Or to make sure she was safe?

Damned if he knew for sure himself.

CHAPTER SEVENTEEN

SARAH BYPASSED THE liquor store.

Funny how sitting in the parking lot and waiting to find a guy to buy her drinks had seemed daring and grown-up a couple of weeks ago.

Now? She felt ten times more grown-up for keeping her distance. Anyhow, it wasn't as if she ever really needed the drinks. She merely enjoyed the attention they brought her when she got to a party. Here in Heartache, she had attention. Erin looked at her as more than just a kid on the verge of a breakdown because her mother died. Erin saw her as a person with a life that wasn't just defined by one god-awful moment. It had felt good talking to her about the past and her old house. It felt good having a friendship with Ally Finley and rooting for her mom to fix her marriage with Ally's dad.

Sarah's father might still only see her in momentary flashes between the old bouts of grief, but in Heartache, it didn't hurt as much, because there were other people who paid attention.

Circling the village square in her car, Sarah searched for a free parking spot and realized she'd have to do a bit of walking. She should have left the B and B earlier, but she'd taken extra time to look her best.

She'd also spoken to her counselor about the new turns life had taken, and for once, she didn't feel like a fraud when she got off the phone. She'd been honest. Amazing how much it helped to have told her father about the letter from Brandon. She'd deleted her Twitter account like the police suggested so "lockeduplove47" couldn't find her. The cops seemed to think "Becky" was Brandon's girlfriend.

Ew.

Pulling into a free space on a street two blocks from the park, Sarah texted her friends to see if someone would walk with her. Dad harped on stuff like that constantly, and in her effort to be better to him, she figured it couldn't hurt to wait five more minutes. A reply came faster than that, though.

Flash your lights so I can find you.

Lucas.

Warmth tingled along her skin, heated and shivery at the same time. She turned her lights on and off quickly then stepped out of the car. Already, she could hear his footsteps as he jogged toward her on the darkened street.

"I'm going to be ready for track season you've got me running so much, Sarah." He sped past a street lamp and she could see him vault over a fire hydrant, the reflective stripe on his tennis shoes catching the light.

"Nice!" she called, locking the car behind her. "Your hurdle form isn't bad, but your speed could use some work."

He slowed to a stop in front of her. Only now did she notice that he really could be a runner. He had the lean strength of a track athlete and he hadn't broken a sweat. Wasn't breathing hard, either.

"I'll let my hurdle coach know you approve." He took both her hands in his and looked into her eyes in a way that made her insides melt a little. "But I paced myself so I wouldn't be sweaty for you. I'm hoping I can convince you to take a turn on the dance floor tonight."

"Really?" She stroked her thumbs over the backs of his broad hands and admired how nice he looked in cargo shorts and a polo shirt with wide blue stripes. "Are you sure you know how to two-step?"

The backstreet was quiet even though it was packed with cars for people who were at Lucky's tonight.

"You're asking a Tennessee boy if he can two-step? New Girl, you're showing your Miami side." He hovered closer and she remembered how good his kisses felt.

"I'm a Cajun first and foremost." She let go of his one hand and pirouetted under his other arm.

"I was at the *fais do-do* when I was old enough to walk."

"Is that right? You'll have to catch me up on your bayou-speak, Cajun Queen." He leaned in close enough to nip her lower lip. Gently. Slowly.

She had to gather all her defenses to keep from kissing him senseless in return. Just because she wanted to take her time and get to know him better didn't mean it was going to be easy.

"Fais do-do." She pronounced it slowly. "It's a dance where the mamas leave their babies in the sleeping room off the dance hall so they can dance all they want." She stepped away from the car, keeping hold of his hand. "I'll tell you more while we walk."

"You're awfully sure I'll follow you," he said in her ear, the sound tickling all the way down her neck.

"No. I just hope you will." She was nervous about telling him she wanted to slow things down. What if he was mad he'd broken up with his other girlfriend?

He held out an arm like a real gentleman so she could take it. Maybe because she'd worn a dress tonight? She felt special. Pretty. Talking to Erin had made her think maybe she could go to school in the fall and no one would be the wiser that she'd screwed up her senior year.

There was hope for her yet.

"Like I said before, you keep me running, but I'm not complaining."

They walked in silence along the sidewalk for a moment, her skirt brushing up against his leg as they passed an abandoned flower shop and—unbelievably—a cobbler place. Who fixed shoes anymore? There was a gun and rod store on the street, as well, but everything was dark until they reached the pizza shop on the far end of Main Street. The scent of garlic and oregano wafted out the door along with rock music. She thought she saw a few kids inside who'd been at the soccer game.

A couple of them looked up as they passed the window. Sarah held up her hand to wave, but a couple of them were already bending their heads together and whispering.

"Sarah," Lucas said. "Remember how I said I wanted to talk to you?" He hurried past the pizza shop and they neared The Strand and Last Chance Vintage. "Can we do that first? Before we dance? I know you didn't want to go anywhere private, but—"

"Let's go to the baseball fields past the playground." She'd seen the field the week before when they'd been playing laser tag. It'd been dark there. And quiet.

"Okay." He pointed down the alley near Erin's

store. "Can we go this way? We'll come out on the side of the dugout."

"Sure." She felt nervous. Jittery. What did he want to talk to her about? "Want to run?"

"Seriously? You're in a dress."

"Afraid I'll beat you?" She let go of his arm. Picked up her pace.

"Can you see well enough?" he called. "Sarah?"

But she was already flying.

She wasn't much of an athlete, but she knew how to run. It was her first-response system when times were tough. She ran from the field trip. Before that she ran from her bad grades with bad boys. Then she ran from her therapy sessions by drinking too much.

And, in between it all, she ran her butt off to get sweaty and forget about her mom taking a bullet in her temple one night in March when Sarah was at a sleepover smoking her first and only cigarette.

"Sarah!" Lucas shouted. She slowed down in case she'd gone the wrong way.

She tripped on a tree root, skinning both knees. Heard the fabric of her dress rip.

"Ouch." The pain radiated down her legs as she held herself off the damp grass with one hand.

Not that it mattered. Her dress was probably already ruined.

Footsteps pounded the earth hard and fast behind her.

"Are you okay?" Lucas was beside her in an instant, arms all around her, though he didn't move her. "I couldn't see you in the dark. I'm so sorry."

"Why are you sorry?" She leaned her head into his shoulder for a second then fell the rest of the way into his lap. He fell over and they were a damp messy tangle of limbs. "It's me who wanted to race in the dark."

"You have to be more careful." He sat up, straightening her legs. "What did you hurt?"

"My knees." She didn't want to sound like a baby, but they both stung. "I skinned them."

The twang of a country band floated on the breeze. They must be closer to the park. She thought she saw the baseball field up ahead, but the lights were off.

"You're sure nothing is sprained? Did you make certain the cuts weren't deep?"

She wrapped her arms around Lucas's neck and squeezed. "You look. I don't like the sight of blood."

"You and me both," he muttered.

"Why don't you?" she asked, stopping his hands before he could lift up the hem of her skirt. "That is, why don't you like the sight of blood?"

"Just let me see." He set aside her hands and positioned his body out of the way of the moonlight to see better. "This is important, so I'll get over it."

He folded her dress gently, laying the extra fabric just above her knees. So careful.

Something about the tender way he cared for her made her let go of his neck long enough to watch him. He cradled one knee and slowly moved her lower leg up and down, testing the range of motion in first one knee and then the other.

She winced.

"That hurts?" He stopped immediately, his warm touch vanishing.

"Yes, but only because it pulls at the cuts. Nothing is sprained. I'm sure of it." She felt bad for scaring him. He appeared really spooked.

"I'm fine. They're just scratches. It's my fault for taking off."

"Why did you do that?" He studied her face, his eyes roaming every corner in the moonlight.

She cupped his shoulders, feeling the warmth of his body through the cotton.

"I was nervous about why you wanted to talk. I get antsy and twitchy when I'm scared. I don't know. Running felt good."

His head tipped forward until it met hers, creating their own dark little pocket of privacy.

"What am I going to do with you?"

"Tell me what you wanted to talk about." She toyed with his collar. It would be hard going slow with him when it felt so good to be next to him, his warm strength anchoring her to one spot and scattering every impulse to flee.

"You asked about my reputation once and I didn't want to talk about it." He tensed. "But I need you to know what happened."

"You can tell me." She could feel all his muscles go taut. His nervousness fed hers even as she wished she could reassure him it was okay.

"I got arrested last fall. Well, not really. But that's the rumor."

She stood up fast, ignoring the spike of pain in both knees.

"Excuse me?" She fumbled for her phone. "Is this some kind of joke or something? Does, like, everyone in town know my real father is a felon? Are you trying to embarrass me?"

"What?" He jumped to his feet. "No. My God, Sarah, of course not. I thought your dad was a producer. This doesn't have anything to do with you. I got in trouble last fall and everyone still talks about it like I'm some kind of criminal."

She swallowed back the panic bubbling up her throat. She didn't believe for a second that he'd done anything criminal—only that a cute boy might be tricking her in some kind of school prank. Besides, she already knew she could outrun his butt any day—track star or not. She was tricky, smart and fast.

"What happened?" Keeping her phone in one

hand, she was grateful he gave her space while she thought through what he said.

"Domestic dispute. My mom and dad—same old crap and nothing new for them. But my dad got out of control and shoved Mom. Maybe he got away with that bullshit when I was four years old, but I'm eighteen. Did he really think he could do that to my mother and I would just let him?" He shook his head in disbelief.

"Oh, my God, Lucas." She stuffed the phone back into her purse and scrambled over to him. "Don't say you got involved."

"Hell yes, I got involved. And I'll be proud I did until the day I die." He remained tense as she slung her arms around him. But when she squeezed tighter, he kissed her shoulder. "It's okay, Sarah. My father and I didn't really fight. The neighbors had called earlier when my mom and dad were yelling, so they got there before things got ugly. But I'd pissed my dad off, and he accused me of hitting him. I'd only just pushed him to keep him off Mom."

Horrified to think that that was the kind of home life he dealt with, Sarah didn't know what to say.

"I'm sorry you had to go through that," she whispered.

He shook his head. "It's fine. It's done. I'm living with my aunt now and I'm focusing on school and stuff instead of family drama. I can't fix my parents, but I can make sure I don't get drawn into that shit again."

"Good for you." She admired the set to his jaw and the determination in his gaze. "And can I apologize once again for bringing you more drama?"

"No." He tipped her chin up and cradled her face so she was forced to meet his gaze. "Sarah, I looked at you the first time and—this is going to sound so cheesy—but I swear I saw that same crazy wildness in you that I feel all the time."

"Lucas, I'm going to do you a huge favor and tell you that you do not need crazy wildness in your life anymore." She took a deep breath. "You're right about me and what you saw in me. I'm trying to get a handle on it, though. I don't want to be the wild girl forever."

"You don't get it." He shook his head, a dark wave of hair falling over one eye as he held her steady, his voice certain. "I saw the good kind of wildness, Sarah. You were carrying a pink laser gun and vaulting over kiddie slides while the other girls were rolling their eyes at the game. I knew five minutes after meeting you that I needed to break up with the girl I'd been seeing because I was going to fall hard for you. You're so full of life and adventure. Well, maybe a little too much sometimes. But I liked you right away."

Warm happiness twined through her, and it was

so nice to feel good again after so much bad crap in her life.

"My dad—my real dad and not the felon—he says I have a powerhouse personality."

Lucas laughed. "That's about right. But then, just when I thought I couldn't be more crazy about you, my mom called to give me an update on how she's been doing since she left my dad."

Puzzled, she couldn't imagine how those things connected.

"And?" She threaded her fingers through his hair, wishing she never had to leave Heartache and this boy who saw good things inside her.

"And she told me she met 'the kindest young woman' on a television segment she was asked to film about her struggle to start over again."

Frowning, Sarah tried to make the pieces fit…

She blinked. "Oh, my God. Your mom is Jamie Raybourn?"

Pieces fell into place as she pictured the tiny blonde who'd just gotten an accounting job at Finleys' Building Supplies. The woman who Erin had helped get an interview outfit and a makeover.

"The one and the same. I always wished I had her last name instead of my father's." Lucas's thumbs caressed her cheeks with infinite tenderness. "But she told me all about a beautiful, warmhearted girl who made her feel good about herself on a hard day. Sarah, I almost freaking cried when she told me your name."

Her voice wobbled. "In a good way, though, right?"

"She's my *mom*. I nearly got my ass sent to jail trying to keep her safe. Yes, it's a good thing you were kind to her." Lucas kissed her lips with an intensity that was a whole lot different than the way she'd kissed him under the slide. There was intention in it. A depth of caring she'd never felt with a guy before.

"Oh." She felt breathless. Dazed. "I thought so."

"It's been tough for me to live with my aunt and not be there for Mom, but my heart's been with her, despite having to pull myself out of that whole mess for a while." Lucas straightened. "I hadn't wanted to tell you about me getting hauled into the station and the rumors around town that I'd gotten arrested before I started school in Heartache. But I've wanted to thank you for helping my mother and I couldn't say it until you knew the whole truth about me."

He sighed with the satisfaction of someone who had gotten a lot off his chest, a feeling she could identify with, having experienced it recently herself in the police station. What strange paths they'd walked to one another.

"Now I know you and I like you even better," she admitted.

The idea worried her a little because it put a whole lot of pressure on her matchmaking scheme between Dad and Erin. She wanted to stay in Heartache more than ever. But how could she make her father fall in love in a week's time?

He'd been moving through life at a turtle's pace for months.

"You said you wanted to talk tonight, too," Lucas reminded her as he wound a strand of her hair around his finger.

Right. She'd wanted to tell him about slowing things down, but she knew he'd be okay with that. If anything, he'd been trying to slow her down.

She also needed to tell him about leaving Heartache, but she didn't want to think about that yet. Maybe she should tell him about the violence in her own past. But with this new tenderness in her heart, she wasn't ready for that tonight, either.

"It can wait." She tipped her face into the spring breeze and inhaled the scent of barbecue on the breeze. "We should go dance."

"But your knees must hurt."

"I'm fine and I want to twirl around with you under the stars. Besides, I need to see you two-step for myself."

"Maybe someone there will have bandages and we can clean up the cuts." He turned around so his back was facing her. "I'll give you a piggy-back ride."

She eyed his shoulders, liking the idea though it seemed way too far for him to carry her.

"I don't know…"

Bending his knees, he lifted her, putting her on his back with ease.

"Come on, Cajun Queen. We'll dance sooner this way."

Sarah laid her cheek against his shoulder and wrapped her arms around him. Her legs locked around his waist.

"Let the record show, I tried to warn you it wouldn't be easy."

"You keep right on warning me away." He picked up his pace as they reached the walking path leading over the bridge and back toward the playground. "You can't get rid of me, Sarah."

CHAPTER EIGHTEEN

A WEEK LATER, Erin hummed with excitement and hope as she finished up her workday at Last Chance Vintage. Her episode of *Interstate Antiquer* had aired on Tuesday night, and now, on Friday, she could hardly believe how much business the show had driven her way. Even more, she couldn't get over how generous the viewers had been with donations for Dress for Success.

Remy had been right about that. She still worried about the business growing too fast, but it wasn't as if there were new fast-food restaurants springing up on the main street just because Erin's store had been featured on a national television show. Professionally, everything was sailing along.

On a personal level? She was worried. After her tense conversation with Remy the night of the break-in, they'd backed off a bit. He still came to her house often. They'd shared meals and even a few nights, but there'd been a wall between them. Both of them knew it wasn't going to work after he left. However, he'd promised her a big surprise when she got home tonight, so her mind was already traveling the route back to her house, curious what it might be.

Was there any chance he could still make a big, romantic gesture the way Scott had for Bethany? It was almost hard to be around Bethany and not feel hopeful that maybe a happy outcome waited for her and Remy, too.

"I can't believe this," Bethany said as she stared into the new addition to Last Chance Vintage, which was now packed wall to wall with clothes.

Erin stood beside her, holding back the heavy plastic sheet as Bethany tried to take it all in. Erin felt dazed each time she saw the huge outpouring of clothes and accessories for her cause.

Erin's whole family had gotten involved in helping her manage the influx of items. Bethany and Scott were paying their new bookkeeper, Jamie Raybourn, overtime for extra hours she worked to help catalog the donations and set up an inventory system. Mack and Nina were investigating how to transport the clothes to Nashville for a three-day satellite event at Mack's bar. Even Erin's mom had helped out, coordinating outfit ideas and photographing them with help from Ally and Sarah. And Heather was flying home early from Texas and would be back in Heartache by nightfall. The project was going to help so many people. It went a long way toward helping Erin feel she'd made restitution, of sorts, for the hurt she'd caused Patrick's wife and children.

"Isn't it amazing to see?" Erin had no idea when she would be able to open the expanded square footage now that she needed to sort and store so many donated items, but her commitment to Dress for Success only increased after Jamie's ex-boyfriend had threatened her. Sarah had explained that Lucas's father was the one who'd threatened Erin. "The donations started arriving less than twenty-four hours after the episode aired on Tuesday night and they haven't slowed down since."

"This is a *lot* of fresh starts," Jamie exclaimed, her pencil pausing over the buttons of a portable adding machine. "We're going to be able to give away quite a few mini-wardrobes as starter packages to women who are in the most difficult situations."

Jamie went back to her calculating as she wove her way through the boxes and packages stacked in every corner of the new space that had been empty just three days ago.

Bethany touched Erin's arm. "You and Jamie both kept saying how much stuff was being delivered, but until you see it, you can't really appreciate it." They stepped back onto the selling floor of the regular store, where a few shoppers took photos of themselves out front.

Last Chance Vintage was definitely experiencing

more customers and more sales since the show, just as Remy had predicted.

Unfortunately, the spike in sales hadn't given her much time to spend with him the past few days. All the more a shame since he planned to return to Miami tomorrow. He and Sarah would drive back together in her car after they dropped off his rental. They'd be home before school resumed on Monday. But then again, there was a surprise planned for tonight.

Maybe he'd changed his mind about leaving. Or maybe he planned to come back once Sarah finished school. Erin had been thinking about it all day. Remy had seemed so excited about whatever it was he had planned.

"Thanks for paying for Jamie to help me out this week." Erin wouldn't have known where to start with an inventory project. Lucas's mom had been invaluable. "I'm glad she got to know Sarah a little bit before she goes home. I have the feeling Lucas and her are going to end up seeing more of each other in the future."

The two teens had been talking about schools they could both attend, or colleges in the same state so they could visit each other. Remy was skeptical and—while he'd liked Lucas immediately—he worried about the kid's unstable family.

Of course. Even for someone without Remy's issues, that was a reasonable concern. But Remy had become more vigilant since the arrest at the store, not letting Sarah go far by herself. Erin had tried not to overthink how much it would hurt to lose Remy, telling herself she needed to concentrate on her own needs for a change—her business and her charitable program.

"He's a good kid, isn't he?" Bethany squinted at the front window display and darted into the vignette to straighten a sign that read Go Green—Buy Consignment! "Lucas stopped by Finleys' Building Supplies on Monday to see his mom's new office and he seemed so proud of her. He completely won me over."

"I liked him right away when I met him, too." Erin checked her phone to see if Remy had texted her. She had one eye on the clock, looking forward to spending time with him. "And apparently his father isn't eligible for bail because of some drunk-and-disorderly issues in the past and an unanswered summons, so Jamie doesn't have to worry about him coming around for a while. Plus, once he's out of jail, the restraining order will go into effect for her, Lucas, Scott and me."

"Basically, he'll have to stay out of Heartache when he's released." Bethany gave the thumbs-up sign.

"Amen." Erin gathered her keys and checked her phone for the umpteenth time, still thinking about Remy and whatever surprise he had in store for her.

Was he ready to move forward? "You're sure you want to hang out here after I close up?"

"Positive." Bethany hugged her. "Jamie has an idea for reorganizing and I'm going to help her get started. You know how I like stuff like that."

"You do like a plan, don't you?" She winked at her sister-in-law, so glad to see her happy again. Was it too much to ask for some of that happiness? "I'm grateful to you both."

She backed out of the store with a wave.

Locking the door with her key, she thanked the excited customers milling around out front. After a few minutes, she climbed into her car to head home, where Remy had said he'd be waiting for her. She'd been wondering about the surprise all day.

She'd also been nervous.

The last time she'd gotten excited about a "surprise" from a guy, she'd been looking for a ring from Patrick. He'd actually been buying expensive "I'm sorry" jewelry for his wife. While—obviously—she knew that Remy wasn't deceiving her that way, she did worry about letting her expectations get the better of her only to be disappointed later. And no matter how much she cared about Remy, he had been distracted all week about what had happened with Lucas's father, repeatedly going through scenarios with Sarah on what to do if accosted.

Rolling down her car window, she pulled into her driveway just in time to see Remy pounding a sign into the front yard.

His muscles glistened with a light sheen of sweat, his T-shirt gone missing as he wielded a sledgehammer to get the job done. She admired the enticing show of masculinity without question, but she wondered what on earth he was doing.

She pulled into her driveway and he turned to see her. His broad grin made her smile back. He stepped aside so she could read the sign he'd just installed on a sizable wooden post right where she had planned to plant a peony bush. The sign displayed a logo for a home security company—right underneath the words *This home protected by...*

He'd installed a home security system.

Disappointment deflated her. She'd let herself really hope this time. Now she needed to drum up some kind of response while she sat in her car and stared through the windshield. She felt gut punched and knew she should stir up enthusiasm. It was very kind of him, and had probably taken several hours to set up. But in spite of everything, she had longed for a romantic gesture before he left. An indication that he cared about her enough to make her a priority.

That risking her heart had been worth it.

"Wow." She stepped out of the car and strode across the grass. "This *is* a surprise."

He wrapped her in his arms and squeezed her tightly. Because he missed her? Or because he spent so much time remembering the horrible death of the woman he could never replace?

She blinked, trying not to let this upset her when she'd known…*known*…he was planning to leave her tomorrow. Damn it, she had no one to blame but herself for letting herself hope.

"I couldn't leave here without knowing you're going to be safe." He stroked her hair. "Wait until you check out all the features this thing has."

Circling her waist with one arm, he guided her toward the house.

"Has Sarah seen it?" She wondered what his daughter had thought. "She said she was going to drop by here with Lucas this afternoon to use the internet and search for schools."

"They were here for an hour or two." He pointed to the motion-detection lights around her flower bed and on the potting shed. "But I may have slowed down their project when Lucas gave me a hand wiring a few things. I figured it was just as well he worked with me on this so he'd be able to wire his own house one day."

"You know how to do wiring?" She studied the security cameras trained on the backyard.

A pile of unused fresh-cut lumber remained neatly stacked behind the garage along with some flattened cardboard boxes from a cordless drill, a saw and the security components.

"I only needed to run electricity to a few places." He raised one arm and showed her how the camera followed the movement. In addition, two big floodlights turned on even though it wasn't dark outside yet. "It's deceptive because they call the system 'wireless' since it uses cellular coverage to send information to your phone and to the home security monitoring company. But you still have to run some wires to power the electrical mechanisms."

"Who sees the footage on all the cameras?" How comfortable would she feel in her backyard knowing her every movement was recorded?

Although, the bigger concern was how clearly this system broadcast his intention to leave town. There would be no last-minute change of heart. No declaration that he realized he wanted to spend more time with her or that she meant too much to him for him to be without her. Remy was leaving and taking his daughter with him. She'd foolishly let herself hope for so much more.

"You can send feeds wherever you want. Check the footage on your secured website or access them from your phone." Reaching into his pocket, he withdrew his phone and called up the video feed. "The monitoring service, of course, has access to the cameras, but they wouldn't actively watch any of them. They'd pull up the recordings only if there was a break-in and you needed evidence to prosecute someone. Or if the police wanted a clue how to find the intruder."

"Cool." She tried to smile and be excited about what he'd done, but her heart kept telling her this was all wrong. "I can't believe you went to so much trouble on your last full day in town."

She'd started this day with very different hopes for how it might turn out. She'd told him about a fishing spot nearby before she left the house that morning and pictured him visiting it. Pictured him making himself at home in Heartache or remembering some of his love for nature, which she'd seen in his old photographs. Instead, he'd been leaving her with one final parting gift to keep her safe.

"I've been planning this all week." He pulled her to sit down beside him on the outdoor sofa on her back deck. "So even when you were trying to convince me to fish, I knew how I'd be spending today. I only just finished up and I worked from the second your car pulled out of the driveway."

"Perfect timing." Heart aching, she kissed his cheek. It tasted like clean male sweat. In spite of the empty ache in her chest, she wanted to drag him inside and undress him, to use her last hours with him to make him see how good they could be together.

But if it hadn't worked yet, why did she think she stood any chance of swaying him now when he already had one of his suitcases in the trunk of Sarah's car?

"I hope you like it." He reached toward her purse, which she'd set on the deck, and pulled out her phone. "Do you mind if I set you up with the feeds and then we can figure out what to do about dinner?"

She drew in a deep breath and nodded, telling herself to put on a brave face. "That'd be great. In fact, I'll go look and see what I have in the fridge while you do that."

They could still have a nice dinner at least. And she knew he'd take her out if she wanted to go. Mack and Nina had been looking at properties all over town for a prospective restaurant they wanted to open, and she'd hoped they could make the rounds after dinner and see where they were. Right to the bitter end, Erin kept hoping something about Heartache would make Remy want to stay.

Even if it wasn't her.

She stared, unseeing, into the refrigerator, hoping for inspiration. A miracle to make this day turn out differently.

Until an alarm bell blared so loudly she jumped a foot off the ground.

Confused, it took her a second to realize something had tripped the new security system. Was someone in her house? Fear spiked. Her heart clamored so fiercely she thought it would pound right out of her chest. She saw Remy racing around the front of the house, picking up a two-by-four off the stack of lumber along the way.

"Remy!" Skidding across the kitchen floor, she ran for the front door. What if some neighborhood kid had wandered close to the house? Would that have set off the alarm?

And would Remy be able to think clearly enough to assess a threat?

"Wait!" she screamed over the alarm pealing its high, electronic screech.

A man's shout drew her to the open garage.

"The cops are already on the way," Remy was telling someone.

Her legs couldn't run fast enough, a bad feeling in her gut.

Patrick, her ex-boyfriend, stood in her garage. Cowered in her garage, really. He held up an old lawn chair in front of himself as protection from Remy, who wielded the two-by-four like a bat.

There was a tiny, fleeting moment of pleasure to see Patrick scared out of his mind. He'd deceived her, his wife and—most important—his own children. She could never forgive him for that. But, coming to her senses, she also knew he didn't deserve to be on the terrifying end of Remy Weldon's very real demons.

"Remy." She spoke loud enough to be heard over

the alarm. "Please disconnect the alarm. I know this man."

"What?" He turned slightly her way but didn't put down the weapon.

"Please relax. This is someone I know." She placed a hand on his shoulder, her fingers soothing the cold tension in his muscles.

Slowly, Remy lowered the board. Nodded. Seemed to come to his senses. When he yanked his phone out of his pocket and deactivated the alarm, she took her first deep breath in long, frightening minutes.

"Erin, who the hell is this maniac?" Patrick squeaked in an octave he probably hadn't touched since eighth grade. He kept his hold on the lawn chair, the fraying yellow netting trailing along his T-shirt.

"I don't owe you explanations, Patrick, but you certainly owe me one." She'd told him in no uncertain terms she never wanted to see him again. "What the hell are you doing here? I made it very clear what I think of you."

Remy glanced up, no doubt hearing the frustration in her voice, but he remained calm. "I should call the security people to let them know it's a false alarm. Should I wait, or will you be all right?" Remy's gaze flicked to Patrick and back to her.

"I'll be fine," she assured him. "He's obnoxious and unwelcome, but he's not dangerous. And he's definitely about to leave, but thank you."

Remy nodded, not going far. He stood in the driveway near her car as he made his phone calls.

"Erin." Patrick's voice had returned to semi-normal. He set the chair down. "I didn't mean to scare you. I came all the way here hoping to win you back. I saw you on that television show and it felt like—I don't know—fate or something. I needed to try one more time."

"You don't get it." She leaned on the riding lawn mower, still not fully recovered from the fear of seeing Remy take off after an intruder. "I will never want to be with a man who lies to me or cheats on his wife. Even if you promised never to lie or cheat again, I would never trust you."

"Erin—"

"Nope. Listen. I would also never be with a man who didn't do everything he could to be there for his kids." She ticked off this second all-important point on her fingers, thinking how much better a father Remy was—even when he wasn't at his best. "You missed birthday parties to fly around the country and be with your mistress. It doesn't matter that it was me. That disgusts me." It hurt to think she'd been a part of that. To picture some disappointed child's face—even one she'd never met—and imagine it was her fault his father hadn't been there for a baseball game or a party or some other part of his young life.

"I did put you first," Patrick said. "You have

to know that you are special to me, so much so I risked my family." He stepped around a croquet set to move closer until Erin arched an eyebrow. He stepped back. "That's half the reason I figured I had a shot if I came down here in person. I knew that was important to you. I don't see how you could think I'd ever put you second when I gave up everything for you."

His face was so earnest. He truly didn't understand. And she truly did not want him. She'd been so determined to find a man who loved her above all else, she'd fallen for a guy who said all the right things and made himself available whenever she was free. She knew now that wasn't what she wanted. Sure, she wanted to be important in a man's life. But she needed an equal partner. Someone who could bolster her when she needed it, and someone who could lean on her, too. Patrick wasn't half the man Remy was.

"Surprising as it may seem, Patrick, I actually would never want to win out over a child for first place in any man's heart."

"Okay." He nodded slowly, his neatly combed hair out of place, his T-shirt stained from the rusty leg of the old lawn chair he'd used as a shield. "I'm going. But can I ask you a question first?"

"I can't promise I'll answer." She was letting time slip away. Time she could be spending with Remy. They had a lot to sort out.

A lot more than she'd realized. Nothing had happened the way she had hoped it would today, and her chest burned with the weight of what it meant. The loneliness and hurt that waited on the other side of this day. But now more than ever, she knew she couldn't settle for having only half of a man's attention.

"Why were we together in the first place?" Patrick shoved his hands in his pockets, still keeping one eye on Remy out in the driveway.

Erin watched Remy now, too, his broad shoulders rolling as he walked out to meet her mother in the meadow midway between their houses. They'd met briefly earlier in the week. No doubt her mother had been concerned after hearing the security alarm.

Remy could even settle her mother, his easy Cajun charm going to work on Erin's parent in a way she recognized in Mom's body language. Shoulders relaxing. Feminine laughter ringing out over the meadow as she threw her head back at some shared joke. God, she'd fallen for that same charm despite knowing the darker layers underneath it. Turning her attention back to Patrick, she tried to puzzle together why she'd ever noticed him in the first place.

"We were together because I wanted to be the center of a guy's world and was too blind to look past the time we spent together. Now I've learned to find fulfillment in my own life and in my work. Learning that was a good thing. But being with you also robbed me of the energy and hopeful romanticism I could have used when I met the *right* man."

Patrick followed her gaze.

"Not that guy." His mouth gaped in disbelief. "Come on, Erin. You had to talk him down from the ledge just now. You don't want to spend your time dealing with more crazy people. Didn't you say your mother was nuts?"

"Get. Out." She enunciated, positive she'd never called her mother "nuts" or anything close to it. "Leave now, Patrick, before I call him back and personally hand him the two-by-four."

His face paled. This time, she relished it.

When he took off running, she knew it was the last she'd ever see of him, thank goodness. He'd only come down here because of the television show, to try to enjoy her fifteen minutes of fame with her. He'd always liked her "artsy" side, as he called it.

But he'd gotten the message. Stay away from her and Heartache.

In the distance, she saw Remy tromp back through the tall grass toward the house, keeping an eye on her retreating visitor. She met him in the middle of the lawn, right beside her flower bed where an ornamental tree bloomed tiny pink flowers.

She couldn't put off talking to him any longer. He'd be leaving tomorrow. She had wished for a romantic gesture. She knew it wasn't coming. Even Patrick had been able to see that Remy had problems he still needed to work out. Maybe if she was younger and more naive, she would jump in with both feet and cross her fingers she could help him find happiness.

At first, she'd thought it was simply a matter of taking a risk. She understood now there were calculated risks where you gambled on good odds, and there were foolish risks that were just for the sake of riding the drama roller coaster. She wanted an equal partner. Someone to share the journey with her.

Remy's hazel eyes met hers. They were greener than ever, maybe because of the colors in the sky at sunset or maybe because of the adrenaline from the confrontation with Patrick.

"I wish you could have seen all the emotions crossing your face just now." He shook his head as he used his fingers and thumbs to make a square frame in the air. "Even if I had my camera, I'm not sure I could have captured them, they slid by so fast."

Her throat clogged. Those emotions he talked

about were that close to the surface, ready to bubble over.

"Remy—"

"I screwed up, didn't I?" His arms dropped to his sides, golden muscles making her wish she could have seen him paddling his pirogue around a bayou. "Not just going after that guy." He barely spared a gesture to dismiss Patrick. "But installing the system without asking you. Setting up so many gadgets like it's my house and not yours."

"No." She corralled his gesticulating hands in hers. Held them. "I don't mind the security. It was sweet and thoughtful and I can't believe you spent all day working so hard to do something really nice for me."

He studied her face, and lights popped on all around them, flooding the grounds with a halogen glow.

"I might have gone a little far," he admitted, blinking against the glare.

"The thing is, I guess I let myself get my hopes up when you said you had a surprise for me. I thought it would be tickets to see you in Miami. Or maybe you'd take a page from Scott's book and come up with someplace we could meet the next time you go on a trip to scout for locations." She lifted a shoulder, not sure what exactly she'd expected. It definitely hadn't been an alarm system. "Every day we've spent together, I've fallen a little more for you and I think you've been retreating from me."

"One step forward, two steps back." He hung his head. "I knew it might be like that when I tried to rejoin the living."

His voice was whisper quiet, as if it was some dark admission. Yet, the thing she noticed most was what he didn't say.

"You don't deny you've been retreating from me." She'd noticed it after his bad dream. And it had only gotten worse after the episode at the store.

She couldn't be with someone who lived half his life in an old nightmare.

"I don't want to." He met her eyes again and there was no denying the force behind the words. "But the harder I try to move on, the more the past strangles me. Falling for you means I'm going to be scared all the time. Scared of leaving you. Of someone hurting you. I know you don't want to live that way and neither do I. I thought if I got the alarm set up, I'd relax." He touched her cheek and his fingers came away wet. "Don't cry."

"I find it sad." She swallowed back dreams that weren't going to come true. Caring about Remy had been a huge risk, and if given the chance to do it all over again, she would. But losing him was going to hurt ten times as much as she had feared.

Already the hole in heart ached and he hadn't left yet.

Not physically, anyway. But he'd been fading a little more every day this past week.

"I never wanted to hurt you." He stepped closer, bringing all that physical comfort she needed so damn badly and couldn't afford to take.

"*I* hurt me, Remy." She stepped back, needing that space between them before she fell into his arms, made love to him all night long and lost the rest of her heart to him forever. "That's on me and I own it. I'm glad I got to be with you, and be special to you, even for a little while. I hope you find peace with…everything."

Tears welled in his eyes, too. And oh, man, that was going to just break her.

She rushed to finish before she lost it. "I need to say goodbye to Sarah. I don't want her to be upset about this. Maybe in the morning I could stop by the B and B while you…I don't know…fuel up the car or get breakfast or something."

He nodded, the movement jerky. He was holding back as much as her. "Of course. I understand."

There was so much more to say, but it would all just end with the same two words, and she couldn't speak knowing they were coming up. Knowing they had to say them.

"Goodbye, Remy." Leaning in to kiss his cheek, she didn't let herself look at him.

She ran into the house and locked herself in her bedroom. The pain of losing him was too big to face any other way. She hugged her pillow and cried, wishing she'd been the kind of woman who could make him smile again.

CHAPTER NINETEEN

No wonder Sarah hated Miami.

Remy had been back for four weeks and was already considering putting their home on the market. What the hell had made him choose a city where just driving home from work required the aggression of an Indy car driver and was guaranteed to elevate his blood pressure? He hung his keys on a hook in the kitchen as he entered their apartment. A hook Sarah had installed, now that he thought about it. It was shaped like a daisy with a ladybug on one petal.

Since he'd returned from Tennessee, he'd noticed a lot of stuff she'd taken care of in the past two years. These days, his eyes were open to all the ways he'd put his head in the sand for too damn long. Knowing Erin had shown him how narrow his world had become. Meeting her had been like an electric shock to the senses, zinging him alive after he'd walked through too much of his life in a daze.

He missed her so badly he ached with it. Too bad he hadn't been able to give her the kind of happiness she deserved. But each day, he was trying to do better. Be better.

He'd taken Sarah back to Louisiana the weekend before to visit her mother's grave. For the first time, it hadn't ripped his heart out. His counselor had suggested it might be a good thing to do. And it had been really...important. They'd brought flowers and arranged the blooms on the grave site in the rough outline of Liv's cypress tree painting. Remy had photographed it and put the photo with the others—his original photo of the tree and Liv's painting of the photo. He'd felt a new sense of peace ever since he'd been able to say goodbye in a way that was meaningful.

Permanent.

Now, laying his jacket over a kitchen chair, he switched on a light above the stove and pulled out a pan to make dinner. That was one of the ways he was living in the here and now—he'd divided cooking duties with his daughter. His nights sucked more—obviously—but he was proud to have expanded his repertoire to include poached eggs. He could grill salmon. And there'd been a time when he did *not* burn a roast, although that dish was far from mastered. Tonight he would Cajun fry some speckled trout his brother had overnighted him, packed in ice.

Fresh caught in bayou waters, the fish was an old

favorite, the recipe something he could make in his sleep. There wasn't anything he couldn't Cajun fry.

When he'd first returned from Tennessee, he'd been primed to return to his therapist and work harder to make progress. Get through those grief stages. Find a way to be a better father and maybe—just maybe—be the kind of man who wouldn't hurt Erin Finley again.

But it had been slower than he'd hoped. His "one step forward, two steps back" theory seemed like a big fat joke these days. At first, he'd stepped so far back he'd actually had a day where he'd been speechless at work. Stuck in a meeting and unable to pull his thoughts together to form a coherent sentence. But then, the guys in the meeting hadn't known that discussing home renovations would put him over the edge. Just the words *air nail compressor* damn near sent him into a meltdown with missing Erin.

Things had gotten better recently. Especially after the visit to Liv's grave. He could feel new hope brewing inside him.

His phone rang while he seasoned the fish.

"Armand," he answered, looking at the caller ID. "You are the hero of the dinner table tonight. I'm cooking the trout as we speak."

Sarah would be home from graduation rehearsal any minute. Mathilda had driven her and—bless that girl—she was helping Sarah with some application essays for late registration.

His daughter had applied to some schools in Tennessee and a few in Louisiana, inspiring Lucas to send out a few last-minute applications himself. The kid was obviously crazy about Sarah, and who could blame him? Remy had been keeping a close eye on that situation, but he had to admit, the guy made Sarah smile a lot. Hard to begrudge her the daily Skype time with Lucas when the boy made his girl laugh so often.

"I only sent the fish to make you come home. The bayou, she misses you." Armand was the most colorful net maker in all of Houma, his stories as prized as his good knots. "I heard her calling out for you while I reeled in the trout, and I said I would try to lure you back with the taste of the delicacies you love best."

"You're not lying about that part, anyway." Remy coated the trout in black pepper and red pepper mixed together. "All the rest of your lines might work on the tourists, but not on me."

"That's because you gave your heart away to the gods of money and you forgot about the sea, you old dog." Armand must be approaching the dance hall because the sound of accordion music swelled until Remy could almost see the skirts swaying and the old-timers sipping their one beer for the night.

Remy turned down the heat under the pan. "Did

you put Mom on the phone while I wasn't looking? 'Cause you sound just like her, brother man."

"Funny how the parents get smarter as we get older, no?" Armand chuckled before he called out greetings. "Enjoy the trout, Remigius. I keep your boat ready."

Remy hung up the phone, surprised how much the last bit had gotten to him—a whole lot more than accusations of selling out to money.

I keep your boat ready.

It made him wish he'd gone fishing that day Erin had given him directions to a nearby river. The place where she'd dropped a line as a girl. For that matter, why hadn't he taken her with him to see the water again?

Maybe frying the fish made him nostalgic. Or maybe it was that old zydeco tune "Quelle Étoile" that had him thinking about things he hadn't shared with Erin. He'd bet she'd love to dance to "Quelle Étoile" in a sweaty dance hall. Or fish for speckled trout. Hadn't she said she wished he'd done something more romantic than install a home security system?

A rustling outside the door warned him Sarah was home a second before her key turned in the lock.

"Hey, Dad," she called, cheery but still not as happy as she'd been a few weeks ago. "Something smells yummy."

She missed Lucas, of course, but he knew for a fact she also missed Erin and all the Finleys. She'd grown deeper roots in Heartache in a few weeks' time than she'd put down in Florida in two years.

"We got a treat from your uncle Armand." He lifted the pan to show her.

"Awesome. Too bad there are no lemon-berry cupcakes for dessert." She hung up her keys on the daisy hook and moved to set the table. "I heard Ally's uncle Mack bought a spot for a restaurant in Heartache, by the way. There will be lots of cupcakes, I'll bet."

As if he didn't miss the place enough on his own, he had Sarah to help him remember how much he was missing.

He tried to recall what his counselor said about doing the hard work. If he put in the hours of dealing with the setbacks, there was no reason he couldn't emerge happy and whole. Ready to start over. If nothing else, he could always do like Scott Finley, who'd poured his heart out on six chalkboards when he couldn't figure out how to make Bethany happy. At least the guy had shown he'd tried.

What had Remy done to show Erin he was trying? He'd been so busy fixing himself and trying to patch together his own issues, he hadn't taken any time to show her he could make her happy. A damn shame since he loved her so much he thought he didn't know how he'd get through another week without her.

He'd known it as soon as he'd left Heartache, but it wasn't fair to tell her until he knew he could uphold his end of what that meant. But as he fried his fish and ticked through all the ways he'd failed her, he figured he might have enough of his act together to try again. No, try his ass off now that he knew how far he'd fallen short.

"Maybe we'd better take a look at the place." He slid the fish onto a serving platter and put it on the table in front of his daughter.

Sarah simply stared at him.

"Excuse me?" she said finally, eyes wide.

"It sounded to me like you want to check out the new restaurant. And I'm agreeing. Maybe it's a good idea." He was setting the pan in the sink when the tackle hug came.

It didn't incapacitate him as much as the squeal that pierced his ear. Partially deaf but definitely pleased with himself, Remy hugged his daughter tight.

No matter what else happened, he'd made one special girl happy today. But he knew it would take a lot more than cupcakes to convince Erin to take another chance on him. For the first time, the words *hope springs eternal* didn't tear him apart when he thought about them. If anything, he hoped that whoever said them knew what he or she was talking about because he needed Erin to have some small hope left. Some lingering faith in him.

ERIN HAD EVERY faith her highlights were going to look amazing.

She straightened from the wash sink at The Strand where Trish had just rinsed out the solution that would put ombré highlights in her newly caramel-colored hair. Of course, her hair was one of the few parts of her life that was working out for her these days. Well, that and her professional life.

Last Chance Vintage had just opened the new addition last weekend with double the inventory. Heather was back in town splitting time with her, so she didn't need to be there as often, giving Erin more time to develop her Dress for Success initiative. She was raising funds to buy a small bus to take their huge inventory on the road so she could bring the mini-shop to women in rural parts of Tennessee who couldn't get to the store. The project had taken on a whole life of its own now that it wasn't just about her making up for hurting Patrick's family. Now it was a way to help other women make their dreams come true. It fulfilled her on a soul-deep level.

Professionally speaking, anyway. The personal part of her life still missed a vital piece.

"Girl, you look smoking hot," Trish observed as she blew out the damp strands, taking the time to curl the ends under with a fat round brush. "You were right about this color combination. I'm loving it on you."

"It looks great, Trish. I really needed a pick-me-up." Erin didn't bother to hide her broken heart from her friends this time. With Patrick, she'd known he wasn't worthy of her anyhow, so moping around and being upset afterward had felt wrong.

But who could blame her for wishing she'd worked things out with Remy Weldon? Half the female population had fallen for him while he'd been in Heartache.

"I can't even watch another episode of *Interstate Antiquer* now. Or *American Voice*, for that matter. How could he just head back to Florida without a word?"

In spite of everything, she felt the need to defend him.

"He's texted me a few times since he left." Four short messages telling her he was trying to get his life together. She hadn't responded as she couldn't afford to take another chance on a man who hadn't made any promises.

"Humph." Trish concentrated the hot air on the ends of Erin's hair. "I really thought I could size a man up better than that. Everything I saw said he was crazy about you."

As if her heart wasn't tender enough, well-meaning friends poked at it regularly. She wanted to believe he'd texted her with some great purpose—that he had hopes of coming back one day.

But for all she knew, the only reason Remy was trying to work out his issues was so he could be a better father to Sarah. While she applauded that in theory, the reality was, it wouldn't fix the ache inside her.

"He's been through a lot." Logically, she understood. Still, she needed to stop making excuses for a man who simply hadn't been able to put the past behind him.

It was as straightforward, and as heartbreaking, as that.

"Well, I say you'll have no trouble turning heads whenever you're ready to date again." Trish spun her chair to face the mirror as she shut off the dryer. "What do you think, sexy woman?"

Erin smiled. The hair did look great, even if what stood out to her the most was the sadness in her eyes. With an effort, she blinked it away and tried to be positive.

"You're a hairdressing genius in addition to being a good friend." Standing, she left her apron in the chair and followed Trish to the register.

Outside, she could see her car parked on the street and—strangely—a basket beside it. She'd been planning to stop by the store before going home for the day, but the basket made her curious.

"Want me to make an appointment for you in

six weeks?" Trish asked, already checking her appointment book.

"Can I call you?" Erin left extra cash on the counter. "I just remembered. I have to get going."

"Well, sure, hon," Trish was saying. "Hey, Erin, you left way too much…"

But she was already out the door, drawn by a basket that looked like a picnic hamper. And it wasn't just sitting on the street as if someone had left it by accident. The red-and-brown woven container was balanced on the hood of her car, close to the windshield.

She looked up and down the street to see if anyone was around. Main Street was quiet for midday, however. The front door of Last Chance Vintage was open, and she could hear the country music Heather liked floating on the breeze, but other than that, the storefront was still.

As she crossed the street and neared the car, she could see a note taped to the top of the basket— "I have a much better surprise for you this time."

The words were scrawled in thick black marker in—she was almost positive—Remy's handwriting. Besides, who else would leave a note about surprises?

Her pulse kicked into high, hopeful gear way too fast. She should be careful about this. Cautious. Wary. He'd hurt her before, after all.

Yet, her trembling hands didn't care what her

head said. She lifted the hamper lid. Taped inside
the top was another note. But this one was scrib-
bled in her handwriting, the very same instruc-
tions she'd left for Remy that last day they'd been
together—directions to the Harpeth River for the
fishing trip she'd suggested.

What on earth? She had only a moment to wonder what he had in mind. Inside the picnic basket was a bottle of wine—the same Chianti he'd
brought to her house that first night. Cheese and
crackers—the cheese was still cool—and some
grapes. There were glasses and silverware, plates,
napkins and a bakery box that could contain only
one thing.

Cupcakes.

A small gasp escaped her lips. Hopeful tears
burned her eyes, the feeling so much different than
all the tears she'd shed in the past four weeks.

Underneath all of it, she found an MP3 player
with a note taped to it. "Play me."

The note was in Sarah's handwriting. The letters were colored with purple stripes of ink. So,
gathering up her basket and the tattered remains
of her hopeful heart, she put everything inside her
car and headed for the Harpeth River.

Hands still shaking, she plugged in the MP3
player and hit the only icon on the screen, labeled
"Erin's Songs." There was a short list of titles in

French. Or more likely, Cajun. But the first on the playlist was labeled "From Sarah."

"Hi, Erin." Sarah's voice filled the car as Erin drove east out of town. "I sneaked in a quick heads-up to you because even though Dad is super excited about his surprise, I know he's also really nervous. And I'm excited and nervous, too, and hate it that I can't be there to see how things turn out. But—amazingly—I have a college interview this week."

Erin smiled as she listened, her heart in her throat to think about Sarah and Remy planning a surprise for her.

She missed them so, so much. She put on her signal light for the left-hand turn.

"Anyway, I want you to know I miss you and love you no matter how today goes, okay? I'll tell you about my interview if you'd like to hear. But the main thing I wanted to tell you is this. Dad is trying. I'm not just saying that because he's my dad, either. He's, like, *really* trying."

Erin listened for a few more minutes as Sarah chatted about how much she missed Tennessee and Lucas. About how she wanted to decorate her dorm room with mirrors like the one Erin had given her. And also about her graduation ceremony and the creepy teacher who tried to hit on her dad and how Sarah had to throw herself between them to prevent the woman from using the occasion as an excuse to kiss his cheek.

By the time she reached the pull-off for the fishing spot, Erin felt she'd had a good pep talk from a friend. A friend she hoped would be a much bigger part of her life.

The parking area sat empty except for one white Lincoln with out-of-state plates that had to be a rental car. Still, she remained in her seat with the doors locked while she took in the scene. Bayou music played on her MP3 player—fiddles and accordions that would make her feet tap if she wasn't so nervous.

A canoe floated in the water, tied to a short wooden dock. A mouthwatering man sat in the boat, his profile so achingly familiar she knew every nuance of expression on his face as he turned his gaze to her. A blanket had been spread on the seat facing him. An antique parasol, which happened to be for sale at Last Chance Vintage just yesterday, rested at an angle to shade the empty seat. Fishing poles and a small silver tackle box were tucked behind him.

Standing carefully, he stepped out of the boat and jogged up the hill toward her. Her heart beat with new purpose, as if it had been in a state of suspended animation for the past four weeks and only just now recalled how to function the right way.

"You came." He stopped just short of her, his

hazel gaze roaming all over her. "Thank you for that."

He seemed relieved. And yes, nervous.

That made two of them.

"I like surprises more these days." Her voice sounded odd, as if she hadn't spoken in a while.

"I messed up the last one, but I worked really hard on this one." He sidestepped to the passenger side of her car and pulled out the picnic basket.

"You sure came a long way for a picnic." She felt so uncertain, she wasn't sure she could get in the canoe until she understood what he wanted. What he hoped to gain from coming here.

In the trees, birds chirped and whistled. The water gurgled around a small cove, but for the most part, the river provided a calm, easy place to paddle a boat or fish. The weather had turned warmer and Erin's bare arms were hot from the sun.

Remy's cargo shorts and T-shirt showcased lean muscle. He eyed her as if he wasn't sure where to go next. But then, apparently coming to a decision, he put the picnic basket on the ground. His hands caressed her shoulders.

"Erin. I love you. I came all this way to say that, but I am ready to show you in every way possible, if you'll give me another chance."

Speechless, her mouth fell open.

"It's okay. You don't need to answer or anything.

He stroked her hair and tenderly kissed the back of each hand.

He kissed the ring finger on her left hand longest and she melted.

"Yes. Yes." She lifted her voice to shout it. "Yes!"

Startled birds took flight as she jumped into Remy's arms and let him spin her around.

"Yes to all of it," she whispered in his ear, barely daring to believe her dreams were coming true. "I want to be with you forever. I'm going to make you so happy."

He scooped her up off her feet. "Starting right now." He grabbed the picnic basket with the other hand and marched them down the hill toward the canoe. "We're going to have the best damn picnic ever. Right after we catch the biggest fish."

"You mean right after you kiss me." She arched up closer to brush her lips over his.

"That part is a before, during and after kind of thing," he said, pausing long enough to kiss her thoroughly. Kiss her senseless. "I picture a lot more of that happening."

She still felt as if they were spinning when he settled her onto the blanket in the canoe.

"This is the best surprise." She stared up at him as he situated the picnic basket between them.

Sunlight limned his shoulders and his golden-brown hair, reminding her what he must look like paddling his pirogue through the bayou waters.

She'd found a smart, charming, thoroughly devoted man she could trust with her heart forever.

"And the good news is, it's only just started," he reminded her, sitting down and stretching out his long legs. "We've got a lot of plans to make, Erin Finley-soon-to-be-Weldon."

Oh, she liked how that sounded.

"But you know what we need to do first, right?" She pulled her phone out of her purse and opened up her messaging screen.

Remy grinned. "I have a good idea."

"Can we take a quick picture?" She leaned toward him and held up the camera for a romantic selfie. At the last second, he turned and planted a kiss on her cheek.

It was, quite possibly, the cutest picture ever.

Erin attached the photo to her text message to Sarah and typed out three words—I said yes.

* * * * *